A Ravel

"Methought I heard a voice cry 'Sleep no more!
Macbeth does murder sleep', the innocent sleep,
Sleep that knits up the ravelled sleeve of care
The death of each day's life, sore labour's bath,
Balm of hurt minds …"

William Shakespeare

Books by Julia Jones

The Strong Winds Trilogy:
Volume I *The Salt-Stained Book*
Volume II *A Ravelled Flag*
Volume III *Ghosting Home*
(forthcoming 2012)

The Allingham Biography series:
The Adventures of Margery Allingham
Cheapjack by Philip Allingham (edited
with Francis Wheen)
The Oaken Heart: the story of an English village at war by Margery
Allingham (edited with Lesley Simpson)
Fifty Years in the Fiction Factory: the working life of Herbert Allingham
(forthcoming 2012)

Books by Claudia Myatt

RYA Go Sailing: a practical guide for young people
RYA Go Sailing Activity Book
RYA Go Cruising: a young crew's guide to sailing and motor cruisers
RYA Go Cruising Activity Book
RYA Go Inland: a young person's guide to Inland Waterways
*RYA Go Green: a young person's guide to
the blue planet*
RYA Go Windsurfing (forthcoming)
Log Book for Children (new edition)
Buttercup's Diary and other tales

A Ravelled Flag

Julia Jones

VOLUME TWO
OF THE *Strong Winds* TRILOGY

GOLDEN DUCK

First published in 2011 by Golden Duck (UK) Ltd.,
Sokens,
Green Street,
Pleshey, near Chelmsford,
Essex.
CM3 1HT
www.golden-duck.co.uk

ISBN 978-1-899262-05-2

All illustrations © Claudia Myatt 2011
http://www.claudiamyatt.co.uk

Design by Megan Trudell

Printed and bound in the UK
by the MPG Books Group Bodmin and King's Lynn.

This book is dedicated to Francis and to Frank
with gratitude for all their good advice – whether I took it or not.

Contents

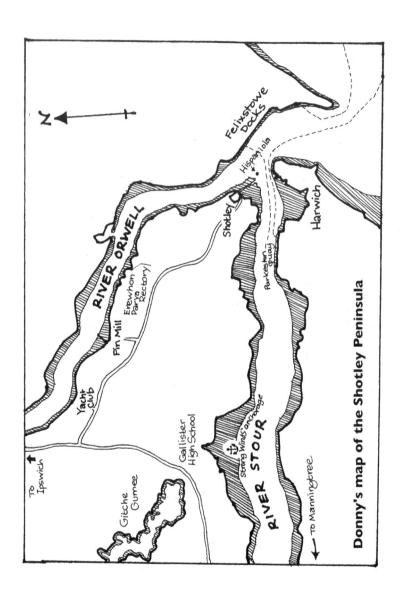

Donny's map of the Shotley Peninsula

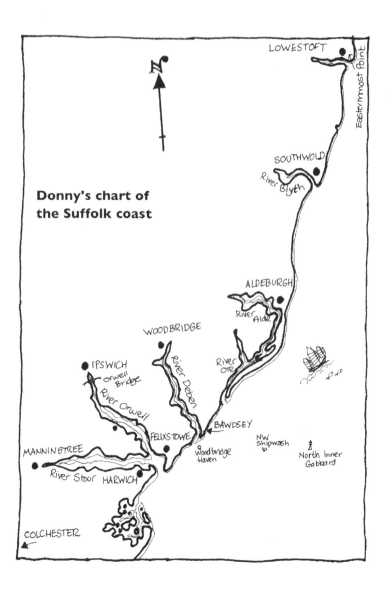

Donny's chart of the Suffolk coast

LOWESTOFT

Easternmost Point

SOUTHWOLD

River Blyth

ALDEBURGH

River Alde

WOODBRIDGE

IPSWICH

Orwell Bridge

River Orwell

River Deben

River Ore

MANNINGTREE

FELIXSTOWE

BAWDSEY

Woodbridge Haven

NW Shipwash

North Inner Gabbard

River Stour

HARWICH

COLCHESTER

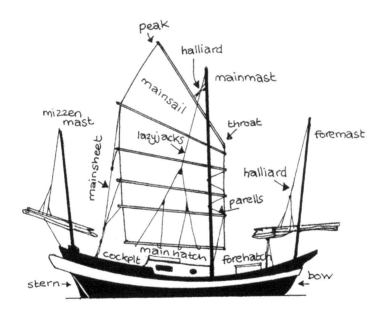

Strong Winds – rigging diagram

CHAPTER ONE

Ship Wreck

Tuesday 26 September 2006, morning

Donny woke slowly and luxuriously that first morning on board *Strong Winds*.

He felt the fragments of a dream evaporating from his head. He was waving from a boat to an island. And his friends were waving back. No, not waving. They had been signalling. With flags. Somewhere else in the dream he sensed two children, outcasts on a deserted shore, sharing their last few crumbs.

Donny shook the dream away. This was the first day of his new life. He didn't need distraction.

When he'd woken yesterday he'd found himself lying on the hard deck of a schooner, soaked by fog. It had been his fourteenth birthday but he'd been alone and frightened.

He shifted one shoulder experimentally against the softness of his bunk. Yes, it ached. And so did the other. The palms of both hands felt chafed but not blistered any more. The salty water was definitely toughening him up.

So good to be here. To be together again. To be safe.

He let himself re-live the moment – also yesterday – when he had first seen this boat, *Strong Winds*, scudding in from the open sea with the afternoon sun glowing golden in her sails. Bringing Great Aunt Ellen home.

It was his second best birthday present ever.

Getting his mum back had been the best.

Donny rolled over, ignoring his aches, and peered across the cabin at Skye's sleeping heap. Her long dark hair was un-plaited and tangled across her face so he couldn't really see her properly. It looked dank and greasy as if it hadn't been washed all the time she'd been away. There were no bright ribbons twisted in its strands and the bits of her skin that he could see were as dull as unworked clay. Her mouth was open and she was snoring slightly.

She was there. The person who mattered most in the world.

Last time he'd seen her had been in the dim light of a hospital ward. She had been sedated. The time before that, she had been screaming.

It was over.

Push it deep down into the nightmare bag and pull the choke-strings shut.

Donny stretched his legs out with a sigh of pleasure and lay on his back watching the pale sun as it danced across the cabin roof. It was almost worth having a few aches and pains. They sort of spiced-up the comfort.

He hadn't felt anything so good for … months? There was a fleecy blanket underneath him, so thick it must be doubled; an unzipped sleeping bag light and warm on top; and a blissfully soft cotton pillow smoothed beneath his head.

Skye had the same. Gold Dragon must have put them there. That's what she liked to be called, his new great-aunt.

She was a small woman, more than eighty years old, with a hook instead of one hand. She had spent yesterday and most of the day before sailing solo across the North Sea from Holland. And she was famous. Polly Lee, pioneer yachtswoman. There had been a TV camera waiting by the lock gate when she and *Strong Winds* had arrived.

Donny wasn't sure where Gold Dragon slept or what time of the morning this was. He definitely didn't want to disturb her if she might still be asleep. So he carried on lying there, basking, as he watched the flickers of light chasing like minnows across the cabin roof. The air in the cabin felt clean and slightly chilly. There must be a breeze outside, a breeze fresh enough to ruffle even the sheltered waters of the marina.

Donny could hear halliards tapping against masts. He was surrounded by boats. Better than any dream. And the yacht that was moored closest was beautiful *Snow Goose*. His friends, Xanthe and Maggi, and their parents would be sleeping there.

If people were still asleep?

He didn't have a watch so he listened harder, hoping for clues. He caught the cry of a seagull, a passing engine and then, from across the harbour came the round-the-clock rattle of cranes loading and unloading container ships in the Port of Felixstowe.

Donny shifted less comfortably.

Cranes and halliards wouldn't waken Skye. When he'd been younger his granny, who was dead, had sometimes put her hands over his ears so he could feel what it might be like in his mother's silent world. But his head hadn't really been silent at all: it had rumbled and buzzed as if it was a machine on stand-by.

There'd been one bad shock among his birthday surprises, gate-crashing his happiness like a cackling black witch. He'd discovered that Granny hadn't been Skye's mother: that she wasn't, in fact, his granny.

They said that babies in the womb could hear their mother's

voice, muffled and far-away like whale music. Skye had been deaf ever since she'd been born but presumably unborn babies didn't hear in the same way. It was probably more like feeling sounds than hearing them. But if Skye had felt her mother's voice, it hadn't been Granny's.

Granny – Miss Edith Walker, who had looked after Skye and him for all their lives – had been an aunt, a senior aunt. Gold Dragon – Miss Ellen Walker – was the junior one. Skye's birth mother wasn't Edith or Ellen but a middle sister called Eirene. Someone who, until yesterday, no-one had ever mentioned.

Great Aunt Ellen had told him last night that Eirene had 'gone' soon after Skye was born. How could this Eirene have gone away and left her baby – a tiny, deaf, brain-damaged baby who wasn't expected to survive?

Donny looked fondly at his mum as her eyelids flickered in dream-sleep.

Eirene! What sort of a stupid name was that?

The cosy waking-up feeling had gone. Donny urgently needed a pee. There was a toilet block somewhere at the end of the pontoons and a keypad with a serial number that he hadn't managed to remember. He pushed his sleeping bag off and sat up. Glad he was still wearing socks. No time for shoes.

Skye moved restlessly as Donny hurried up the companionway. He couldn't wait. He could see Joshua Ribiero about to get into his car.

Donny ran along the pontoon to catch him. He didn't notice the limited edition electric-blue Mercedes parked strategically overlooking *Strong Winds*.

"Good morning, Donny. We thought that you would never

wake. June has taken the girls to school and your great-aunt has walked to buy groceries. We offered to help but … she's a very independent lady."

"Yeah, right. Er, sorry, what's the code for the toilet block?"

"898132. You reverse the telephone number. And, Donny, please don't linger. It's best for your mother that she's not left alone until she has completely understood where she is. She has been given a large quantity of medication and it'll take some time for her body to readjust. We can expect physical symptoms as well as considerable disorientation. Possibly distress."

"Yeah, sure, I'll be really quick. Er, thanks a lot," said Donny and sped away. Eight nine eight, one three two, eight nine eight, one three two. That seemed about the most urgent information right now.

Joshua hesitated, then left. He had patients waiting.

A blond woman in a Gucci business suit swayed briskly towards *Strong Winds* in her Louboutin shoes. Making bad worse was her special gift. You could call it mal-fare.

Donny punched the numbers into the keypad and heard the automatic lock click free.

It wasn't so easy to exit. Someone else was fumbling with the lock, outside. Didn't seem to understand the combination, wouldn't listen when Donny tried to help. All he could do in the end was stand back and wait until the man, or whoever it was, got fed up trying and went away.

Donny didn't see anyone when he finally got out. He didn't really look because now he could hear shouting.

Something was happening on *Strong Winds*. The junk couldn't be ... moving?

Donny ran.

"Mum!" he yelled, as he hurtled down the access ramp.

That was a waste of breath.

Skye was standing on *Strong Winds'* foredeck in her old jersey and her long dark tie-dye skirt. She was pushing against the wooden staging with a boat hook. The junk's mainsail was half unfurled and the mooring lines were loose. There were trailing ropes everywhere.

She was looking towards the lock gates and the wide spaces of the harbour and sort of howling as she shoved the boat fiercely away from the pontoon. The fresh breeze was already catching the top section of the unfurled mainsail, threatening to make the heavy junk unmanageable in this confined space. The next row of expensive moored yachts was only metres distant. Donny knew he must do something quickly if he were to avert a massive collision.

But what?

Snow Goose, the Ribieros' pride and joy, was lying just ahead of *Strong Winds*. Both boats had been moored in the central area of the marina, where there was room to lie alongside instead of having to manoeuvre into narrower, car park-style spaces.

Donny ran to *Snow Goose* and vaulted on board. As he'd hoped, there was a spare coil of mooring line, neatly positioned on the yacht's aft deck, ready attached to her starboard samson post.

"MUM!" he shouted again. And hurled the line straight at her.

His aim was good. The rope snaked out and hit Skye hard on her shoulder and the side of her head. She stopped shoving and looked to see where it had come from.

Then she saw Donny.

He could use sign language now. "Tie the rope onto something! Quick! Tie the rope on!"

The middle section of the mooring line had fallen in the water but Skye had caught its end. She dropped the boat hook and began to pull, hand over hand, heaving herself desperately back to her child as if this rope was some super-sized umbilical cord.

She was pulling much too strongly. The slack was lifting too quickly out of the water. This could be another disaster. *Strong Winds* hadn't stopped moving backwards. She'd never be able to take the strain once the full weight of the boat came onto the rope. It'd burn the skin off her hands, pull her overboard.

"Tie the rope on!" Donny kept signing. "Wrap it round something!"

He saw her look about, then bend forward and wind the rope round and round one of the solid wooden cleats, which were positioned inside the bulwarks on either side of the junk's high bow.

Not a moment too soon. The curve in the line was straightening. Could slender *Snow Goose* bear *Strong Winds'* full weight?

The rope twanged taut, shaking off drops of water in sparkling curves on either side. Donny felt *Snow Goose* shift under him as she took the strain. She pulled back hard on her own mooring lines. A moment of tension. Ropes and cleats creaked.

Everything held. It was going to be okay. *Strong Winds* stopped slipping backwards. She was several boat-lengths away from *Snow Goose*, momentarily at rest.

Another section of her big mainsail tumbled free.

Donny was trying to work out angles. Should he attempt to winch the junk back to her berth? Would she swing in against the pontoon? The space behind *Snow Goose* was empty and *Strong Winds* had plenty of fenders to minimise the impact. He could be there in seconds and get a rope to her stern. Skye would be there too. They could hold the junk steady; then sort out the mooring lines in safety.

Was that what was going to happen? For a moment Donny hesitated.

Skye was uncertain too. She looked at the rope, then looked at her child, still parted from her by a stretch of rippled water.

Skye wasn't used to water. This separation frightened her. The lies she'd been told were dripping poison through her head. She began again to heave on the rope that linked her boat to his.

"No, Mum, NO! Don't do that!" he signed.

Hurried footsteps on the staging behind him. "Here … son … you look as if you could do with a hand."

One of the men from the marina office had seen his plight and was running to help.

It was too late. At that moment an unlucky gust caught the top sections of *Strong Winds'* loosened mainsail and set her sailing. The tide-less water offered no resistance and she picked up momentum in a couple of metres. The high strong bow, which yesterday Donny had thought so beautiful, was coming at him like a battering ram.

Straight towards the pointed stern and varnished spars of the elegant *Snow Goose*.

"Pairrfect," murmured the Mal-fairy, selecting one of the stored numbers in her BlackBerry. There had been all that unfortunate publicity yesterday. This should put the record straight. Or skew it, naicely.

Donny was searching for something, anything, he could use to stave off the impact. He knew his own arms would be too short: his boy's strength not enough. Was there an oar, a boat hook even? He pulled at *Snow Goose's* tiller in the futile hope that it would come free and he could use it to avert disaster.

The tiller was fixed in its position. There was nothing he could do.

CHAPTER TWO

Striking the Colours

Tuesday 26 September continued

The impact was crushing. Instinctively Donny leapt backwards onto the pontoon in the last second before the heavy junk struck the aft end of the yacht. It was only later he realised that, if he'd stayed where he was, he'd probably have been seriously injured.

Strong Winds' bow was so much higher than *Snow Goose's* stern that it caught the yawl's mizzenmast first and forced it backwards with a rending crack. The mizzen boom was triced up close to the mast so both were caught between the flaring bulwarks on either side of *Strong Winds'* broad stem. The mizzen shrouds were wrenched out of their fastenings with an audible ping. Everything – mast, boom, shrouds, halliards and bundled sail – crashed to the deck in a tangled mess.

Even this didn't completely halt the on-coming junk. The impact shook out her entire mainsail so the wind drove her forward all the stronger. Once the mizzenmast had collapsed, the lower section of *Strong Winds'* bow was forced directly against *Snow Goose's* stern, shouldering it towards the pontoon.

The yacht tried to twist away but was held rigid by her own mooring ropes.

"Let go her bow-line!" Donny shouted to the man from the office.

Then he ran a few strides along the pontoon and leapt up again onto *Strong Winds*. The junk's deck was in chaos. Skye appeared to have undone every rope she could see – and three-masted *Strong Winds* had plenty to undo. Halliards, sheets, parells, warps, lines, hawsers – ropes, thick and thin, trivial and essential, were trailing, snaking, tangling from all sides.

It was lucky that Donny had helped his great-aunt to stow the mainsail as they'd approached the marina yesterday evening.

In fact it was better than lucky. The man from the marina office might have thought that it was chance that had led the boy unerringly to find the main halliard amidst the chaos, but Donny sensed that there had been something guiding him. Something Ancestral?

A few hard pulls and the junk's mainsail meekly disappeared.

Donny fastened it firmly but didn't waste time coiling the halliard. He dashed to the stern ready to catch one of the mooring ropes. Two neat loops made a clove hitch knot over the samson post and *Strong Winds* was finally secured.

Slowly, silently and hopelessly, Donny and the man began their vain attempt to pull the junk back from the mass of wreckage that had been *Snow Goose*'s stern.

That was when his new great-aunt returned from the village shop.

His social worker arrived as well. Her name was Sandra. She had come to tell the family that the Statutory Service Care Review & Assessment Meeting, which should have been taking place that afternoon, had been rearranged for Friday morning.

"We hoped that a later date would … allow everyone time to … re-assess," Sandra stuttered, her rosy face blanched by the sight before her. "I think I've come at a bad moment." She paused again, gulping on her understatement. "Should I call … medical help?"

Skye had collapsed. Her body sagged against the junk's high side. Her brown eyes were open and appalled, gazing at the wounded yacht, beginning to comprehend the damage she had caused.

"Not unless you know a good boat surgeon," said Great Aunt Ellen grimly, not averting her own eyes one second from the tangle of spars and rigging and splintered wood. She'd seen water hosing from an outlet in *Snow Goose*'s white hull. Donny could hear a faint whirring that he guessed was some kind of automatic pumping system.

What would she think of them now? On their first morning!

Then June Ribiero came hurrying down the pontoon. She'd taken Xanthe and Maggi to school. She bent forward towards *Snow Goose* and stretched out one arm as if to ask … but words failed her.

"Uh, I'll be off then," said Sandra. "If there's nothing I can do. Donny, there's a bus that you can catch from outside the Shotleygate Stores tomorrow morning. It leaves at about quarter to eight. I've got you a temporary pass."

Donny took the pass and put it in his back pocket. Gallister High School seemed worlds away. "Goodbye," he said.

June stepped neatly on board. "I'll check her bilges. There may be damage below the waterline."

"I'll begin cutting her free." Gold Dragon's good hand was reaching for the wire cutters that she kept in the rigging pouch permanently strapped to her side; her hook was teasing out the first of the shrouds that would need to be severed. "There's a yard here, isn't there?" she asked the man from the office. "That water's coming in fast." She pointed to the continuous arc pouring from *Snow Goose*. "She needs hauling out PDQ. Get them to send a launch."

He nodded and spoke urgently into his hand-held radio.

June reappeared. "She's filling. There's a plank sprung. Maybe two or three. We need to get her out. The automatic pump's not coping."

"Message sent."

Great Aunt Ellen was back to Polly Lee now, Donny thought. She wasn't bothered about him and his mum. You could see that she was a round-the-world sailor who'd got used to coping with things. Like sinking ships were her daily bread.

She'd found an extra-thick, tarry rope, which she and the marina man were fixing under *Snow Goose*. It worked like a sling: one end fastened to the mooring stage, the other to *Strong Winds*. It kept the yacht supported either side, though Donny didn't reckon it would last for long if *Snow Goose* was really going to sink.

The eighty-year-old was moving fast. Now she was cutting away more of the wreckage that snarled the two boats together, then she looped a thin, strong, length of line around the tangle of mast and rigging, so it could be hauled back on board for repair later. She got the marina man to help with that.

"Okay," she said, allocating jobs to a couple of other boat owners who'd come along to stare. "You take the forrard mooring line and you stand by aft. Then I could do with a hand amidships…"

She looked at Skye. Shook her head, irritably. No room for land-lubbers. That was what she'd said.

"Sinbad. Hand-pump and bucket in the port cockpit-locker.

Get aboard with Mrs Ribiero and get pumping."

There was already water spilling over the cabin floor and rising up the sides of the berths when Donny joined June on board the stricken yacht.

"I'm … sorry."

She was putting all her energy into pulling up and down on the manual bilge pump. Her tailored trousers were rolled clumsily up to her knees; there was a sheen of sweat on her dark face.

"I've brought another pump. Where would you like me to go?"

To hell, perhaps? The Ribieros had been so unbelievably kind and now he and his mum had wrecked their beautiful boat. He wanted to cry but he hadn't got time.

"That depends on its hose. A long one? Good. It'll reach right over her side. Take my place while I lash it in position."

No shouting or recrimination – yet – just focused and practical, determined to save *Snow Goose*.

Donny put all his feelings into his pumping. Up and down until his lungs were heaving and his shoulders howled. Up and down. His stomach hurt; his breath was roaring in his ears. If he died doing this he wouldn't care.

They got the water level back below the cabin sole and managed, desperately, to keep it there. Then June went on deck and Polly Lee press-ganged another spectator to replace her at the second pump.

Donny pumped on. It was all he could do. His chafed hands burned.

He heard the launch arrive and then *Strong Winds'* engine started. He felt *Snow Goose* begin to move as she was half towed, half lifted to safety.

He and the other man didn't speak. There wasn't much Donny wanted to say.

Only Skye was out of place when Donny eventually left *Snow Goose* and came back on board his new home. *Strong Winds*' decks were clear, her boat hook had been re-stowed, ropes fastened and coiled, fenders positioned for use.

His mum, however, was lying on the foredeck. Her knees were pulled up to her chin, her arms clasped over the back of her head. Her hair covered her face, her eyes were hidden. They would be shut.

This was Skye's terrified shape. Donny wished that he could curl up next to her. What was Great Aunt Ellen going to say now she had time? How could he face his friends?

He knelt down awkwardly. He guessed from the damp patch on her skirt that she had wet herself. This must be what Joshua had meant when he said 'physical symptoms'. What a start to their new life!

"I've never been good with people." Gold Dragon had come up behind him. She was carrying one of the blankets from the cabin and a large bar of milk chocolate. "Unlike Edith. She'd have produced hot tea for all and sets of dry clothes half an hour back."

She dropped the chocolate abruptly in his lap and let the blanket cover Skye. Then she began making violent shooing gestures. "They're cacking themselves watching. Human shite-hawks! Can't you get your mother below?"

She was right. There were knots of people standing on the pontoons and along the seawall. Some were straightforwardly staring; others chatting and glancing furtively in their direction or happening to pass by, carrying their water cans or refuse bags. Some of them had cameras. One looked really professional.

"I'll try. Honestly she's not always like this."

His great-aunt stopped shooing. She looked old.

"I didn't know how to begin. I could see I was scaring her worse. So I left her. I had to think of the ship. That's my responsibility." That faint Australian lift at the end of her sentences made it sound as if she was asking him for understanding.

"I know," he said. "I really do." A captain's duty was to his ship. That was something he'd accepted years and years before he was born. "I bet your brother Greg never wrecked any of his boats though."

She laughed then. "He most certainly did. I wasn't there but I heard all about it. Now eat some chocolate yourself and do what you can for your mother." And off she went, over *Strong Winds'* side and down onto the pontoon.

The spectators shifted out of her way. The people with cameras mostly hid them behind their backs. Just one person pushed a microphone in her face and asked whether she had anything to say.

She didn't even glance at him. Donny watched her striding resolutely to the boatyard: a small, determined figure, facing another unpleasant task.

It didn't get much more pleasant when Xanthe and Maggi came back from school that afternoon and Joshua from the hospital.

"You're saying that your mum untied everything and started trying to go somewhere – in *Strong Winds*?" Xanthe was trying to understand. She wasn't making much headway.

"Yup," said Donny.

"She untied … like *everything?* Whether she knew what it did or not?"

"Yup."

"She's never been on board a boat … not before last night?" said Maggi.

"Nope."

The sisters fell silent, frowning furiously with the effort of not being angry. They were both skilled sailors. They couldn't imagine why anyone would so randomly unfasten a deck's worth of ropes. They'd looked without speaking at their own lovely yacht, high out of the water, with two planks sprung from her stern and the mizzenmast snapped jaggedly away at the base.

Donny looked at his feet to avoid looking at his friends. Their mother had gone home without speaking to him and he'd thought he was going to puke when he'd stood there watching their father's clever fingers feeling round the ugly slit where the planks had burst away.

"It is possible that there was already a weakness. Perhaps the fastenings should have been replaced before now."

"There was nothing wrong with her mizzenmast." Xanthe couldn't stop herself.

"Accidents happen, Xanthe, you know that. Sometimes we can learn from them and sometimes we can only accept."

The accepting bit wasn't going so well.

Xanthe and Maggi had known that Donny's mum was different. They didn't have any problem with the idea of disability or mental illness. It was the reality that was hard to deal with.

"Is this what she's like?" asked Xanthe. "Your mum. Twenty-four seven?"

"No! No way. Not hardly ever. She's … beautiful. Okay, so she very occasionally gets panic attacks. Who wouldn't?"

"Do you think she was trying to escape?" asked Maggi, frowning harder. "Take *Strong Winds* and just go? I mean, she's been in … a mental ward. If that was me, I might …"

"Maybe," said Donny. "No, I don't know what started her off. I'll try and ask her when she's better. Probably she'd woken up and I wasn't there and she didn't know where I was … and then she saw all those ropes tying things down. Like she'd been tied down. So she started setting some of them free. Your dad said I shouldn't leave her. It's totally my fault."

"You only went to have a pee. You weren't exactly sightseeing."

"I did notice she moved when I was leaving. I could have found a bucket. Then I was slow getting out. There was some bloke in a muddle with the numbers. I couldn't explain to him."

"Donny-man, I know she's your mum but you're gonna have to stop beating yourself up. It was that loose mainsail that really caused the damage. And the wind, catching it."

He wished they'd chuck him into a piranha tank.

"You weren't there, Xanth, you didn't see. I want you to take *Lively Lady* back before I wreck her too."

Xanthe shook her head. She looked cross and tired and his good friend all at once. "We're Allies, right? We want you to have the dinghy. You can't know what's going to happen next."

"Anyway," Maggi added, "the man from the office told Dad you'd acted like you were twice your age. Dad's a doctor, remember; he understands about sick people. Him and Mum, they're kinda reliable …"

"Yeah," agreed Xanthe. "Mum can be stressy but she gets over it. Look, Donny-man, we need to get home and do stuff. You know – homework and music practice and supper. Go easy on yourself. Okay?"

As he watched his friends go loping off towards their father's car, Donny wondered, for a moment, what it would feel like to have parents who were 'kinda reliable'?

Skye was sitting in a sleeping bag when Donny returned to *Strong Winds*. Her wet skirt was swirling around the marina laundrette and she hadn't anything else to wear.

"A crooked tongue told me you were gone. I sought to follow."

She must have been having a bad dream.

"It's okay, Mum. We're going to be okay. Be a family again."

"We'll get your camper-van back," said Great Aunt Ellen. "Then you can decide what you're bringing on board." She didn't understand signing. "Your foster-carer dropped by with your school clothes, Sinbad. I told him today wouldn't be such a good day for those other children to visit." She gave a wrinkly grin. "He wasn't shedding any tears. Said he'd have to fit them all with safety harnesses first. Name's Gerald. Bit of a dry bob is he?"

"Um … probably."

He'd no idea what a dry bob was but it seemed unlikely that Gerald, the health and safety fanatic, and Gold Dragon, the nautical adventurer, would ever view the world through the same pair of binoculars.

He remembered Gerald's bleachy clean kitchen at Erewhon Parva vicarage. Then he looked at *Strong Winds'* glowing varnish work, her oil lamps, books, the gleaming barometer and alluring compass.

If only she'd allow them to stay. If only they didn't mess up again.

He'd like to have seen the others – Luke and Liam and baby Vicky – and he *had* to see Anna. He'd got his mother back: she needed to find hers.

His great-aunt was looking at him. Her eyes were bright and hard. He'd better offer to do something helpful. Didn't know what. Peel potatoes or something? Wash up?

"You look land-sick, Sinbad. Go for a sail, why don't you? I'll stand the watch with Nimblefingers. We'll eat later. If we can't wait, we'll probably save you some. Or we might not. Then you'll have to make do with weevils and hard tack."

"Could I really? Go for a sail?"

Donny knew that Gold Dragon would be proud and fierce and not a bit like Granny Edith. He was learning that she was also trustworthy and kind. So you could see that they were sisters.

He explained to Skye what he wanted to do and took her on deck, still wrapped in her sleeping bag, to show her *Lively Lady*. He absolutely promised he wouldn't be away for long. She even sort of smiled when he told her that, in this new place, her name was Nimblefingers.

Then he scrambled into the dinghy and rowed out through the lock behind a small motorboat setting off for an evening's fishing. The cross-harbour ferry was tying up for the night. The river lay before him, wide and quiet.

He set his sails and headed for the old red and white schooner, the one they'd nick-named the *Hispaniola*.

When he and the Allies hadn't met Great Aunt Ellen, they had used one of the schooner's three tall masts to run up a warning message for her, in flags. They wanted to put her on her guard against Inspector Jake Flint, the gross policeman, and his devious accomplice, Denise 'Toxic' Tune. The gruesome twosome had been out to get Gold Dragon – Donny didn't know why.

The flags had been Anna's idea: a red and gold one for China because that was where Great Aunt Ellen had been living and a red and white quartered 'U' flag. In the international code of the sea that meant 'you are standing into danger'. Best of all was a double-headed dragon ramping across a black silk background. She'd found it on the Internet when she'd googled *Strong Winds*. It even had the right number of toes.

The evening breeze was warm and steady. *Lively Lady* was pulling forward and heeling slightly. She tempted him to hold his course – across the harbour and out to sea. When Flint had come at him – was it still only yesterday? – Gold Dragon had stopped his powerboat as neatly as if she'd been lassooing a galloping bullock.

He could see that the flags weren't flying any more. The *Hispaniola*'s signal halliards had been dirty grey with age. They must have frayed. He ought to climb aboard and collect them. Otherwise it was like forgetting about your balloons when the party day was gone. And anyway, he'd promised Skye …

The signal halliards hadn't frayed: they'd been cut.

Someone had severed the cod-line and the entire hoist had tumbled down. Two of the flags – the stars of China, and the 'U' flag that spelled danger – were lying neatly on the deck. A piece of planking had been placed over them. It had a message in fresh black paint:

SHIP PRIVAT.
KEEP OFF.
GO HOME LÓNG.

The third flag – Anna's resplendent dragon on its rippling black background – had been slashed into tatters. Not torn or cut but ripped, again and again, with an extremely sharp knife.

Donny stood still a few moments. Shocked. Then he bent down and began to pick up the small pile of jagged strips that had been blowing out so bravely only twenty-four hours before. There was no fragment left more than a centimetre wide. No-one, apart from him and his Allies could have identified these remains as Great Aunt Ellen's 'house' flag.

Xanthe and Maggi had told him that the dragon flag had been copied from a famous pirate called Miss Lee. They assumed it was a sort of tribute.

He hadn't asked Great Aunt Ellen yet if that was right. Hadn't had time. Only met her yesterday. Didn't properly know anything about her. She was his family. He felt that she was kind. But why copy a flag from a pirate?

And what did pirates do anyway? In real life and the twenty-first century?

As he began, reluctantly, to pick up the bits of flag, Donny struggled not to blame his granny (Edith, not that cheat Eirene) for not telling him more about her youngest sister. He knew that Edith and Ellen had quarrelled over baby Skye. Edith had won: Ellen had left.

All those people cheering when *Strong Winds* arrived at the lock gates last night – they'd known about her. Perhaps the person who'd done this was jealous? People who were famous did have to deal with freaks sometimes. Or maybe this nutter simply didn't like dragons?

Donny shivered and his hands felt clammy.

Be honest. He was scared.

GO HOME LÓNG

He didn't totally understand the words but he definitely got the message.

Donny didn't want to think what a knife like that would do to human skin.

CHAPTER THREE

Who's There?

Wednesday 27 September

"You're telling me it's not over? You're saying that there's still someone out there who's trying to get at you or your great-aunt?"

"At her … I'm sure. There must be something I don't know that's in her past. And as I don't know anything …"

He'd been waiting all morning to get Anna's brain focussed on his problems. She was in Year Nine, the same as him, but Gallister High was a big school and their timetables were completely different. She and Maggi were in most of the same top sets and Xanthe was two years above. Donny was sort of middling academically and he hadn't been there very long.

He hadn't seen either of the sisters today. He didn't mind too much. Obviously he still felt terrible about *Snow Goose* but he didn't want to talk about her any more. He wanted to talk to Anna about the *Hispaniola* and the flags.

At lunchtime he grabbed his chance: used his plastic meal card to buy a sandwich and a drink from one of the vending machines and headed upstairs to the library. Anna was in her usual corner, skipping food to get maximum time on the Internet – or as much of it as the school's system would allow her to access. She didn't look entirely pleased to be interrupted but Donny wasn't taking any notice. He needed her to help him understand what had happened.

"It was her flag that they attacked. She copied it from some

Chinese pirate – you know that, it was you who designed it. And if it is me they're getting at then it works the same. Threaten someone I care about, it scares me off, doesn't it?"

"*Do* you care?" Anna hadn't yet bothered to look away from her screen.

"Of course I do! She's my family."

"Yes … but you didn't even know she existed until your granny died. And you've only actually been living with her for two days. Plus she looked to me like someone who was pretty capable of taking care of herself."

How to put this? Donny floundered on. "Gold Dragon's really tough and all that. She was excellent when we thought *Snow Goose* was going down. I wish you'd seen her … except, of course I don't wish that, because I wish the whole thing never happened. But it's not totally one way. She doesn't have a clue how to talk to Mum for a start and I can't think how she's going to learn. You really need two hands to sign. Not one and a hook."

Anna carried on working.

"She's come here because of us and so far all we've done is give her grief. So I sort of feel responsible. It might be to do with what happened before – you know, when they were children and all going off sailing and that. Great Uncle Greg and Granny were like the grown-ups and she was the baby. They were always leaving her behind."

"I don't get all that playing at *Swallows and Amazons* stuff. Or your weird dreams. The point is what happened on that boat yesterday, not what was in some book a couple of lifetimes ago." She looked at her screen again and scrolled impatiently through a couple more pages. "Are you saying that you haven't even told her what happened to her flag? Your great-aunt is a round-the-world sailor, for godssake – not some ship's baby!"

"I couldn't even decide whether to take the scraps away. If I did, it would show that I'd been there again. If I didn't … well, then I realised I didn't want to leave them behind. The *Hispaniola* didn't feel like a safe place any more."

"So? You didn't exactly make it safer by taking a few bits of flag away."

"I suppose not."

His explanation wasn't going very well. Maybe it wasn't a very good one. Donny couldn't always understand the way that boats made him feel. Yesterday the *Hispaniola* had felt sad and wrong and cruel. He wasn't sure he'd reacted all that sensibly.

After he'd found the tattered flag and read the KEEP OFF notice, he'd forced himself to walk all the way round her deck. He'd slept there once but it had been dark and he'd been exhausted. He hadn't looked at it, not properly.

The deck was metal, riveted together, he guessed, and with ridges to stop you slipping over maybe – if you were running to action stations in your regulation rubber-soled shoes, crouched beneath the gunwales and with the decks awash.

Why did she make him think like this?

It must be the paint. From the outside the *Hispaniola* was a dull crimson and white. The red was almost the same colour as the redundant light vessels scattered around the harbour. Her upper works were white too, the bits that people passing by would see. She was eye-catching, if a bit eccentric.

But the deck paint told a different story. It was a very particular shade of grey, blue-grey, battleship grey – the colour his great-uncles Greg and Ned would have lived with all the years they served in the Royal Navy. Before they had both died. It looked as though the person who had re-painted the outside of the schooner to look like something out of a fantasy film hadn't bothered with the decks – or had been working from an alternative script.

The more he looked, the more puzzling the *Hispaniola* felt. Everything was metal. A bit rusted in places, where the rivets had wept, but tough as armour. Almost war-like. Except that you surely couldn't go into battle with those three telegraph-pole-style masts? He couldn't even see how the sails were meant to work.

Then Donny had thought he heard … fluttering?

Trapped wings, frantic, beating against cage bars. Prisoners from far away, terrified and desperate in the cold dark.

But when he'd stopped and looked around there was nothing.

Not even a few late swallows gathering along the crosstrees to begin their long flight south. You could think of birds like spirits. He and Granny and Skye had always especially looked out for swallows but this year the birds had gone without him noticing them at all.

He tried peering inside the *Hispaniola* through her deck-lights and cabin portholes. But all the glass had been painted over with thick black paint, including the wheelhouse. That didn't seem quite normal, even for a boat that wasn't being used any more. There were padlocks on the forehatch and the cabin door, metal bars as well. More notices in black paint. They looked fresh.

TRESPERCUTERS WILL BE PROSACUTED
TRESPARSERS WILL BE PROSERCUTERS

Donny began to ask himself why all this was necessary? Okay, so he'd kipped on board two nights ago and here he was again. But he was only calling to collect his flags: he hadn't been planning to move in. All these padlocks and notices – talk about overkill!

Maybe it was the dodgy spelling, maybe it was his feeling that this was all way over the top, maybe he'd simply run out of energy for being scared. Whatever reason, Donny had stopped being frightened and turned awkward.

He didn't try explaining to Anna why he'd done what he did next.

He went back to the base of the mainmast, where the flags had fallen, and picked up the KEEP OFF plank. He turned it over and pulled Xanthe's rigging knife out of his jeans pocket. She'd sort of said he could keep it and it had a marlinspike that he could use to scratch a message of his own.

"Croeso," he wrote. "Wilkommen, bienvenue, fáilte, ola!" – as many words of greeting as he could remember from the multicultural welcome poster that had been on the doors of his primary school in Leeds. He couldn't properly remember the Urdu or the Arabic but he was sure he'd got the Chinese welcome right. He liked character writing so he made it his main feature: spent extra time gouging out the graceful lines and curves with the rigging knife's flat blade.

Then he had spread out the red and gold national flag like a mat in front of the main cabin door and put the plank on top of it – *his* side up.

He stepped back and looked at his installation. Okay, it definitely wasn't as funny as when Maggi had painted jaws on Flint's shark-boat but it was the best he could do for now. Whoever'd cut the signal halliards, put all these padlocks on the doors and daubed the threatening notices needed to lighten up a bit. Get more fun out of life. Make a few friends.

Then he'd picked up the 'U' flag and the shredded gold dragon and scrambled down into *Lively Lady*. Shoved the flags into his bosun's bag, hoisted the dinghy's jib and let the flood tide and the evening breeze waft him easily back to the lock. The gates were standing open and the man in the office waved at him as he rowed through. The marina was beginning to feel positively home-like.

Or it would have done, if he hadn't happened to glimpse *Snow Goose* high out of the water like a tall, white, wounded bird.

"Has Gold Dragon said where you're all going to live?" asked Anna, bringing him back to the present with a jolt.

He knew that the only reason she wanted to know about Great Aunt Ellen's plans was because she needed somewhere she could come and use her computer. Even before he'd met her she'd been searching missing persons' websites and asking careful questions hoping to find some information about her mother. She'd assembled her own computer in school DT club, but at the moment she couldn't use it. Her carers, Gerald and Rev. Wendy, had found it and there'd been a big, totally unnecessary, row. They still didn't know that she'd been using it to surf the internet.

Anna had asked Mr McMullen, the DT teacher, to store her computer in his department. She was terrified of anyone checking its memory and discovering which sites she'd been visiting. The machine was incredibly slow and she'd only used dial-up but "Some of the best sites are a bit 18-plussy," she'd told Donny. "I couldn't encrypt. Didn't have the memory. If someone like Flint or Toxic found out where I'd been searching … "

"Well, has she?" Anna asked again. "Is she going to rent somewhere? Or can she buy?" She just about managed to look at him this time. Then she pressed 'save' and wrote something on her scribble pad.

Donny glanced over. Another web address. Gold Dragon hadn't said anything about houses. But he hadn't asked her. To be honest he hadn't even thought about it.

What to say?

"Maybe she thinks she ought to wait until after the SS meeting. I'm still officially in Wendy and Gerald's care, remember, and they only got Mum out of that hospital by pretending she'd be living hygienically at the vicarage as well as me."

Anna smiled. (First time that lunch-break.) "It was such a great moment! When Rev. Wendy told us that she'd told the SS that humungous lie."

"You could have sunk me in a baling pan, as Xanth might say I'm feeling really bad about the Ribieros. Did … did Xanth or Maggi say anything on the bus this morning? About … *Snow Goose*?"

Anna stared back at her screen again. Pressed her lips together as if she was trying to keep something trapped inside. "Not really. They told me what had happened. Um, how is your mum?" It sounded like a polite enquiry. Not as if she cared.

"Dunno. Bit obsessive-compulsive. She keeps on trying to

undo things. I only just stopped her pushing us off again this morning. I think Maggi was right. She's sort of fixated on escape. She wants us all to leave. Says we're surrounded by snatchers and crooked tongues."

"Do you think she should have stayed in the hospital?"

"Course not! It's the hospital that's made her like this. All I need to figure out is how to help her stop. She could get us into so much trouble. Especially if she starts casting off anyone else's boat. Gold Dragon's going to have to watch her all day while I'm here. There are some really expensive yachts in that marina, you know."

"Boats, boats, boats!" said Anna, standing up suddenly. "That's all any of you ever talk about. Don't you realise that I've used practically the whole of this lunch-break listening to you talk about you and your family and *boats*? This is the only chance all day I have to get on the Internet and you've … stolen it!" There were red splodges on her cheeks and the words came bursting out. "I *wasn't* talking about boats when we were on the bus this morning – or I was trying not to! I was asking Maggi if I could maybe go round hers this weekend and use their computer. I wouldn't have gone on any of the dodgy sites. But no, they're going sailing all weekend. Sailing! There's some dinghy racing championship and that's going to take them all their time. Both days! Even though Xanthe's got GCSE coursework." Her fingers were shaking as she logged herself off. "I hate boats! I hate sailing! I need to get *my* mother back. Just as much as you needed to get yours. More, in fact. There's the kids as well as me. Luke and Liam and Vicky – remember? You might *try* to give them a thought, if you've any water-free space in your head. Which I doubt. I know

I was getting closer. I know I was. So what if Flint ripped up that silly dragon flag? I wish I'd never wasted my time making it."

The librarian had got up from her desk and was coming over to tell them to be quiet but Anna had closed down and was walking to the bag-park.

Donny hurried after her. Her head was turned away from him and she missed the first time she tried to swipe her card through the monitoring system.

He guessed she might cry but he didn't care. As soon as they reached the corridor he grabbed her arm and made her stop. "What do you mean, getting closer? Have you made contact with your mum?"

She took a deep breath, dashed a fist across her eyes and seemed to will herself to calm down. "No. I haven't." Every word was crisp and vehement. "I would have told you that. Even when you were going on and on about your bloody sailing. But I've discovered there's someone else who's looking for her too."

"How? Who?"

"I don't know. I met him in one of the places that I shouldn't visit. I'm sure he's a man and I think he's seriously old. He was asking for 'Lottie' – that's her real name! So I have to find out more about him, without him finding out anything at all about me. It's not particularly easy. Especially when I only have forty minutes a day in a firewalled secondary school library. And then you come along and waste it talking about BOATS!"

CHAPTER FOUR

Just Formalities

Friday 29 September, morning

Anna certainly knew how to get her point across. After she'd finished chewing him up in the corridor that day, she'd spat him out with an ultimatum:

"If you get me un-supervised, un-filtered Internet access, I'll tell you about this man – if there's anything to tell. I might even tell you a bit about my mum. Until then it'd be a waste of my time. And you'd be another person who might leak."

She hadn't spoken to him since.

Donny was thinking about Anna as he sat in the back of Sandra's car being driven to the SS meeting. It was in Colchester, maybe about forty minutes from Shotley. Great Aunt Ellen was in the front and Sandra was doing her kindly best to make the journey interesting for someone who hadn't been in England for the last fifty years. Skye was in the back with Donny. She couldn't hear and he wasn't listening.

He still hadn't any idea where Gold Dragon was planning for them to live and nothing she'd said had given him any clues. Until then he didn't see what he could do to help. They didn't have Internet on *Strong Winds*. If nothing was said in the meeting about houses, then he'd have to ask straight out on the journey back.

Sandra kept insisting that this meeting was purely a formality.

She told him that he didn't have to come but Donny wasn't taking any chances. If this was such a formality why did anyone have to go? Why were they bothering to have a meeting at all? There must be other things they could be doing.

His tutor, Mr McMullen, had said that he should insist on his right to be present at meetings but it wasn't always that easy. Anna had been in the system longer. She knew that they didn't even invite you if they thought you had an 'attitude problem' or their decisions might 'upset' you. Then it was Professionals only.

Statutory Services Care Assessment Meetings, Anna had said they were called. SSCAMs – scams! They'd had a bit of a laugh checking out the different acronyms: Statutory Services Care Review and Assessment for Professionals – SSCRAP or without the SS it just spelled CRAP. He couldn't remember what this one was called. There was Review in it somewhere, he thought.

He'd got to find some way of fixing up their friendship again. Okay so he had an attitude problem but, well, so did she.

Donny squeezed his mother's hand. If anyone should have been allowed to stay behind it should have been her. But they couldn't have left her on *Strong Winds* on her own and Sandra had said that the whole point of the meeting was to recognise officially that Donny's situation had changed: his great-aunt had arrived, his mother was out of hospital. He wasn't on his own any more so he could come off the SS register. That would be a result!

This looked like a town. Time he tuned back into Sandra.

"There'll be a chairperson who'll explain everything and make sure you're comfortable with the procedures. They'll try to make everything as informal as possible. I'm not entirely sure who else will be there. Your tutor said he'd be teaching so he didn't want to come unless it was urgent. I told him it was okay because we're just signing you off. Mr Ribiero had a theatre list that he couldn't reschedule but Mrs Ribiero said she'd be attending as your supporter."

"Maybe Flint won't bother coming either," thought Donny, with a sudden surge of optimism.

But the first people they saw as they arrived at the big, slab-sided SS building were the Gruesome Twosome, Flint and Toxic. It wasn't surprising that they enjoyed each other's company. He was a massive bully: she was twisted and clever and liked watching children get hurt. Donny and Anna were certain that they had something sinister going on behind their official disguises. Something that allowed him to own his million pound shark-boat stuffed with state-of-the-art equipment and her to indulge her taste for designer outfits and multiple pairs of seriously expensive shoes.

What was worrying was that the man walking in between them turned out to be the Committee Chairperson. They were coming out of the 'No Admittance to the Public' area and all three were smiling broadly as if they'd had a jolly good chat and were absolutely the best of friends.

Donny's heart sank.

Then Great Aunt Ellen set off the metal-detector alarm.

Sandra had led them to the reception desk where some woman was distributing visitor badges from behind floor-to-ceiling toughened glass. As soon as Gold Dragon stepped forward, a siren sounded and red lights began to flash.

Everyone turned to stare at her. Flint took several giant strides forward and positioned himself dramatically between the octogenarian and the receptionist – legs apart and arms wide – as if to shield the latter from violent attack.

Great Aunt Ellen looked puzzled for a moment. Then she half smiled and raised her hook. "Is this the problem?"

"No, madam," Flint lunged towards her. "This is."

Gold Dragon was wearing her shore-going togs: navy-blue jacket and trousers with a politely formal cream silk shirt. She'd even twisted her long straight plait into a bun. Unfortunately she'd forgotten to leave off her sailor's leather pouch, with a set of tools for emergency repairs. He'd watched her using them that day on *Snow Goose*.

Flint pulled out her broad-bladed knife, leapt back and held it up for all to see.

Denise Tune gasped in well-faked shock. A *knaife*!

"Oh, you don't have to worry about that," Great Aunt Ellen explained. "It's old. The whole set's old. I wear it all the time. Sleep with it sometimes. I'd have left it on board if I'd thought." She unbuckled the belt and pouch and stepped around Flint towards the sealed-off desk. "Why don't you take care of my tools while we're here?" she asked the receptionist. "I didn't realise you people were so jumpy. I'm a sailor, not an international terrorist, you know!"

If she was trying to help everyone relax it didn't work.

The siren and the flashing light were switched off. Then a man in security guard's uniform came unsmilingly out from behind the reception area with a clear plastic bag. He took the equipment without a word and placed it in the bag as if ready to be used in evidence.

Flint did not hand over the knife. Instead he reached into his black briefcase and extracted a padded zip-lock into which he sealed it with exaggerated care. Then he brought out a triplicate pad, wrote Confiscation of Offensive Weapon, filled in the date and place and passed it to Great Aunt Ellen for signature.

"This item will be available for reclaim at your local police station after not less than three working days, to allow for processing," Flint intoned. "It may be returned to you on presentation of a certificate of occupational need signed by your employer or other suitably qualified professional person."

Gold Dragon stared at him as if he were a Wellington boot dragged out on the end of a salmon line. Then she extended her hook and scratched a mark that crumpled and tore the top leaves of Flint's pad.

"Sorry," she said, unconvincingly. "I've never quite managed to get the hang of writing no-handed."

The fat policemen flushed crimson around his stubbly jowls but Donny noticed the brief and satisfied nod that he directed at Toxic Tune over the head of the Chairperson. He didn't like the look of it.

Skye was also watching this strange scene. "These are crooked tongues," she signed. Then she put her arm around Donny's shoulders to give him a quick hug. It was strange. They'd only been separated for a few weeks but her arm seemed to reach him at a slightly different angle. He'd grown taller since he'd been down here.

This was good but kind of awkward. Great Aunt Ellen hadn't

been able to persuade the people at the car pound to let them take the camper-van away and get all their stuff out. Apparently there were still problems about the insurance and the MOT and finding Skye's driving licence. Plus a fine and something called an impoundment fee. So Sandra had gone there for them and picked up a couple of bags of clothes. That morning Donny had climbed grumpily into his old best jeans – only to find that they were now half way up his ankles and decidedly tight around the waistband. Considering how many meals he'd missed recently, that didn't seem fair.

He felt even more irritated when Sandra said that the SS would be wanting him to have another height and weight check before they signed him off. He didn't see why they should take any credit for him having a growth spurt over the time he'd been on their register.

Skye had also got fresh clothes from the van and Donny had persuaded her to wear a plain dark shawl over her long dress instead of one of Granny's man-size home-knitted sweaters. She'd washed her hair and allowed Donny to braid it but she hadn't wanted him to twist in any of the coloured ribbons that she'd used to love.

Donny could feel his mum trembling slightly as she held him close. This seemed to go on all the time now. She was taking about six pills a day because the new doctor said it would be dangerous to come off medication all at once. They were anti-depressants but the doctor kept calling them her 'happy pills'. Donny thought he was a complete idiot.

After Flint had shut the knife into his case, and done something ostentatiously complex with the combination locks, Toxic glared at the Chairperson. He cleared his throat and looked a bit shifty; then said that everyone needed to come straight to Room M1. He said there were some matters of procedure he needed to run past them.

Run straight over them more like. Leaving Donny, Skye and Gold Dragon spluttering and splintered in his wake.

Room M1 was a large room with a huge table. They found themselves at one end of it, sitting opposite the line of the Professionals like prisoners in the dock. Sandra changed places to be near them. Someone, who she introduced as the Gallister High School nurse, moved with her. The rest stayed solidly where they were. Flint and Toxic plonked themselves either side of the Chairperson as if they were his minders.

There was a secretary taking notes and a small Asian-looking man in a suit and two other women who were not introduced and who never spoke. Their function seemed to be to nod at everything the Chairperson said and to glare disapprovingly at the misfits opposite. There was no Mr McMullen, no June Ribiero, no Rev. Wendy even.

First the Chairperson thanked everyone for coming – his cheesy grin flashed from side to side at Flint and Toxic and the support team and somehow fizzled out when it reached Skye, Donny and Great Aunt Ellen. Then he got his mouth full of words and announced that this inter-agency meeting had originally been convened to enable the Statutory Services to be discharged of the responsibility of accommodating John Walker, aged thirteen, a young person discovered homeless.

'Originally convened?' thought Donny. What does he mean by 'originally'?

The Chairperson gave Donny a patronising smile to show what a nice kinda guy he was. "Hi John, I'm Tony, by the way. I'm called a Service Manager but you don't need to worry about that. Good to meet you, John."

"Thanks. Actually I'm called Donny, not John. I'm fourteen now not thirteen and I wouldn't have been homeless if the police hadn't grabbed my mum and taken our van away."

"Happy birthday to you then … But you know, er, Donny, in this part of the world we think our young people should be looking to live in something, you know, a bit better than a van. We're signed up to delivering a society where Every Child can have high material expectations."

Tony tried another grin but it was Denise Tune's lip-sticked leer that bothered Donny. Maybe he'd best shut up.

Tony carried on. "As most of you know there was a certain amount of orchestrated media attention when Miss Walker – hello Miss Walker!" He gave Gold Dragon a flirtatious little wave.

(Don't wait for her to wave back because she isn't going to, thought Donny.)

"When Miss Walker arrived in our country publicly announcing that she was going to take charge of the boy." Tony's voice grew stern. "Miss Walker has, I understand, enjoyed a certain measure of celebrity in the past and perhaps she assumed that this would be sufficient to smooth her through the safeguards of our Caring System … "

"I didn't give it a thought. Your system, I mean. I'm Donny's great-aunt. My sister died so I came to take her place. They're my family: where's your problem?" She gave her sudden, rippled smile to Skye and Donny. "Besides, I've seen a bit of weather now.

I reckoned it was about time I found someone to raft up with."

It was obvious to Donny that she was trying not to sound as if she was taking them out of duty, but she'd said the wrong thing as far as Tony was concerned. His cheesiness turned positively rancid.

"Ah, that delicate matter of a lady's age … So you're intending to take up residence here? Make use of our Health Service, perhaps? But Miss Walker – or may I call you Ellen? – I don't believe you hold a current British passport?"

"No, no and no! From what I've seen of your health service so far I wouldn't touch it with a full-length quant." She glanced at Donny to make sure he was signing for Skye. "No, I'm not sure exactly where we're going to fetch up. I think my niece needs to take some time to get to know me first. And no, I don't have a British passport. Handed it back years ago. I'm an Australian citizen. My mother was Australian … though she raised five children here." She paused for a moment, then she fixed Tony hard with her bright blue eyes. "One final negative – I certainly do not give permission for you to call me Ellen!"

"Thanks for the family history, Miss Walker," Tony wasn't trying to sound nice any more. "Though I'm afraid it's irrelevant. My point is that we have Procedures for Inter-country Adoption and we can't simply set those aside when someone arrives at our shores with the TV cameras running. You'll need to return to Australia and make your initial application there. And, you know, Miss Walker, I fear you'll find that your age is against you. In our country we ask that our prospective parents should not have reached retirement age before the young person ceases full-time education. It can be a tiring business raising a youngster."

Gold Dragon looked surprised. "Eh? You can't have been listening, Mr Chairman. I'm not planning to adopt Donny. He has a mother. She's here. Look."

"Ah, yes." There were no fake grins for Skye. "Ms Skye Walker … who can give the support agencies no information about the father of her child. Ms Skye Walker … who has herself required intensive support from the day she was born and whose most recent release from hospital was not conducted precisely according to the provisions of the Mental Health Act. You know, Miss Walker, it should have been you who signed those discharge forms. Not some misguided foster-carer."

So Rev. Wendy was in trouble. Maybe that was why she wasn't here?

Gold Dragon shrugged. "I wasn't asked to sign any forms. I'd have gone over as soon as I found where she was. I guess I'd have managed to use my good hand if I were signing for my niece."

There wasn't a cat's-paw of amusement.

Tony carried on as if he was a prosecuting lawyer on prime-time TV. "But Miss Walker, events that next day surely confirm that your niece would have been better staying where she was? In Hospital where she was being Professionally treated and was prevented from endangering herself, or the public, or other people's property."

Donny saw that there were newspapers at Tony's end of the long table. A local evening paper with photos of the wrecked *Snow Goose* and Great Aunt Ellen looking old and inadequate. That must have been when she was saying that she wasn't as quick as Edith when it came to dishing out dry clothes. There weren't any photos of him but there were plenty of Skye. Not

Skye looking terrified and panicking but Skye looking deranged and … dangerous.

The secretary handed them out like they were class worksheets.

Toxic tutted. Flint hrrmphed. Tony looked smug.

Gold Dragon got angry. "Listen here, hobo, I don't see you as a marine insurance assessor, I don't see you as a doctor. I'm having some trouble even seeing you as a human being. You say you have a responsibility for accommodating Donny? Good. Now get this into your log book: I intend to share my home with my family for as long as they want to share it with me. Sleep easy, Mr Chairman, your problem's solved."

"Not quaite … " Toxic cut in as if she'd been waiting for this moment. "Denise Tune, Educational Welfare in a Multi-Agency Context, Every Child Matters, Lead Worker."

Donny's hands froze. He couldn't sign that lot to Skye. Couldn't even make jokes from it. He'd forgotten how sick Toxic's sugar-coated voice made him feel.

"Aim tasked with assessment of Appropriateness and Risk Factors. Tell me, Miss Walker, where exactly are you living?"

"On board my boat, *Strong Winds.*"

"And is … *Strong Wainds* … a British boat?

"No, she was built in … Southern China and flies the Australian flag."

Did Great Aunt Ellen hesitate? Maybe she was surprised to find someone like Toxic taking an interest in her boat.

The small man raised a finger as if he had a question to ask. Toxic tipped her head to one side. Her caring side.

"You've had quaite a long day, Miss Walker. Research suggests that, in the older person, even maild fatigue may exert a negative influence on the ability to retrieve fact. Especially in a context of personal disorientation. Ai don't expect you're able to recall more preçaisely where your vessel originated?"

"I'm not ga-ga yet, Ms … er. *Strong Winds* was built in Bias Bay."

That meant something to the small man. Looking at him, he was probably Chinese so maybe this Bias Bay was his hometown.

Toxic carried on working through her phoney check-list.

"Has *Strong Winds* a permanent postal address?"

"Yes. When we're in Shanghai."

"Ai see … And what steps have you taken towards purchasing some suitable Property in our area?"

"Property? You mean … a house?"

Toxic tilted her head the other way. She looked pitying this time.

"Yes, Miss Walker, a house. A place where people live. Normal people, that is. Not *un*-invited travellers causing a public nuisance in their *un*-insured vains. Or bringing in their Chainese junks, which run amok and wreak devastation to an English Yacht."

She gestured towards her own copy of the newspaper. Picked it up in her long-taloned fingers, smailed without cracking her make-up.

Great Aunt Ellen ignored the taunts. She was still playing it straight: still trying to explain her perfectly reasonable intentions to these strangely hostile people. Donny remembered how he had felt when he first hit the System. He felt sorry for her. But he wanted her to give an answer to this question – even more than Toxic did.

"I haven't any plans at all to buy a house. I've not owned a house in my entire life. I'm a sailor. But I'm ready to drop anchor for a while, see how we rub along. If Donny's happy with this school he's at, I thought maybe we might make Harwich our home port."

"Ai see," Toxic repeated. "Ai see that you have no intention of buying a Property. You intend to remain an itinerant traipsing around in your Chainese boat … sorry, your Chainese *junk*. And you're seriously proposing this *junk* as suitable accommodation for a family! Has it been … quarantined?"

Gold Dragon's eyes grew hard. Her voice was steely. "Doesn't need it. Paperwork sorted in Rotterdam. EU country. *Strong Winds* is my *home*, Ms … er. The place where I've lived the last fifty years. She's sound and she's seaworthy. She'll last my niece and great-nephew another half century if they find they like the life."

Of course, thought Donny. Of course Gold Dragon hadn't been planning to buy a house! How could he have thought it? The moment he seriously tried imagining her piratical figure walking sedately up a garden path to go ping-pong on a front-door bell, he knew he'd been living in Neverland.

He didn't mind – a home on board *Strong Winds* sounded great to him. Could be a bit tricky till Skye learned the ropes – at least how not to *un*tie them all of the time. But Internet access, telephone lines … how was he going to break this to Anna? He'd promised to help her in her quest: Anna never forgot promises.

"John may consider your old junk an improvement on his mother's van," Toxic sneered. "But I doubt anyone else will share his view."

"Personally I think living on a boat sounds rather romantic," said Sandra.

Tony turned on her like a spitting cobra. "As your manager, Sandra, I have to remind you that this is a Professionals' meeting. We don't speak *personally* here."

Sandra shut up.

Tony carried on. He was looking mainly at his secretary who was taking the minutes. "Clearly we need to Professionally assess whether the proposed accommodation meets our minimum standards criteria. Separate bathroom facilities, his own bedroom, study and recreation areas – the things we caring parents Want for our children. But, you know, what we all have to think about first is the Risk to John."

"Risk, what risk? *Strong Winds* is in Shotley marina, not the South Atlantic!"

"The risk, Miss Walker, of Significant Harm. I do not believe that your niece is a fit person to be entrusted with parental responsibility for this troubled young person. You have ruled yourself out as a potential adopter and have failed to put forward any credible alternative. I therefore declare this Statutory Services Care Review & Assessment Meeting closed."

Donny was too shocked to work it out and Tony carried right on. "I am convening an immediate Child Protection Conference and I move that John be accommodated in one of our secure Units. As previously arranged."

One of the silent women removed the cling-film from a plate of home-baked cookies and placed it before Tony like a votive offering: the other draped a napkin over her arm and fetched the cafetière. Then she looked around the table and selected seven bone china cups.

Donny did a count-up: none for him and Skye and Great Aunt Ellen, obviously. None for Sandra and the school nurse either, he guessed.

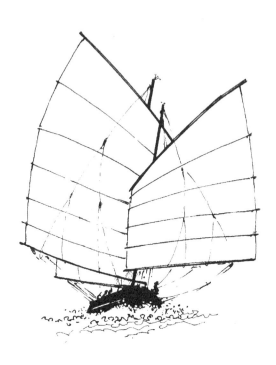

CHAPTER FIVE

S.S.C.R.A.M.

Friday 29 September, afternoon

Tony's Conference didn't last long. It was almost funny when Donny looked back. Except it wasn't funny in the least. It was about as hilarious as running your dinghy onto a submerged rock on the first day of a holiday.

Tony started out by reminding them all that the rules for the Conference allowed any participant who felt intimidated by anyone else in the room to ask for that person to be removed.

Gold Dragon had got herself together now. "That's okay, Bunter," she said to Flint. "You're not bothering us. But you can take yourself off if you like."

"No," said Tony smoothly. "You misunderstand. Inspector Flint has already advised me that he is not comfortable with you remaining in here, Miss Walker. Possession of an Offensive Weapon. I have to ask you to leave. There's a chair outside."

Gold Dragon didn't move.

"Aim additionally suggesting that John's presence is no longer Appropriate," smiled Toxic. "Research suggests that young males in his situation lack the emotional maturity to accept the judgement of Professionals."

"We get stroppy when we're pushed about, you mean?"

Her smile became even wider and more wolfish but Tony wasn't going to use up any more charm from his limited supplies. "Get up and get your great-aunt out, John. There may be a chair in the foyer for you as well."

"Leave my mum on her own with you lot? I don't *think* so."

Donny knew that Skye would be picking up fast on the body language. Sometimes she was so quick that he hardly had to bother signing but she wasn't well now and he remembered what Joshua had said about disorientation. He leaned close to her and began explaining in a way she'd understand.

"You were right, Mum. They're all of them crooked tongues. And snatchers. We're in enemy territory and it isn't looking good. We three have to stick together if we're going to get out of here alive."

He had no actual idea what they were going to do. Gold Dragon had hooked herself to the back of her chair, daring them to force her out. Donny wondered whether he should hang onto the table leg or punch someone. The problem with the second option was being spoilt for choice.

Skye stood up, tall and stately. Then she made her sign of peace to everyone around the table. It was a bit like a bishop's blessing. Hand held high, she backed carefully out of the double doors.

Donny and Great Aunt Ellen followed.

Gold Dragon scowled; Donny managed a quick thumbs-up all round. As he passed the secretary's seat he caught sight of her agenda paper – Statutory Services Care Review & Assessment Meeting. S.S.C.R.A.M – scram! Too right, they were out of here!

Skye turned away and walked through the foyer, out into the street. Gold Dragon used her hook to push the visitor's badge under the screen to the receptionist.

"I'll have my belt and pouch now," she said, in the sort of voice that you didn't argue with.

Donny, meanwhile, had an irresistible, straight-to-video idea.

He saw that there were indeed two solid, high-backed chairs positioned outside the meeting room. Perhaps people were always being chucked out of Tony's Conferences and had to wait there in disgrace while the Professionals rearranged their lives.

The double doors of M1 opened outwards. Donny was the last of his family to leave so he shut the doors behind him, grabbed the nearest chair and stuck it neatly under both handles.

It might have been made for the job.

The receptionist yelled at him but she was trapped behind her security screen. Donny gave her a smile that he tried hard to make as cheesy as Tony's. Then he was out of there and legging it along the pavement to catch up with the others.

The street curved sharply away and led them into a shopping area. Skye took them down a side lane; through an arcade and back to the bookshop that she and Donny had visited when they had first arrived in Essex.

The Goth with black clothes, purple hair and a nose stud recognised them at once. She asked Donny whether his mum had enjoyed *Swallows and Amazons*.

"Oh, er, she was buying it for me." Donny didn't usually tell people that his mum couldn't read words.

"So what did you think of it?"

"Yeah. It was cool." Maybe this wasn't the way to describe a book that had helped to change his life but … where to start?

Great Aunt Ellen asked whether the shop stocked any of the other volumes in the series. She bought *Swallowdale, Winter Holiday* and *Missee Lee*.

"These are the ones that happened next in time," she said,

showing Donny the first two, "but *Missee Lee*'s always been my favourite. I thought of her as my pirate godmother. She had three islands and a patch of sea. If you decide to live full time on *Strong Winds*, you ought to read her story."

"I don't ever plan to live anywhere else," he said fervently. Then he remembered *Sailing*, the book that had been her brother Greg's most treasured possession. He'd written a list in the front of all the boats he'd ever captained. "At least, I plan to live on *Strong Winds* and sail *Lively Lady* until I'm old enough to have a ship of my own," he amended.

Gold Dragon added a local bus timetable to her pile of purchases and they left the bookshop. There was enough money left for some filled baguettes, which they ate on their slow bus journey back to Shotley.

The small man did not stay for the talking that followed the family's escape. It was time he returned to his base. They would need him now to keep lookout on the harbour. They could not have Hai Lóng staying here.

When the small man discovered the welcome mat he was very angry. This was defiance. Someone would suffer. He kicked the plank aside and went below.

"There's sure to be someone waiting," said Donny, as they walked down the steep hill towards the River Stour. He remembered, only too well, how Flint liked to hunker down in his police car until his victim came strolling innocently within range. Then he'd be out and snatching his prey, ruthless as a conger eel in a rock pool.

Donny was right: there was someone. But it wasn't the person he'd expected.

Rev. Wendy was sitting in *Strong Winds'* cockpit. She had a slim black laptop perched on the downhill slope of her knees and was holding it rather awkwardly with one hand while she tried to make notes with the other.

"For Sunday's sermon," she explained, closing the machine with obvious relief. "I often need to make changes. It's having so many different parishes. What suits one is almost certain to upset the rest."

None of them knew what to say to that. Skye was looking speculatively at the aft mooring line. She scooped her long skirt into one hand and climbed aboard, stationing herself strategically close to the samson post where the end of the warp was knotted. Donny stayed on the pontoon. He didn't know whom he trusted least: his mother or his former foster-carer.

Rev. Wendy slipped the laptop into its case and came ashore to join him.

"Beg Nimblefingers to hold off for few moments," Gold Dragon said to Donny. "She'll get her chance soon enough but I need to pay our harbour dues. We can't afford to stay here any longer – even if we wanted to." She nodded to Wendy and set off to the watchtower beside the lock.

"Um, hello," said Donny, after an awkward pause. "Why are you here?"

"To offer my assistance …"

He didn't give her a chance. "Thanks but no thanks," he said. "I've had your assistance before, remember. You do what Toxic Tune tells you. That's probably why you didn't bother turning up at the meeting." He was surprised how much he'd minded about that: not one of their so-called friends showing up. Typical adults! His friends would have come – if they weren't all locked away in school. "You knew you'd get your orders afterwards. I expect you've come to drive me off to some SS boot camp. Well, I'm not going."

Rev. Wendy sighed. "I understand your anger," she said. "I want you to know that I did attend the meeting. So did Mrs Ribiero. But we both attended in the wrong town. We went to Ipswich, not Colchester. Unfortunately there'd been some mistake in both our letters."

"Everyone else got there," said Donny. "Flint and Toxic and a bloke called Tony, who looked like a lawyer, and his posse of hags and enforcers. *We* all got there. Wish we hadn't."

"Yes. The mistake was only in our letters. They were sent from Denise Tune's personal office. No-one could quite explain it."

"You missed a treat. All the sort of stuff you really like – talking in gobbledygook; risk-assessing anything fun; slagging-off Skye 'cos she can't answer back; forgetting that the only thing that matters is people loving each other. Not whether they have the right size bathroom and five portions of veg for breakfast."

Donny'd been boiling up to let rip at someone. In the absence of the real villains Rev. Wendy was the perfect target. She just stood there in her drab clothes and dog collar taking it. Her cheeks got a bit blotchy in the wind and she held her laptop closer to her thin chest.

Donny found quite a few more things that he wanted to say. He forgot he should have been keeping watch on Skye and he didn't notice that his great-aunt was back already from the marina office, looking shocked and extremely cross.

"That's enough," she said. "Apologise at once! How can you have forgotten who rescued your mother from that … bin and brought her here? I'm ashamed of you."

Donny went very red. "Sorry," he mumbled, kicking a bollard. Then, "No, Mum, don't!"

Skye had lost no time turning the deck into a spaghetti heap of loosened ropes once again. Now she was undoing *Strong Winds'* fenders and very obviously preparing to leave. Donny did notice that she hadn't (as yet) cast off any of the mooring lines. Had she actually learned something from last time's disaster?

"Godssakes!" muttered Gold Dragon, as she sprang on board to try to restore order. Donny knew he ought to follow her.

"All right," he said to Wendy, "It's been a bad day. But you did get my mum out. Never mind what you and Gerald said about her all those other times when you thought I couldn't hear."

"Oh! I can't deny – I have been a sounding brass and a tinkling cymbal. But I have seen the error of my ways. It's why I've come."

"You're too late: we're off. Maybe you don't already know but they won't let Great Aunt Ellen look after me 'cos she's too old and she won't buy a house and they think I need protecting against my mum. So they're going to get some sort of Order and meanwhile they want to bang me up in a Unit."

"No, no, they don't."

"Yes they definitely do. They said so, in the meeting. You weren't there."

"But we were."

Donny stared at her. Had the vicar finally lost it?

"Mrs Ribiero was most … upset when she discovered what

had happened. No, let me speak with truthfulness … she was furious. I give thanks that she is also knowledgeable. She insisted that I had an inalienable right to be consulted as I am your named carer – at least I was your carer then. The Statutory Services have since relieved me from my duty."

Rev. Wendy sacked!

"So, at that point … when I was … any decision made without me could be open to legal challenge. Mrs Ribiero said that she was ready to instigate such a challenge. They were forced to reconvene. First she tried to have the meeting postponed so that she and I could drive to Colchester, then, when they said that wasn't possible, she demanded that they use a video conferencing system." Rev. Wendy shook her head. As if she still found events rather hard to believe. "I have to say they weren't immediately keen. In fact they said that, because they were in Essex and we were in Suffolk, they didn't think the systems were compatible. Something to do with bandwidths?"

"Oh," said Donny. Technically he didn't have a clue but he didn't want to put her off, so he nodded, knowingly.

She looked relieved as she continued. "You youngsters are such experts. Fortunately – providentially, even – I was able to offer a suggestion. The Diocese is currently piloting a new initiative. We have a target to reduce the mileage undertaken by those of us in rural districts. So we've all been issued with these." She touched her laptop. "And I've recently attended a networking course where we practised talking to colleagues as far away as Chelmsford. I was therefore able to point out that compatibility between the counties is possible. In fact, once the system was set up, we aditionally managed to contact your tutor at Gallister

High School. That was another of Mrs Ribiero's ideas." Wendy paused again. "I'd expected Denise Tune to have been keener. But she wasn't. She seemed to think he wouldn't have much to say. He did though. Once he understood what was proposed, he became most … eloquent."

Donny began to get the message. "So am I okay to carry on living with my mum and Gold Dragon? Did the three of you fix it? Have I been signed off from the SS?"

Her shoulders drooped. "Not really. Your name's on the At Risk register and there's a Care Plan, which you must follow if you're not to be sent to … the Unit. We – that's June and I and your tutor – continued to disagree but the vote went against us. Six to four. They wouldn't let June vote – or speak – but, because it was only my face on the screen, they couldn't see the notes she was writing for me. That was also providential. I'd never have achieved a deal on my own."

A deal? Previously when Denise Tune had told Rev. Wendy to jump, she'd only wanted to be advised the recommended height. Had his ex-foster-carer really changed?

Donny could hear *Strong Winds*' engine running. A deep, purposeful sound. Wouldn't it be simplest to head out to sea and not come back?

"I entreat you to listen," the vicar said urgently. "They expect you to leave the country. It's extraordinary but I got the impression that some people would welcome that outcome. No-one will to try to stop you. Then your great-aunt will be charged with child-abduction. She'll never be able to return."

"She might not mind …"

"And they'll charge your mother as well. You must stay. We

fought for you. Sandra too … as far as she could. Her job was threatened."

"Look lively there, Sinbad." Great Aunt Ellen was Polly Lee again, a seafarer ready for adventure. She'd loosed two sections of *Strong Winds'* foresail, angled so that the wind was already pushing the junk's bow away from the pontoon.

"Why? Why should I trust you? You might be okay now but they're monsters. We don't have to come back – ever. *Strong Winds* is an ocean-going vessel."

"What about the other children?" Wendy asked, desperately. "Little Vicky might forget you but Anna, Luke and Liam won't. I wonder how you'll feel about yourself if you blow off and leave them without saying goodbye? They've been abandoned once. Deserted – by their own mother! At least come and see them before you go. Please."

Anna, he'd forgotten Anna!

It felt bizarre to hear his former foster-carer saying pretty-please, instead of laying down the law as if she'd been personally entrusted with the SS commandments in stone tablets. But if she could do deals, so could he.

"Okay," he said. "It's not my decision. Gold Dragon's the captain. And my mum's got a point of view – except nobody takes any notice. But I might just tell them what you've said and we might decide to stick around a bit. Or we might not. Meanwhile, you're always on about Trust so I'm going to dare you to give it a try. I want you to let Anna use that laptop to access the Internet whenever she chooses. I want you to trust her to go wherever she wants on the web. And not even ask her where she's been unless she wants to tell you."

Rev. Wendy looked horrified. "Inappropriate content … guidelines …danger …" was all she managed to splutter.

Donny had cast off the bow-line now and was back on board with the stern warp in his hand, ready to slip as soon as the junk had swung towards the lock gates. "No trust: no deal," he called. "I'm not even going to ask."

She opened her mouth and shut it again. He slipped the line and Polly Lee put the engine into gear ahead. The light above the lock showed green. They could go straight in.

The vicar had to run. Back along the pontoon, past the slipway and the marina office, until she was leaning over the safety rails as water poured in through the sluices and *Strong Winds* rose steadily to the level of the river beyond. She was breathing heavily as she called across to the captain. "Miss Walker … and Ms Walker … I'd like to invite you to supper tonight. Donny will explain … Please tell him that I'm going to trust … I'm going to do as he's asked … as soon as I reach home. Whether you come or … whether you don't."

Gold Dragon looked surprised. "It's a fair wind," she thought aloud. "We could pick up an overnight mooring at Pin Mill. But I was set for sea."

"Gerald's making fish pie," Rev. Wendy was begging. "From sustainable stocks …"

The gates at the far end were opening. Donny cast off once again and Skye pushed energetically on her boat hook.

Polly Lee hesitated as *Strong Winds* nosed out towards the broad grey river. As they passed the ferry pontoon she reached her decision. "I'd prefer to get that dinghy up in davits for a sea passage. It's freshening already and the twenty-four hour forecast's not good. We're not shipshape and I've an inexperienced crew. No harm in a run up the Orwell first."

"Donny," she ordered, "Dip our flag to the Reverend. We're accepting her kind invitation."

CHAPTER SIX

Hawkins

Friday 29 September, evening

When leaving Shotley Marina in all but the smallest boats, you have to keep quite straight in the narrow, dredged channel for about fifty metres until you've passed between the two tall entrance beacons. Keeping straight is not always as simple as it sounds: tides can run strongly over the mudflats on either side of the channel and it's easy for a boat to be pushed off course and ground in the shallows whilst still apparently pointing towards the beacons. The easiest way to counter this is to pick a mark on the far side of the harbour and keep it in line with the beacons. Or you can keep looking astern to check that the leading light by the lock gate indicates your course is steady.

Skye was standing on *Strong Winds'* foredeck as they motored steadily out into the Stour. She gave a shout of joy and spread her arms like wings.

Polly Lee looked a bit startled to have her tuition interrupted and sent Donny to check that his mother was okay.

"The big sea water," she signed, looking ecstatic. "Kayoshk!"

Sure enough there was a pair of seagulls perched one on each of the entrance beacons watching them depart.

"Is Nimblefingers all right?"

"Very!" Donny shouted back. "It's her first time, remember."

He saw his great-aunt's face change just for a moment. He didn't know whether she was going to laugh or cry. Then the motorised foot-ferry came pushing past in the narrow channel. The handful of passengers stared curiously at *Strong Winds* who was crabbing slightly under engine and foresail as she kept her ruler-straight course between the lock and the beacons.

"Of course she's all right," said Gold Dragon, as if it had been Donny who had questioned this. "She's Eirene's daughter! Ask her please to come here and stand with me. We should have done this years ago."

They passed the beacons and the junk swung 90 degrees to port. They were all three of them together in the cockpit and Skye seemed to drink in the wide grey harbour scene as if it was an elixir. She was alert and confident, gazing ahead. She took Donny's hand first then reached out towards her aunt. She wasn't even shaking.

Almost at once she needed both hands back to sign a question. "Hiawatha's chickens?"

She gestured towards the *Hispaniola*. Donny repeated what she'd said but it took a moment before he understood what she meant.

There were budgies wheeling above the schooner's deck and perching on her crosstrees. Or were they canaries? He wasn't very good on exotics. There were at least a half dozen of them, maybe more.

It was a strange and troubling sight. The birds seemed confused, fearful of the open space. Donny watched first one and then another make tentative flights away from the schooner then hesitate, turn, flutter back.

There was a chill in the freshening breeze and the late September light was fading.

Gold Dragon reached for her binoculars. "Crazy little kites. Harwich Harbour's no place for them … They've escaped from somewhere. Or been tipped out. Cages, most likely. Now what's Nimblefingers wanting?"

Skye was signing urgently.

"She wants you to head over to the schooner. She says there's something wrong. Mum's got brilliant eyesight."

Another shredded flag? More black-painted signs? Donny felt a squirm of embarrassment when he remembered the childish message he'd left outside the *Hispaniola*'s wheelhouse.

But it was nothing like that.

His mother had spotted one of the small bright birds tumble exhaustedly from the schooner's gunwale. A wave had caught it before it could fly back to safety. Now it was struggling in the water, a frantic yellow speck being carried away by the rushing tide.

Polly Lee swung *Strong Winds*' bows in the direction of Skye's pointing arm and reached down to slow the engine. "Man overboard, Sinbad. Tell your mother to keep pointing. She's not to let up for a moment. Shrimp net by the foremast. You cut along and stand by ready to use it. Look lively. You'll only get one chance. Port side."

She took the junk down-tide of the weakening bird, then brought her head to wind before she stopped the engine.

The handle of the shrimp net wasn't quite long enough. Donny crouched as low as he could behind the junk's high gunwale ready to cling to a stanchion and reach his whole body out. So close … not close enough?

Then everything seemed to go quiet and he could only wait

70

for the drowning bird to drift the last half metre. It was scarcely moving and its eyelids were half-shut. Donny was certain they were too late.

He scooped it on board anyway and gave it, dripping, to his mother.

Skye wrapped it quickly in a corner of her shawl and carried it down into the main cabin.

They were only a boat's length from the *Hispaniola*. The other birds flew up in alarm as Gold Dragon restarted *Strong Winds'* engine and swung the junk away.

The foresail filled with a snap. The birds flew higher, still uncertain. Then the wind took hold of their weak and ragged flock and blew it across the harbour to Felixstowe.

Donny wondered how many of them would reach the shore – and what would happen if they did? The skyline of gantries, girders and vast container ships didn't look like a welcoming place for such fragile escapees. He remembered something he and Anna had seen happen there.

The *Hispaniola*'s wheelhouse door was open. Was the owner on board?

Polly Lee called to him to hoist the mainsail and Donny lost no time unfastening the main halliard from its wooden cleat. The sooner they were gone, the better. The mainsail ran easily up the tall mast, each battened section unfolding in sequence until the full sail was ready to take the wind.

Polly Lee sheeted it in and turned off the engine. Donny hoisted the mizzen and they went winging up the River Orwell with the tide.

Skye had kept the rescued bird folded in her shawl until its feathers were completely dry and its bright dark eyes watchful. Then she'd stroked its tiny head with the tip of her finger until she was quite sure that it was a tame, not a wild, creature. By the time Donny and Gold Dragon had reached Pin Mill and picked up a mooring close to the end of the Hard, Skye had persuaded the canary to take beakfuls of fresh water and to grip her forefinger with its slender claws.

When Donny came below it turned its head sharply to regard him and tensed as if about to flee. Then it began to chirrup and to preen as if anxious to expunge every last trace of the waves that had so nearly killed it.

Now that the little bird was well it would soon be hungry and they had no food to offer. Skye wrapped the canary softly back in her shawl and carried it with them as they rowed ashore in *Lively Lady* and walked up the lane to the vicarage. Donny was sure Gerald would have something seedy in his macrobiotic kitchen.

It was odd – but definitely good – to be arriving at Erewhon Parva as a visitor. The vicarage had never felt like home and he'd promised himself that, whatever happened, he wouldn't live there again. He'd run away, go AWOL.

Skye's step faltered as they turned into the gravelled drive behind the dusty laurel hedge and, as she looked up at the grey stone façade, she held the canary closer. Great Aunt Ellen tapped lightly on the front door with her hook and Donny braced himself to resist the familiar atmosphere of disapproval and suspicion.

But no dull adult voice told Luke and Liam that it wasn't safe to run, as the two boys hurtled out of the sitting room into the cold bare hallway, shouting. Anna was close behind them. She was carrying her red-headed half-sister, Vicky. She didn't say anything – she wouldn't have been heard if she had – but she looked … as if she might have hugged him!

Donny guessed this wasn't personal. It could only mean that Rev. Wendy had been true to her promise and had told Anna that she could use the new laptop. It was the www Anna wanted to embrace, not him. She could continue her search.

Skye smiled with relief. As soon as the front door closed behind them, she unfolded her shawl and set the canary free.

Rev. Wendy stifled a small scream as the yellow bird flew joyously up to the railing around the upstairs landing and perched for a moment on the dark wood before taking off on a series of energetic explorations.

'You see?' Skye signed, 'He is not a wave-wanderer but a house-friend.'

Gold Dragon began to apologise for her niece but Skye couldn't hear her. Donny didn't try to interpret. He'd be wasting his time trying to explain to his mother that letting a rescued bird fly free in the first safe house you found wasn't the most natural and sensible thing in the world.

Gerald had slammed the kitchen door and was pulling on his rubber gloves, muttering about hygiene regulations and avian flu. His wife, however, had recovered remarkably fast and now seemed as entranced as the children.

The canary took a skimming flight down the long upstairs corridor, then returned to the landing rail. It paused, chirruped and launched out again to circle the wide space above their heads. It didn't cannon into walls or hurl itself against the high windows. It was investigating, Donny realised, not trying to escape. Suddenly the hall and landing began to transform into good solid empty space where anyone could have fun, instead of a gloomy no-man's land to hurry through on your way to somewhere else. Skye was right: the little bird was a house-friend.

Rev. Wendy was smiling. He didn't know her cheek muscles could do that. "Oh, bless …" he thought he heard her mutter.

Skye signed to Donny that he should ask Gerald for some food.

The foster-carer looked flustered. No change there. He blinked a bit and slipped back into his kitchen, opening and closing the door behind him as if he were being pursued by hornets. Donny and Anna rolled their eyes at one another. Gerald was *so* hopeless.

But they were wrong. When Gerald reappeared he was carrying a plastic plate with carefully tea-spooned heaps of sesame seeds, mung beans, sunflower seeds, pine kernels and brown rice, plus an up-turned Horlicks lid filled with fresh water. Surely a canary's five-star delight?

Skye stretched one arm towards the bird, as if she were calling it back.

It paused, turning its small head from side to side as if each eye wanted to be sure that the other eye had seen correctly. Then it shuffled a few steps sideways along the balustrade, made up its mind and skimmed down as if it were surfing solid air.

"Bless …" said Rev. Wendy again, as she watched the canary pecking, considering, swallowing or discarding Gerald's haute cuisine.

She didn't look quite so certain when Donny explained that Skye thought that the canary should live with them in the vicarage because it had been fearful on a boat. Gerald's mouth dropped soundlessly open and Anna had to bury her face in Vicky's warm tummy to hide her giggles.

Luke, however, went pale with longing. "Please, oh please can we keep him? Li and me's always wanted a budgie. Or any pet but a budgie would be best of all. We'll do all the work, won't we, Li? He won't be any bother. We love him so much."

He turned to his brother for confirmation but it wasn't needed. Liam had already crept right close to Skye and was watching the canary as it supped up water with its short black tongue. Slowly, very slowly, the younger boy touched the bird's soft feathers with the tips of two fingers. Skye wrapped Liam in her free arm as if he too were a salvaged fledgling. He leant against her as if he'd known her all his life.

Wendy and Gerald stared at each other. "But …" they croaked.

"It's a very tame canary," said Great Aunt Ellen. "I've no idea where it's come from but I don't think that need worry you. It's not as if it were a dog … I knew a man in China once – greedy, cruel, treacherous, despicable in every way … but his songbirds were delightful. He came to a bad end of course … so completely irrelevant here … forget I mentioned him. The bird'll be fine. You'll need a cage though – for visitors."

The vicar was pulling herself together. She walked across the hall to her study but didn't completely close the door. A moment later they heard her on the telephone.

"Environmental pest control most likely," muttered Anna to Donny.

When Wendy came out she was still looking cheery. "Mrs Everson has something we can use," she said to Gerald. "Luke can come and fetch it with me now. I'm sorry about the supper."

"Completely ruined. I don't know why I bother."

Even dried-out fish pie going brown around the edges tasted wonderful to Donny once they were all squeezed round the kitchen table. There was locally-pressed apple juice for the children and Rev. Wendy produced a bottle of Essex white wine which she claimed to have won in the harvest raffle.

"I notice some of the same gifts being re-donated time and again," she commented. "So I thought perhaps we should take this one out of the system."

Donny saw Gold Dragon blink convulsively after she'd taken a single sip. Skye, on the other hand, was thirsty. She swigged her portion as if it too were apple juice and held out the glass for more. Donny couldn't remember Granny buying them anything stronger than ginger beer.

The canary had settled contentedly into the tall narrow cage that had formerly housed Mrs Everson's daughter's chinchilla. They covered the cage to help him sleep – or her. There were gender issues. Once Luke had discovered that the bird had been rescued near the *Hispaniola,* he and Liam insisted that it should be given a name from *Treasure Island.* They'd wanted Jim but Anna objected that they didn't know whether the bird was male or female.

"If you call it Hawkins," said Donny hastily, "It could be Jim or his mother. They would have had the same surname."

"Not necessarily," said Anna. But she didn't go on about it for long. It was Friday evening; House Meeting had been cancelled;

her little sister had fallen asleep sucking her thumb and she had the weekend ahead with the promise of a new, fully-enabled laptop with wireless broadband.

Toxic and Tony arrived just then. Walked straight in without bothering to knock.

"Unannounced Monitoring as per schedule 666 sub-section 13," said Toxic – where anyone else would have said good evening or I hope we're not disturbing you.

Though, coming from her, both would have been lies.

"They've accepted the Conditions?" said Tony to Rev. Wendy. He sounded surprised.

"I haven't told them anything. Can't you see we're having our family supper?"

She'd betrayed them. Lured them here so that he could be re-captured at Toxic's convenience. Anna's Internet access hadn't been worth this much.

Donny looked for his two companions. Gold Dragon had been telling Luke and Liam round-the-world adventure stories and making plans for everyone to come sailing with her on *Strong Winds*. Clearly she'd completely forgotten the bizarre SS meeting and Tony's incomprehensible threats.

She was up and out of her chair now, as ready to run as he was.

Skye wasn't going anywhere. She'd slumped forwards onto the formica table and was fast asleep and snoring, a third glass of raffle wine spilled beside her. It had been a long day.

Toxic nodded to Tony. He nodded back as if she had jerked some invisible string attached to the back of his head.

She picked up the wineglass and took a deep, slow sniff of its remaining contents. Then she extracted her BlackBerry from its snakeskin case and took a photograph of Skye.

"Witnessed?" she said and Tony nodded once again.

"Not such a good moment perhaps," she purred to Wendy and Gerald, smiling with extreme delight. "Ai'll pop back in the morning. With Inspector Flint. Ai had no idea you would be exposing the children to Alcohol on these Family Occasions."

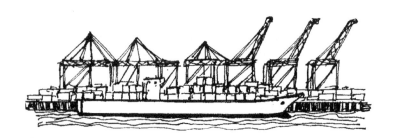

CHAPTER SEVEN

Shipping a Hostage

Saturday 30 September

Flint's shark-boat was already moored in the Port of Felixstowe No Admittance area as *Strong Winds* slipped through Harwich Harbour in the pale light of morning.

It gave Donny goose bumps to see it there. He'd almost rather its owner had been bullying the kids in the vicarage. Ever since he'd seen those tiny birds blown towards that quayside, he'd been trying not to remember the day that he and Anna had watched that fat policeman and a small man in overalls wring a cage-bird's neck.

Then stamp on it. At the top of those exact same steps where the shark-boat was now. He wished he could have forgotten that delicate blue feather still sticking to the sole of Flint's boot as he guzzled lobster and slurped chilled wine. Stuck with dried blood probably.

They hadn't said anything to anyone. They'd been too churned up.

And they'd been scared.

Donny's immediate impulse was to veer away, take *Strong Winds* over towards the Stour, cross the deep-water channel someplace else.

But he'd had his orders. Besides, changing course now would take him directly across to the *Hispaniola*. Even at this distance he could see that there was a black two-man speedboat attached to the same dangling rope he'd used for *Lively Lady*. That must be the owner on board. The owner of the knife?

Wasn't there some old myth about someone having to take his ship between a whirlpool and some clashing rocks? Donny felt a kinship with that bloke, whoever he was. He couldn't ask Polly Lee what to do. She was checking charts. The rest of the ship's company was still asleep.

They'd had a struggle getting Skye back on board. Two and a bit glasses of Rev. Wendy's raffle wine had knocked her out completely. He guessed it hadn't mixed so well with the happy pills. He didn't think she'd ever had wine before.

He was glad she hadn't seen Toxic and Tony; glad too that she'd missed the grim conversation about the conditions under which he wasn't going to get sent immediately to an SS Unit. He hadn't had to tell her – yet – that she'd been judged a 'risk' to his emotional well-being and likely to 'abuse' him through neglect.

Apparently the people at Tony's meeting reckoned they could make a better job of helping him grow up sane and happy. Ha ha.

Anyway, there was a new Care Plan that said that Donny would be allowed to live with his mother and great-aunt for as long as he achieved 100 percent school attendance and 'challenging' academic targets. Skye had to 'engage' with the local health service – which probably meant carry on taking the tablets – and Gold Dragon was bound over to keep the peace. Flint wasn't.

There was more … much, much more. Rev. Wendy had been forced to take them through it clause by clause after the crooked tongues had driven away, still smirking.

Donny had shouted at her of course. But eventually he'd had to realise that she hadn't deliberately let them down; that she had been trying to do her conscientious best. He couldn't see how Rev. Wendy could bear to allow Toxic into the house. Then he had remembered that she and Gerald were responsible for all the other children. If Wendy fell out with the SS, what would happen to Anna, Luke, Liam and Vicky?

Nevertheless her faith in the System had been badly shaken.

"At first June and I thought that our video contribution had made a difference – until we began to wonder how it was that they had all the Conditions so clearly arranged in advance?"

"You think this might have been their Plan B all along?"

"That was our impression," she answered sadly.

The worst of the Conditions was the one that said *Strong Winds* had to become a 'fixed abode' – permanently attached to the shore with an address and postcode. This was to enable the SS bureau-rats to swarm aboard as often as they liked in order to check up on Donny's 'saifety'. Once the site had been selected any attempt to move *Strong Winds* would invalidate the Care Plan and Donny would immediately be sent to the Unit. No wonder Tony had seemed surprised to find them still here.

"Mr McMullen tried to make the point that that this was a completely unreasonable request to make of a sailor such as yourself. He and Mrs Ribiero thought that you would head out to sea at once."

"They'll have to send a gunboat to stop me." Gold Dragon growled.

Rev. Wendy looked exhausted. "Then I think you'll be acting exactly as they wish and they'll make sure that none of you can ever, legally, return. I believe that this is their preferred option. Their Plan A, if you like."

The way he had been feeling last night, Donny didn't much care. He guessed Gold Dragon felt the same.

Except that it seemed so totally unfair that she was being ejected from the land of her childhood when all she'd done was return to try to help him and Skye. And she'd hardly seen anything yet. There might be things she remembered from when she was young. People maybe? She'd come all the way from China. Not even allowed to stay for a holiday. And they'd hardly begun to be a family.

Gradually, rather cleverly, Rev. Wendy had managed to persuade them not to leave at once but to try living under the new conditions for just a few months. "I believe boating people often do come ashore for the winter …?"

"Not my sort."

"And Donny's mother is so very recently out of hospital …"

They had all looked at Skye then … head down, mouth open, one braid sopping up the spilt wine, the other partially unravelled. One of her hands flapped and groped among the crockery like a suffocating flounder. If she was dreaming the dream was not good.

Gerald cleared the table and fetched a j-cloth: Donny took his mother's hand and stroked it without speaking. She'd been so well earlier. He'd thought she was going to be okay again. Be her real self.

"Well, Sinbad, what do you think we should do?"

"Dunno … except that, if us staying *isn't* what they want us to do … then I think we probably should. Just to wind them up."

"And to find out what *is* going on," said a quiet voice from an unobtrusive corner.

Anna had put Vicky into her cot upstairs and had come down again to listen to the discussion.

Luke and Liam were still there, sitting either side of the covered cage. Liam was chewing his fingers and Luke was making knots in the corner of the sheet. Donny knew, suddenly, that this wasn't only about him and Gold Dragon and Skye: the kids needed them to stay as well.

"We all know what it's like having our lives mucked up by adults," Anna continued. "But you can usually see a few reasons – even if they're rubbish ones. What the SS is doing to you lot is completely *un*reasonable. I don't even think they're obeying their own rules. So it's logical to assume that there must be something else going on in the background. Something crooked and foul."

Wendy, Gerald and Great Aunt Ellen had stared at her but said nothing. Donny felt his spirits lift with relief. Anna was on his case again.

"It sounds to me," she carried on, not really looking at any of them, "as if Flint and Toxic had put the squeeze on that Tony before the meeting even started. They obviously badly want to get rid of you," she said, directly to Gold Dragon. "That's why they're making it so hard for you to stay. If it were me they were pushing out, I'd want to know why. Then I'd make up my mind whether I was going. Not before."

"We could live here at Pin Mill," Donny said. "With the houseboats. *Snow Goose*'ll be in the yard so we can maybe help with the repairs. Then I've only got to turn up to school each day and do my homework and all that stuff and I don't see that they can complain. As long as you don't scare poor Flint-ums with your rigging pouch."

Gold Dragon had struggled to raise a smile. It was obvious that she longed to be hull down over the horizon waving her last farewell to life on British shores.

"Son of a sea-cook," she snarled at last. "If I were back in the Islands I'd have him chop-sueyed or sweated down to caulking tar. That's that then. I'll run the old lady up the beach for Monday morning and hand 'em my landing card. But I'm going sailing first. All shore leave cancelled for forty-eight hours. Tip a bucket over Nimblefingers. She'll soon sober up when she gets a sniff of spray."

"You're … going? And we can't never come?"

Great Aunt Ellen looked at the younger boys. Then turned to Rev. Wendy again. "I could ship an extra hand or two from your crew here if you think they'd enjoy a voyage?" She didn't seem to hear Gerald's reflex hufflings about lifejackets and homework, thermal underwear and waterproof shoes. "If I've got one or two of yours aboard, then you'll know I'll have to bring 'em back."

Luke's eyes were wide. "You mean we'd be like … your hostages?"

At last Gold Dragon grinned. This was her kind of talk. "And work your passage too or I'll feed you to the fishes."

Liam had a Saturday morning football match – which was of course un-missable – so he chose to stay behind and be the first in charge of Hawkins.

Anna said that, this weekend, she'd prefer to stay ashore as well. Donny knew why. He'd help her after this weekend, he really would. He could learn to sit there in the library checking websites all through lunchtime.

Gerald refused utterly to let them take Vicky on board *Strong*

Winds. So it had only been Luke who'd climbed aboard in the glistening darkness with a biodegradable plastic bag slung over his shoulder like the dunnage of a jolly Jack Tar.

Thus far all was quiet. It was still early and *Strong Winds* made very little sound when she was under sail.

No movement on board the shark-boat.

They were close now.

The shark-boat's aft end looked different. Donny stared as the ebb tide hurried them past. Then he understood. The aft end was open because it included some sort of docking station. There'd been another small boat concealed between the powerful twin engines.

And you didn't have to be Sherlock Holmes to guess where it was now. Even the young James Bond could have worked that one out. Flint *did* have a connection to the *Hispaniola*. His speedboat was tied alongside her now.

Donny supposed that meant that it must have been Flint who wrote the signs and sliced up the dragon flag. Though he would have thought that, if the fat policeman could spell anything at all, he'd have been a hot-shot at PRIVATE and TRESPASSERS WILL BE PROSECUTED. Also, the *Hispaniola* hadn't felt like Flint's sort of boat.

Well, he'd obviously got that wrong.

The hulls of the container ships towered high above *Strong Winds* as Donny held his course.

"Pufferfish's out visiting early," said Polly Lee, coming back on deck and staring across at the *Hispaniola* through her binoculars. "Ah, I think he's spotted us. Now we might have some fun." She sounded as if that was exactly what she wanted. Once she was on the water, no-one intimidated Gold Dragon and survived.

"No, he's going back into the wheelhouse. Doesn't want to play. Learned his lesson last time, maybe." She took another look and frowned. "You know, Sinbad, there's something not quite A1 at Lloyds about that *Hispaniola* of yours. For one thing her stern's all wrong. That boat was never designed to sail."

Flint had seen them and had turned away. That was spooky. *Lively Lady* was up in davits with her mast down and sails stowed. They were obviously heading out to sea. So why wasn't he hurtling after them bellowing threats and orders? He had his speedboat.

Anna and Rev. Wendy must have guessed right. Flint and Toxic wanted them off their muddy patch … evicted, banished. History.

They'd be in for a surprise on Monday morning, then. When he turned up scrubbed and shiny ready for a new week at school. He was almost looking forward to it.

"Where're we going? Why didn't you tell me we was gone?" Luke's tousled head appeared from down below. He was wearing his pyjamas and trailing a sleeping bag behind him.

"Thought you might need your watch below. Midnight was pretty late for shrimps."

"I ain't a shrimp, I'm a hostage." Luke sounded offended. "Where're we going?" he asked again.

"As far as Donny's policeman friend is concerned we're setting off across the pond – that means crossing the North Sea – maybe back to Rotterdam. He thinks we're runaways you see, not raiders."

"We could be," said Luke. "I wouldn't mind being runaways.

Not if it meant crossing a sea."

"One day," she sighed. "But this time we're bluffing. Partly because I've promised to deliver you back by Sunday: mostly because we want to make him sick as a parrot when he finds out he was wrong. We'll have to settle for raiders, this voyage."

"Explorers," said Donny. He could add stuff to the map he'd been drawing.

"So where're we going to raid? I mean, explore." Luke looked quickly towards Donny, wanting to fit in, say the right thing.

"The most easterly port in Britain," said Gold Dragon.

"Great!" said Donny "Where's that?"

"That's just Low'stoft," said Luke. "We even lived there. In a sort of caravan place 'cos we didn't have no money. My dad were born Low'stoft. And his dad were born way out on the Dogger Bank. He said my great-nan got caught there, unexpected. I wasn't sure … They was fishermen."

"Then we'll hire you as our native guide and you won't have to work your passage swabbing out the bilges after all."

Luke hugged his sleeping bag a bit tighter. "I told you. I ain't never been to sea. We was always waiting for my dad to come home. Bilges is okay."

"Born on the Dogger Bank, eh?"

"That was them. I ain't never been there."

"Well we'll have to see how you shape up. One day, if you sign ship's articles, I'll take you there – and your brother too, if he's got salt water in his veins. But before I let these wreckers beach me I've a piece to business to attend to. Now skip off below and put some clothes on. I can't have my hostage catching his death; it'd be bad for trade."

"Right, Sinbad," she said briskly. "Time you learned to steer a compass course. We'll be standing out to sea for the next few hours in case they're tracking us on radar. And we'll keep a listening watch on channel 16. Though they'll probably keep their scuttlebutt to themselves or use a harbour frequency."

"You think there's more then one person there?" Somehow Donny couldn't imagine Toxic being out on the water at this time of the morning.

"If he's the Moloch our vicar seems to think, he'll have an enforcer or two in the shadows. Someone anonymous and unscrupulous who puts the frighteners on in private while the big men pace the bridge-deck in their official caps."

The blue bird? Was that some private scare?

"Your friend Anna was a little too quick spotting the lie of their land. Knows too much for a girl her age. Made me wonder how she'd fetched up here?"

He couldn't answer. Anyway, what did he know? Anna kept her secrets as securely as if they were chained into heavy lead caskets and sunk in the deepest sea-rifts.

He shrugged. Gold Dragon nodded.

"No need to tell your mother or the hostage but one of the reasons we're setting our course for Lowestoft is so I can see a man about a knife. A rigging knife, you understand."

CHAPTER EIGHT

Night in a Foreign Port

30 September-1 October

He almost told her about the slashed flag then. But there was so much else to think about: crossing the deep-water shipping lanes, then holding *Strong Winds* steady for the North West Shipwash and on towards the Inner Gabbard. Once Luke and then Skye were back in the cockpit it wasn't something he wanted to talk about anyway.

When they were about sixteen miles off shore they altered course – northwards. He could feel the strong tide and freshening wind picking up *Strong Winds* and sweeping her along with them.

His great-aunt was in a hurry and so, it seemed, were the elements. Donny and Luke got used to a seascape furrowed with tumbling waves, their crests curling over into foam in their apparent haste to overtake the junk and race her to the horizon. They got used to the motion too. As each roller passed beneath her, *Strong Winds* lifted and surged, twisting slightly as if she was frustrated by her inability to keep up with the rushing water. The waves sluiced out from underneath her hull, temporarily flattened by her weight, then hissing and bubbling as they hurried on.

When Skye appeared on deck, she wedged herself into one corner of the cockpit. She seemed isolated and even more silent than usual as she watched the weather building up and passing over them, and the occasional sea birds dropping by hopefully to check their wake. When Great Aunt Ellen offered everyone toast and Marmite and mugs of tea she shook her head and looked away.

By mid-morning they all needed wet-weather gear. There was nothing big enough for Skye so she had to have an old tarpaulin. Great Aunt Ellen found her an ancient sou'wester and her dark brown eyes stared fixedly from underneath as if she were seeing for miles. Only her fingers were busy picking and pulling at a complex knot on the end of a piece of hemp. It wasn't long before she had completely deconstructed it and was reducing the rope to fibres.

"I wish Sandra'd got more out of the van instead of just clothes. Mum has sets of worry beads when she's feeling like this. And she's got a rain poncho. It was summer when they captured us: it's about to be October now."

"Another reason not to cut our cables too soon. Why let those scoundrelly swabs scoop the rest of your possessions? That's a Turk's Head Nimblefingers has undone. If I could teach her how to knot it up again she'd be invaluable."

"Like in the book," said Donny. "Your brother Gregory's book. I gave it to you that first night."

The salt-stained handbook that should have brought good luck: the book which had slipped out of his great-uncle's duffel-coat pocket before he plunged to his death in the Barents Sea. Gold Dragon had taken it without a word. And then Donny had fallen asleep.

She must surely have been pleased? She'd said that she'd had nothing to remember him by. And her other brother, as well, Great Uncle Ned. He'd died the same day. His ship torpedoed.

They thought Greg might have been trying to save him.

Knots and splices. The book was big on them.

Great Aunt Ellen nodded. "You're right. I didn't really thank you. It was a shock but … I'm glad."

Donny grabbed his chance. "Sometime … will you tell me about your other sister … Eirene? The one who went away? And I'll sign it to Skye. Eirene was her mother. She ought to know."

"In that case, remind me to provide a locker-full of rope fenders for her to deconstruct."

It wasn't exactly an answer but he didn't take it as a no.

The tide had turned against them by the time they reached Lowestoft. The flood was running strongly north to south across the harbour entrance whilst the wind was blowing fierce in the opposite direction. Shoals on either side of the main channel set up complex cross currents and the whole area seemed a mass of broken water and white spindrift. The pilot book advised against entry in these conditions. They did it anyway.

"There's HOLES in the water!" yelled Luke. He didn't seem at all frightened. Polly Lee found safety harnesses for everyone and showed them where to clip on. Luke's hair was bristling with salt, his face stinging pink with spray. "This is WICKED! Way better than the death ride at Pontin's!"

Donny wasn't so certain. *Strong Winds* was plunging like a bronc and the task of holding her steady as they waited outside the harbour for the entrance lights to turn green was taking all his inherited skill – and then some. Polly Lee stood poised beside him, saying nothing. Skye was being miserably sick.

It was hard to find words for his relief when they finally slipped between the white pagodas on the pier heads and into sheltered water.

They moored in an enclosed space presided over by an old-fashioned clubhouse. As soon as she had spoken to the duty manager, checked all the warps and seen the sails neatly stowed Gold Dragon changed out of her oilskins into her shore-going jacket. She needed to get to the shops before closing time, she said. She was as matter-of-fact as if they'd arrived by bus.

Luke, Skye and Donny had a quick look round then settled in the main cabin eating apples and heaps of bread and jam and drinking hot, sweet tea. They felt as if they'd been half way around the world instead of forty miles up the Suffolk coast. Luke said that even the amusement arcade and the candy-floss stall looked different when you came to them off a boat. And those white pagodas were awesome. He seemed a lot more cheerful about being here since he'd arrived with spray on his face.

There was a gentle tapping on the ship's side. When Donny went on deck he found a Chinese girl smiling and dimpling and offering him a take-away menu for some local restaurant. He wondered whether she'd come because of *Strong Winds* being a junk so he took the leaflet and asked her if she'd like to come on board. She shook her head and stepped back looking, for a moment, terrified.

Then she paused and smiled again and ran away from the harbour and down the esplanade giving out her leaflet to the few excursionists who were wandering around now that the rain had cleared. Donny glanced casually at the mass-produced flier. He was glad to see he'd got his welcome sign pretty well spot on.

✳

The restaurant was called the Floating Lotus and it seemed they were expected. There was a map on the back of the flier that led them away from the main street into darker, narrower lanes. Luke hadn't wanted to leave the harbour but Donny persuaded him that explorers always had to venture inland to seek fresh water sources and replenish their supplies.

Gold Dragon was going anyway. If they wanted any supper they'd better put their best feet forward.

"Anna's mum didn't like us goin' down this way. It was all right for her an' Dad but not for us."

"Hostages go where they're dragged."

That reassured him, of course and he cheered up completely once they had reached the Floating Lotus and met its owner, Ai Qin Pai.

Ai Qin was probably quite old but she didn't look it. She was as petite and erect as Great Aunt Ellen herself. But where Great Aunt Ellen's skin was weathered by years at sea, Ai Qin's face was peachy smooth and her black hair gracefully styled. She wore pressed black trousers, a crisp white shirt and a silk embroidered waistcoat with matching bow tie. She placed herself at an angle to their table where she could supervise her restaurant whilst also talking quietly.

A waitress brought them a pot of jasmine tea and five tiny cups, which Ai Qin offered with her compliments. Then she helped each of them to order their meal – all in perfect English – and sipped her tea as she began a long, incomprehensible, exclusive conversation with Gold Dragon.

Sometimes one or other of them wrote something on a paper napkin. Ai Qin covered the writing when any of the waitresses came near and, at the end of the meal she tore both napkins delicately to shreds. Then she teased the remnants into two randomly sorted piles, took one for herself and offered the other to her guest. Donny got the odd impression she might be worried about security.

It was a strange way to have a meal together. Skye, Donny and Luke talked to each other – Donny began to teach Luke how to sign – but they were mainly just repeating things they'd already said. They were all pretty tired.

There was one moment when Ai Qin had to tell a man to leave. He'd upset one of the younger waitresses and had had too much to drink. He was with a couple of friends and looked as if he could be planning to argue with the small, female proprietor. Gold Dragon was half out of her seat to go and assist when the Floating Lotus chef appeared from his kitchen.

He was an enormous man with a scarred face and he happened to be carrying a seriously scary cleaver. There was something odd about the way he walked but the troublemakers didn't stop to discover what it was. They were gone, apologising urgently and shoving money at Ai Qin to pay for their unfinished meal.

"Son of a Chinese sea-cook – she's got her personal Long John Silver!" said Great Aunt Ellen appreciatively.

Donny laughed and so did Luke a couple of seconds later. Skye smiled too when Donny translated. *Treasure Island* was one of the classics Granny had read to them when she was alive. When she was still, uncomplicatedly, his granny.

Somehow the evening went better after this even though Ai Qin came back to their table to continue her private conversation. The man with the prosthetic leg could definitely cook as well as providing such an immense back-up service. Donny's stomach felt soothed and filled by the bowls-full of sweet and spicy noodles curled inside him as contented as a warm cat.

As the four of them walked homewards to *Strong Winds* he decided that there couldn't be any harm if he asked his great-aunt about the language she'd been speaking.

"It's Mandarin. It has many different dialects. Ai Qin and I both speak a rather old-fashioned version so we understood each other tolerably well. When we were unsure we used the character alphabet."

"Were you telling her news from Shanghai?"

If she tried to pretend they'd been exchanging favourite recipes for shark's fin soup he wasn't going to believe her. Skye wasn't the only one who could pick up on body language. Gold Dragon and Ai Qin had been discussing something that had made them angry and upset.

The cold air had blown Luke's sleepiness away and he looked interested too.

"Do you know anything at all about China?" she asked them.

"Er … nope."

"Then it's not a story for tonight. And it's certainly not a story anyone would ever have told me when I was a child your age."

She quickened her steps. Donny hadn't heard her speaking like a traditional great-aunt before. He swiftly revised his priorities. "Tell us about Eirene then. Tell us about Skye's real mother."

The Chinese stuff didn't matter: it wasn't anything to do with them.

There were always watchers near the Floating Lotus. When news of the Dragon's visit was passed to the Tiger he spoke at once to his friends among the Ghosts. These visitors were dangerous. They must discover the place of greatest weakness and use it to make the sweet waters of life turn to poison in the strangers' mouths. Hai Lóng must be driven out.

Great Aunt Ellen didn't answer Donny straightaway. After they'd returned to *Strong Winds* she said she needed to watch the stars for a while. He looked out after about ten minutes and saw her sitting alone on a bollard, smoking an old-fashioned tobacco pipe as she gazed across the harbour towards the deserted trawler basin.

There was nothing to look at and no stars either. The basin was empty and the former fish-packing sheds were shuttered and silent.

He and Luke played a game of cards: Skye was fiddling with one of *Strong Winds'* boxes within boxes. When Great Aunt Ellen finally rejoined them, she turned off the main electric light and lit the oil lamps so the saloon cabin shone like a story-telling cave.

Caves have dark places. Gold Dragon chose to seat herself in the shadows of the cabin corner so her face couldn't easily be seen. "My sister Eirene was the special one," she began. "The heart of our family. She could be sensible with Greg and Edith or go make-believe adventuring with Ned. I loved Ned." Her old voice softened. "I miss him even more than I miss her. They almost drowned me when they were crossing the Red Sea and then Eirene forgot me while she was inking in a map. I was captured by savages, then chopped into the pot to make eel stew."

"Wish I'd been there," said Luke.

Great Aunt Ellen nodded. "The best holiday I ever had. There was another friend who was always writing stories but she didn't let other people into them with her like Eirene did." She paused for a moment. "It was strange. Their friend grew up to be famous. Whereas Eirene …"

"Yeah, Eirene, what happened to her?" Donny didn't give a toss about these friends: he wanted to know what had happened to Skye's actual mother.

"Eirene grew up very beautiful."

"Did she look like Mum?" Donny hadn't meant to interrupt again but this time he couldn't help it. Even when he was little he'd sort of noticed that Skye and Granny didn't look like each other at all. He didn't look like Skye either, and Gold Dragon looked exactly like her sister Edith – except with a hook and a plait and her wrinkles in different places. Maybe this Eirene was the missing link?

"No. Not in the least. Skye looks like her father."

"Her *father*?" He'd failed to hoist in that a newly discovered grandmother must mean an unsuspected grandfather as well.

"Yes. Skye's father, Henry. He was an Ojibway Indian from Ontario province. The resemblance is powerful. It gave me quite a shock when I saw your mother that first night in the marina. Henry was a sachem."

Donny looked across at Skye. It was so completely obvious. How come he'd never seen it? Not that he knew what a sachem was.

"Your father was Ojibway," he signed to her. "Gold Dragon says you look like him. She says he was, um, a great man …"

"Mudjekewis," she answered, but Donny wasn't really listening.

"So how did Eirene meet this … Henry?"

"Henry had joined the Canadian army. After the war he stayed in Europe working for the UNHCR."

"What's that?"

"United Nations High Commission for Refugees. Eirene was with the Red Cross. I can't explain how much she suffered. Especially at the end when they were going into the camps. The few times she came home she looked like a victim herself – all skull and bone but still those blazingly expressive eyes and her lovely way of moving. I thought she should have been a dancer if we'd all had different lives."

"I sometimes think that about my mum. Except she should have been an artist."

Gold Dragon looked curiously at Skye. "Maybe that's my clue. I've been trying to find my sister in her but I get stuck. Eirene was such a word-person and …"

"And you think Mum isn't," Donny finished for her. "But you don't know whether she is or not because you don't understand her words."

Donny wasn't necessarily as confident as he made out. Some things always got lost in translation.

"Gold Dragon says that your real mother had deep feelings. She loved stories. She could have been a dancer."

"Beautiful Wenonah was my mother," Skye signed back unhesitatingly.

This time Donny noticed. "Beautiful Wenonah? Eirene … but Granny!"

Donny stopped. This was *Hiawatha*-land. His mum had got

into a complete muddle. She was in the wrong world, not just a different language. Mudjekewis and Wenonah were characters from her favourite poem. They weren't his long-lost relations.

Yet her father had been an Ojibway. That was weird. How could he explain it? Gold Dragon might as well have handed him a stack of Turk's Head knots and ordered him to knit them into lambswool jerseys.

Skye didn't miss many of Donny's expressions. She leaned forward and took one of his hands, signing straight into it in the special way they'd worked out when he was very small indeed. "Beautiful Wenonah *was* my mother. Not Nokomis."

Nokomis had been her word for Granny.

"You knew? That Granny wasn't your birth mother? All this time?"

"In my dreams," she signed back.

"So why didn't you tell me? I'm your son! Unless I've got that wrong as well." He felt angry with her now. He pulled his hand away.

"*Who is this who lights the wigwam, with his big eyes lights the wigwam?*" she signed, quoting.

"Okay, okay. I didn't mean it. But that was just a poem."

"Poems are like my dreams. In my dreams I know things differently. Too many of them are bad dreams. I try to guard us from them."

By making dream-catchers or not telling me things? Donny wanted to ask. He felt he'd been excluded. Treated like a child.

Then he noticed the concern on Great Aunt Ellen's face and the bewilderment on Luke's. He remembered that finger-spelling was as incomprehensible to the others as Mandarin had been to him.

"It's okay. Mum says she knew. About her parents."

Great Aunt Ellen looked relieved; then she frowned again. "Does she know what happened to them? Why they left her?"

"What happened? To Wenonah and Mudjekewis? Why were you living with the old Nokomis?"

"They took the longest road. They never returned or sent a sign."

"Yes," Great Aunt Ellen agreed when he translated. "That is what happened. She does know. But I don't know if she knows why. I don't suppose it matters."

"It does to me," said Donny.

Luke nodded too. "We doesn't know why Anna's mother went. So we doesn't know if she's coming back."

"*Wahonowin! Wahonowin! Would that I had perished for you, Would that I were dead as you are! Wahonowin! Wahonowin!*"

Donny shivered. Had to shake himself alert. Skye was right. Poems were a bit like dreams, the way their words came blowing back to you. Made you think of outcasts, far across the lonely waters.

"We knew we wouldn't see Eirene and Henry again. Not in this life." Gold Dragon shifted further back into the cabin shadows. "They met and married in the camps. Then they went home to Ontario. To Henry's people. Soon after they arrived the Ojibway were attacked by a virus. A European virus. It was only a strain of rubella, only German measles, but Henry's people had little protection. Several of them died. Eirene got a slight temperature and a few spots but …"

"But that was when she was pregnant with Mum?"

"In those first crucial weeks."

NIGHT IN A FOREIGN PORT

Donny should have stopped signing then. Should have guessed that this new knowledge would be too much for Skye. She was not yet strong enough. But Great Aunt Ellen's story was answering questions that he hadn't ever thought to ask. His hands just kept on going.

Henry believed that he and Eirene had brought the fever to his people, Gold Dragon explained. That they were responsible for the deaths.

He was almost certainly right.

Then he began to experience a series of dreams that convinced him that he and Eirene should set out again across the oceans, carrying away their contagion and their burdens of guilt and grief.

"Some Native American people take dreams extremely seriously," she said. As if Donny didn't know that!

So Henry had begun to build a sea-going canoe, the *Houdalinqua*, and Eirene returned to England to have the baby and say goodbye to her sisters. Ellen was preparing to go abroad herself. She wanted to visit Australia where their mother had grown up. Gregory and Ned and their parents were already dead and Edith was heart-broken at the prospect of being the only one of all their family still left in England.

"But of course she didn't say anything. She wouldn't. It was only after the birth went wrong in the hospital, and the baby was born so weak and ill and starved of oxygen, that Edith pointed out what was howlingly obvious. Skye had no chance at all of surviving a long voyage in a semi-open canoe to an unknown destination. She would certainly die. Her own parents would have killed her. If Henry was determined to go, then Eirene had to choose between him and their baby."

"He wouldn't change his mind?"

"He believed there were some things that had to be done. Duties that you couldn't avoid without losing your soul."

What a freak! Donny felt furious with Henry for putting Eirene in this situation. Selfish git!

"And she chose him?"

"Yes, in the end she did. And you have no right to say that she was wrong. Henry came to bless his daughter before they left. We all met. And then we said goodbye. They knew the baby would be Edith's treasure for as long as she lived. Mine too, perhaps … "

The story was over. Great Aunt Ellen made them all some Ovaltine.

"No dallying tomorrow morning if we're to make Pin Mill at the top of the tide."

Donny and Luke set off to use the facilities at the clubhouse. Gold Dragon began to move around *Strong Winds*, checking all was shipshape for the night. Then she noticed that her niece was silently distraught. Skye was sitting in the cabin, arms folded around herself, Ovaltine untouched, rocking mutely to and fro, grieving for the parents she had never known.

Ellen's heart went out to this big, sad woman but she didn't know what to do. She couldn't communicate without Donny there and she suspected that Skye might be afraid of her. People often were. It had been years since she lived in a family.

She thought of all the sailing yarns she had ever read. She thought of the long cold days and nights she herself had endured with only *Strong Winds* and Eirene's parrot for company. She fetched the bottle of ship's brandy and knelt awkwardly beside Skye to offer her a medicinal swig.

It was the worst thing she could have done.

CHAPTER NINE

Neaped

Sunday 1 October

Some of the waitresses from the Floating Lotus came down to the harbour to see them off the next morning. They were giggly and lively once they'd stopped being shy. They ran along the breakwater waving at *Strong Winds*. Ai Qin wasn't there but Donny noticed the big chef standing somewhere near the RNLI shop, as if he was keeping watch over the girls.

The sea was so much calmer. It almost looked like a different place – except there were still waves breaking on the hidden shoals to either side of the entrance channel. This area of the sea was littered with wrecks, Gold Dragon said. Ships that had gone down within sight of safety, drowning everyone on board. Their families watching helplessly.

The morning sun dried the last patches of damp out of *Strong Winds'* sails. Donny was glad to be sailing again. He reckoned he did his thinking best at sea and yesterday's story had left him with a lot of thinking to do. What would he have decided if he'd been Eirene? Or Henry?

There was no doubt that Granny had been a brilliant mum to Skye. Caring for her, fighting for her, keeping her alive and safe must have gone as far as anything could to soothe the terrible grief she suffered after the loss of her brothers. And then she'd done the same for him as well.

He could understand how Henry must have felt when he

realised that he and Eirene had brought that disease to his people. Far worse than him and Skye smashing up *Snow Goose*.

But he couldn't make up his mind what he thought about Eirene. Mothers should always stay with their children. Shouldn't they?

Skye had already gone to her bunk before he and Luke had come back last night. She had a small foc'sle cabin that Polly Lee had previously used as a storage space for ropes and sails. Lots of *Strong Winds'* spare equipment had been left behind in China so as to make space for him and Skye to bring their possessions on board. It was a pity they had so little to bring.

He should maybe have tried harder to find his mum a dream-catcher. Hers had been forgotten in the hospital and he'd given his to Luke back in the vicarage. He thought he'd heard her moving about the cabin in the very early morning, sort of moaning and searching. But after their long day at sea, and the delicious meal, Donny had slept too well.

They took the inshore passage this time. Sailed past low sandy cliffs and long stretches of shingle beach; past seaside towns and the mouths of unknown rivers. The air was as clear as if it had been rinsed by yesterday's rainstorms: the waves as glittery as if they were auditioning for parts in a holiday advertising campaign.

Donny mostly saw reminders of war – Martello towers with slits for windows, concrete pillboxes that might have housed a gun, radar-monitoring stations which were dead and quiet now.

"Cold War," said Great Aunt Ellen as they passed concentric rings of metal masts on the marshes before Orford. Then, about an hour later, she stared at some low, reddish-coloured cliffs in amazement. "But everything's gone!"

"What's gone? Does it matter?"

"Perhaps not. But it should …"

"What should?"

"Everything that's gone. The people. The technology. The scientific brilliance."

"More war-time stuff?"

"Stuff you call it! Stuff that saved us in our darkest hour!"

"Okay, I guess … Didn't you ever hear from them again?"

"Who? Oh, Eirene and Henry? No. And if you're about to ask me whether I ever went looking, yes, I did. I called in ports that I wouldn't otherwise have chosen and I asked questions that were roundabout and casual. We'd all agreed, you see, that we had to let them go. They were never to look back. It was to be the longest road. Edith had the baby. And I … I had Eirene's parrot. And her flag. It was supposed to be enough."

"They probably died."

"And if they didn't then, they would have done by now. I'm eighty-something dammit and I was the youngest of them all. Fatally much younger … Do stop brooding, Sinbad. Come and take the helm for a while. Better still, persuade your mother to come and take it with you. You can stand in on this tack and get an eyeful of Bawdsey Manor, that's what I was talking about. Then you'll need to bring her round smartly and head out for the Woodbridge Haven buoy. The shoals here are treacherous."

But Donny couldn't persuade Skye even to put her hand to *Strong Winds'* up-curved tiller. Which was a pity because he was sure she'd like it. It gave him such a vibrant, connected feeling.

Luke liked it too. He kept going on about some Viking raiders' project they'd been doing in school.

Skye seemed a bit strange and unfocussed today. He wished he hadn't told her about the camps. Or the deaths from European disease. This evening he was going to have to tell her about the Care Plan and his School Attendance Targets and the SS threat to put him in a Unit if he failed to comply. Not exactly bed-time story stuff.

If they hadn't had Luke with them they could have pointed their bows away from the coast. They could have sailed on and on like Eirene and Henry. He could definitely see the attraction.

But Luke was there and he didn't seem to have noticed the atmosphere. He was still in adventure mode and it was time he had a turn at steering. Why should ancient history mess up all their lives anyway? If he saw Flint or Toxic at the school gates on Monday morning, he was going to give them a V sign: V for Voyages.

The two boys chatted about nothing in particular as the flood tide took them swirling up the River Orwell back to Pin Mill. There was no sign of the shark-boat and no activity around the *Hispaniola*. The only odd thing that they noticed was an empty cage that had somehow got washed up on the saltings.

Gold Dragon wasn't interested in salvage suggestions. "We've got to reach Pin Mill Hard as close to high water as we can. Not a moment later. If I've got to neap this brave old lady I need to make a proper job."

Neaping meant that she had to sail *Strong Winds* as far up the mud as she possibly could, at the highest moment of the tide, and moor her securely. After that the junk would be stranded for about eleven hours out of every twelve. Stuck fast. Access available anytime to Flint, Toxic and their creepy crew. If the grounding took place at the top of a spring tide, like today, the junk could be stuck for a fortnight or even a month until an equally high tide occurred again.

Strong Winds slid to a stop where there was an empty space in the line of houseboats and Polly Lee left all sails up for several moments longer so the junk continued piling on. They laid out anchors fore and aft and took warps to the posts and chains that were already there.

Donny's heart sank when he caught sight of one of the Year Ten bullies who'd had a go at him and Vicky that time. He'd forgotten that they were likely to be hanging around the Pin Mill Hard. The boy lobbed a hefty stone in their direction then slouched off round the back of the pub. Almost as if he'd been looking out for them and was on his way to report their arrival.

Then the tide turned and the water began the six-hour process of draining away.

So did Great Aunt Ellen's good temper.

Skye was told sharply (via Donny) that none of these new knots were to be touched under any circumstances. Luke was marched back to the vicarage and Donny dispatched to his berth straight afterwards. His orders were to check his homework, eat some supper, pack his bag and go to bed. She would set him an alarm so he had all the time he needed to catch the school bus in the morning. No excuses would be accepted.

Monday 2 October

He did what he was told. Would have done it anyway without her needing to be so snappy. He was up and ready in plenty of time. Walked up the lane to his old stop where he used to get on when he was living at the vicarage. Joined up with Anna. All exactly like before. Xanthe and Maggi would be waiting a couple of stops further on. They could have an Allies meeting on the bus. Like they used to do.

Except that the driver wouldn't let him board.

He looked at Donny, checked his list and said that Donny's temporary SS pass had expired. His parent or guardian would have to make a written application to the correct department and that might take several weeks to process. There'd probably be a fee to pay; he didn't know the circumstances. Meanwhile, he said, it was more that his job was worth to allow Donny a place this morning. He'd had a letter. From the Welfare.

"But I've GOT to get to school!" This was where he'd been catching the bus ever since he had first started at Gallister High. Donny couldn't believe that the driver would have even noticed that he hadn't been at the stop last week, let alone demand to see his pass and then refuse him. He could have been off with flu or something. There were loads of spare seats. "I'll be in mega-trouble if I don't."

"Should have thought of that before you started getting yourself picked up from Shotley. This ain't a free-for-all. Whole system would be in chaos if kids started jumping on wherever they felt like. Now step back off the platform, young man, I've my regulars to collect." And away he went with a self-righteous fart from his exhaust.

His first day under the new system and he needed 100 percent attendance! If he tried walking he wouldn't be there till about lunchtime. He didn't know whether there were public buses and anyway he hadn't got any money.

Donny ran back along the road to Erewhon Parva Vicarage.

Gerald and Vicky were in the kitchen with Hawkins chirruping from his tall chinchilla cage. Rev. Wendy had already taken the car and left. She was delivering Luke and Liam to their primary school, then driving on to one of her many meetings.

"I can ring in for you and explain," said Gerald.

"Anna's going to tell someone. That's not the point – I've absolutely got to get there. Dead or alive. Every day. It's in my Care Plan."

"How very awkward. I'd better call a taxi."

"Except I haven't any money."

"Thinking about it, neither have I. Wendy needed the purse ..." Gerald furrowed his brow and thought about it a bit more. He was never exactly quick. "Desperate times, desperate measures, John. I'll write an IOU to the Flower Fund!"

The taxi took forever to arrive. They were always busy at this time of the morning, the driver explained helpfully. Taking children to school.

Donny missed the whole of first period, which should have been tutorial, then dragged himself grumpily round his next two lessons until it was break and he headed to the library to find Anna.

It wasn't good news. She hadn't found Mr McMullen, who might have understood and thought of something helpful. Only a supply teacher who'd marked Donny absent and said she'd have to get the office to send out a truancy call. Apparently he was on a special monitoring system for At Risk children.

"And I haven't a clue how I'm going to get home. That taxi cost fifteen pounds! Do you think you could ask Maggi if their mum would give me a lift? That would get me part of the way back … I don't mind walking the rest."

"Maggi's not in. Someone said they thought she'd had an accident on Saturday – racing in all that wind. I haven't seen Xanthe either. I think she's on a GCSE field trip."

"Looks like I'll be walking all the way home to Pin Mill then," said Donny glumly. "I'd better print myself out another map. It'll be something to do at lunchtime. I've just discovered that my meal card's been cancelled."

"SS really reckoned you'd be gone," Anna commented as they set out together on their long march after school. "I bet they're heart-broken that they can't be sending each other memos about your truancy and getting Flint's policemen out with their sirens and flashing lights."

She'd skipped all her library time to share her lunch and try to persuade the school administrator to get Donny the right forms for a permanent meal card. Then she'd refused to get on the bus herself and said she'd walk back to Pin Mill with him.

"Yeah. It'd have been like their Christmas had come two months early if they could charge Gold Dragon with abduction."

"Before she arrived, Flint and Toxic were forcing you and your mum to stay … "

"It seemed they wanted to get hold of her then."

"But now that they've seen her … "

"And realise what a total star she is … "

"They can't wait to get rid of her!"

Donny's old school shoes were about a size too small. He was going to get such blisters.

"To be fair …"

"Why?" said Anna, "Why be fair? When did that idea ever enter their heads?"

Donny laughed. "You're right! But, it's like you said that night at the vicarage, this isn't normal SS stuff any more. And I understand about as much of it as I speak Mandarin."

It was about five miles from school to the vicarage. They were sticking to the same route that the bus took – on the off-chance that Rev. Wendy or one of the Ribieros might drive along and rescue them. The weather was okay and the leaves on the trees and hedges were turning to their early October bronze and gold.

Donny needed to think about something that wasn't his feet.

"Anna," he said suddenly, "I'm really sorry. I haven't asked you a single thing about your weekend. I mean, how did you get on? Is that bloke still there, the one you thought was looking for your mother?"

Anna's wide grey eyes sparkled, her pale face flushed. It was one of those moments when she looked so amazingly pretty. "Is he there! This weekend it felt like I couldn't click a mouse without scrolling over him! It's like he's a transmitter suddenly booted up to maximum frequency. It's unreal! If I'd been going home on the bus today, I was going to get my old machine out of Mr Mac's cupboard and take it back to the vicarage. I want to look through some of the searches I've saved. Try and see how I could possibly have missed him."

"Oh. Sorry about that."

"It's okay. I probably oughtn't to take the computer without telling Mr Mac. I didn't want to ask that sub teacher."

"So, this bloke. Is he a perv? You said he was on some dodgy site …"

"Dunno. I didn't do any of those this weekend. Didn't want the Diocese accusing Rev. Wendy of being 'inappropriate'. It's another reason for wanting my own computer back. I mean technically it's prehistoric but I can possibly find a way of linking it to the laptop and covering my tracks by creating alternative user identities. If I could have spoken to Mr Mac I was going to blag some extra cabling. I wanted to ask him about adding a USB port as well. If I ever have any money I'm so buying a memory stick."

"I thought ICT was meant to be a boy thing!"

She tried not to look pleased. "I've always been a techie. My dad was. I expect I got it from him. And there was some mega-Prof in my mum's family too – though it certainly skipped her."

She went quiet then. A white van came fast round a corner heading in the direction of the school. It was completely on the wrong side of the road. The driver braked when he saw them, swerved slightly and sped on.

"Bloody idiot!" snapped Anna, who'd jumped up onto the bank. "We could have been a pram or a horse or anything … What a berk! I should have got his number. Answering your question: his screen name's Oboe – though I don't know why he's bothering with it. He's being so up-front I'm surprised that he hasn't given out his address, home phone number and chest size. He keeps on posting the same message 'Signal from Mars for Lottie Livesey. Urgent. Will Lottie Livesey please make contact? My last few crumbs to share.' I bet he's getting some weird replies!"

Signals from Mars – had he dreamed that somewhere? Couldn't think that he had: couldn't see that it mattered. "Have you answered him?"

"I can't not. But I don't trust him. And that's not only because I don't trust anyone – if he actually knew my mum, he'd know that she's *so* not into computers. I set her up a website ages ago, before she had Vicky. I keep checking it in case she leaves a message. But she never used it and she hasn't now. I sent Oboe the link."

"Won't he have found the site already? Surely he'll have Googled her?" Donny was doing his best to think the way that Anna did.

"Obviously." She didn't sound that impressed. "Except the name I used should make him think it's actually her who's made contact – if he does know anything and he's not just phishing."

"What name?"

"Theodora. That was my mum's mum's name. They fell out years ago. Then she died. That was when we were living in Lowestoft. Mum didn't even go to the funeral. Refused to accept any of her money. Never mind that we could have done with it."

"Oh," said Donny. "That seems a bit extreme."

"That's Mum. She's really sweet and caring, ninety percent, but she has these principles. She doesn't compromise."

"Oh," said Donny again. Anna and her mother maybe had something in common. "Um, what did they quarrel about?"

"Politics, I think. My mum was a protest singer whereas her

mum was a romantic novelist. I tried one of her books when I was about nine – *Castaways*. It was rubbish."

"Oh," said Donny once more. "That's strange …"

"What's strange?"

But it had gone. "Oh, I dunno. Thought I might have heard of her?"

"Unlikely. And can you *please* stop saying 'oh'. It's totally getting on my nerves and we're not even half way home."

"Oh … KAY!" said Donny, dodging as she swung her schoolbag at him.

CHAPTER TEN

Inappropriate Behaviour

Thursday 5 October
'What's the good of thinking about them?' said Dorothea. 'They might as well be in some different world.'

Dick started so sharply that he almost dropped his telescope.

'Why not? Why not?' he said. 'All the better. Just wait until dark and we can try signalling to Mars.'

'To Mars?' said Dorothea.

'Why not?' said Dick. 'Of course they may not see it. And even if they do see it they may not understand. A different world. That makes it all the more like signalling to Mars.'

(from Winter Holiday *by Arthur Ransome)*

Anna's old computer had gone from Mr McMullen's cupboard. Mr McMullen was gone too. A succession of cover teachers took Donny's class for registration and supervised their DT lessons. There was a rumour that someone from Education Welfare had made a complaint against Mr Mac for exceeding safety numbers on his open department evenings. Another rumour said he'd been sacked for inappropriate behaviour with one of his students.

"Education Welfare? That's Toxic. This'll be her revenge attack for him sticking up for you at that meeting last week," said Anna to Donny as they grabbed a table for four in the main dining-hall. "The inappropriate bit could mean me because he helped me build my computer and I'm a girl."

"But even Rev. Wendy couldn't see anything wrong in that: she mainly got in a strop because you were using it in the vicarage and you hadn't asked. Don't you remember her coming in and saying 'There has been Deceit in this House!'?"

He thought she'd laugh but she didn't. "I should have known they wouldn't have forgotten about it. Before you and your great-aunt arrived Wendy used to ring up Toxic almost every day to check that it was okay to allow us to breathe. You know, there might have been some new research which advised selective stifling." She sounded bitter. "Of *course* she'd have told her about my computer. And how Mr Mac had helped me with it. A ready-made excuse for a Toxic Special smear campaign. As if anyone would be interested in sex when they could be doing electronics. That woman is *so* evil ... Poor Mr Mac."

Anna sat down. She didn't eat anything. Donny began noticing that some of the other students were nudging each other and looking as they walked past. He wondered whether he should stand up and have a go at them.

"Hey, do you reckon she'll try making trouble for our parents too?" asked Xanthe, clattering her tray onto the table top. "Our mum gave her mega-grief about putting the wrong addresses on those letters."

"Yeah – and they put in that complaint against Flint for breaking speed limits on the river."

The sisters were laden with veggie pasta, garlic bread, side salads and orange juice. Maggi's arm was in a sling because she'd broken her collarbone. She'd been sitting out in her *Laser* dinghy and had been thrown violently across in a squall. She said it had really hurt at the time but it was okay now. She waved at a couple of the girls who were staring at Anna. They hesitated a moment then one of them waved back and they turned away. Seen off by Maggi's smile.

It was great to be eating with his Allies again. Great Aunt Ellen had used her good hand to sign the forms for Donny's replacement meal card and had given him some money to put on it. He couldn't see it was going to last long and he hadn't liked to ask her about school shoes as well. He'd watched her face sort of stiffen when she'd found out how much his school bus pass was going to cost.

There'd used to be help in the system for him and Skye – free school meals, for instance – but that had somehow vanished. An admin problem, Sandra thought, but she didn't seem to know when it would be fixed. She also wasn't able to say when she would be calling on them again. Her work was being re-structured.

Gold Dragon had scowled and said they didn't want handouts. It had, however, been a big relief when Rev. Wendy had remembered that she'd noticed a boy's bike advertised in the village shop. Just £30 – the price of two taxi journeys!

Wendy had bought him the bike and she'd also paid back the Flower Fund out of her own money. She said they'd still some care allowance left from when Donny had been looked after at the vicarage. He wasn't entirely sure this was true. You'd have thought that vicars didn't do lies but he'd once seen Wendy do a really big one. He considered it her Finest Hour.

Then she and Gerald had reverted to type and made an unbelievable fuss about rechargeable front and rear lights, a safety helmet and fluorescent strips. They even produced clips, which he was supposed to put round his trouser legs. Donny's school trousers were now so short that they hardly reached the tops of his socks when he was cycling. Still, he took the clips and thanked them and stuck the strips on his jacket and rucksack and did remember to wear the helmet. In general Wendy and Gerald were so decent nowadays that Donny had almost forgiven their treacherous past.

Anna evidently hadn't. Her face looked hard as she re-lived that day they'd taken her computer.

Maggi and Xanthe were reminiscing much more happily. "It was fun painting Jaws on his bling boat!"

"And hearing Mum bawl him out in the club!"

"It's not that hilarious," Anna snapped. "Your parents won't get done in by the SS: they've got status – and each other. But I'd like to point out life's not such a breeze for us plebs. Never mind that Mr Mac's done utterly nothing wrong: I bet they're giving him a hard time proving it. And humiliating him in front of the other teachers. Meanwhile Toxic's got my computer. You don't know how bad that is. She's such a *witch*! She'll get Flint to get some police specialist working on it. They'll find everywhere I've been."

The sisters sobered up.

"Okay," said Xanthe. "Message received. Hilarity put on hold. So tell us. Where *did* you go?"

Anna put her fork down and pushed her plate away completely. Donny tried not to stare at it.

"Nowhere that I had to pay – and that's most of the proper investigation sites, the ones that say they can access police records and stuff. Obviously I kept checking the National Missing Persons site but I didn't expect to get lucky there. Didn't expect much anywhere. Mum's so not a techie and if she's trying to hide, there must be a reason. I mainly need to know that she isn't dead." Anna's voice sounded bleak. "I've never said that I was me. I've kept trying to find if anyone's seen or heard her over this last year. I've spent a lot of time on music sites – posing as a fan. And on friendship sites, pretending I'd been at school with her, posting lists of her favourite songs …"

"Was that how you met Oboe?" asked Donny.

"I was following a string and it sort of led me there," said Anna. "It was one of those 'eager to meet you' sites."

"Maybe this Oboe set you up," said Xanthe. "Like he was grooming you."

"Sounds well creepy to me," agreed Maggi.

"Maybe," said Anna. "I was mainly hoping that he's another searcher: someone who's getting sort of desperate. Like I am."

Her last three words sounded small and exhausted.

I do know something, thought Donny. There's something here I've read or I've dreamed. Something from another life.

Maggi gulped and reached across the table and put her hand on Anna's arm. "I'm sorry," she said. "I completely hadn't got it."

Xanthe, however, steamed straight in. "Okay Anna. It's well past time you levelled with us. *Why* are you all being looked after by Wendy and Gerald? Why did your mother leave? Someone told me that the other kids' father's in jail. What did he do? And where's *your* dad?"

"My dad's dead. And so's Luke and Liam's mum. My dad was a structural engineer and he was killed in an accident over the North Sea. I'm not sure about their mum. I think she had cancer or something." She moved her arm away from Maggi, folded her hands on her lap and carried on talking, not looking at any of them. "I was almost seven so I remember quite well the night my father died. We had a small house, a mile or two outside Immingham. It was really comfortable, only me and them. The stairs were the best bit. There were thirteen, you see, the number of chromatic notes in an octave so Mum had painted them black and white, like on a keyboard. You could do a different tune every time you went up or down. And she kept adding colours because she hoped that I would learn to hear in colour like she does. She never quite realised that those stairs were more like number patterns than sounds to me. I think Dad understood. Anyway … there was always music in our house but that night the music wasn't right. I'd gone to bed and I could hear Mum trying to work out some phrase. Over and over again. I couldn't sleep because I was waiting for the moment when she'd get it. But she never did. Instead there was a knock on the door and two policemen came and someone from Dad's company."

Anna went a bit quiet then. None of the Allies wanted to speak.

Then she carried on. "Mum went a bit crazy after that. She fell out with her record company and her agent. Just did pubs and clubs and street corners, practically. That's how she met Luke and Liam's dad. He sings shanties. He's not exactly educated. He'd been a trawlerman and the company he worked for had gone bust. He was going to work on the rigs but she persuaded him not to. She thought she could support everyone with her music. I thought she was wrong. We were all living in this dump and Bill, that's their dad, used to drink too much. Sometimes he'd go off to sea and then he'd come back and they'd have a row. But they always made it up again. Once us kids had been sent to bed."

The suppressed hate in her voice would have burned through steel. "Then she was pregnant with Vicky and she couldn't go on giving concerts. So he went to work in Felixstowe docks and got in trouble with the police. And that's when I first met Flint and Toxic. Happy days. Not."

"Didn't you say anything to your mum? You know, about how Flint bullied you and Toxic watched when you were being sick?"

"She had enough to worry about. Bill was in prison ages before he got convicted. That was when Vicky got born. I think they were trying to pressure Mum to dob him in. It would be their standard tactic. Unless they were just bullying for pleasure."

"What had Bill done?" Xanthe was leaning forward, staring at Anna. Her normally loud voice had gone quiet.

"Something at work. Mum kept insisting he'd been set up. She would have known not to bring me into it. I never pretended that I liked him."

Then her cool brain clicked back in gear. "That was my big mistake. I've thought about it since. She liked him so I should have kept my feelings out of it. Then maybe she would have trusted me. We could have set up a communication system."

"But …" Donny was sort of trying to say that Anna had only been about eleven, or maybe ten and why should she have had to pretend to her own mother about not liking this drunken stepfather? And he still didn't think her mum should have left.

The first bell had gone: the dining-hall was starting to empty. Xanthe stood up and began stacking their plates. "You're gonna have to accept this one thing, Anna. Nobody, absolutely nobody, – let alone your mother – could know you for more than five minutes and not trust you." Donny and Maggi nodded as hard as they could: Xanthe carried on. "I swear that it was because she like totally trusted you that she knew it was okay for her to leave. She knew that you'd be looking out for the others. She knew you wouldn't let her down. And you haven't."

Anna pushed her chair back. She hadn't eaten any of her lunch. She knocked her water glass onto the floor and didn't stop to pick it up.

It was the end of that same day and Donny was hurrying after her as she headed for the bus. "Can't you just hang on, Anna? My feet hurt."

She hitched her bag higher and walked faster.

"Please, Anna, I know I'm thick but why are you so uptight about your old computer?" He was sort of hobble-running. "You didn't use your real name when you were on it. You didn't find anything about your mother and you've got Oboe on the new one. How's having your old searches going to help Flint and Toxic? I need you to explain."

She answered in her voice that was like spitting. "Because, if you remember, Wendy and Gerald didn't know that I'd been on the Internet. They thought it was a homework project. That witch'll have my screen names now. All the places that I went and the updates that I posted will give her detail about my mum that she probably didn't have before. Nice for anyone who can visit the paying sites and look at records that I couldn't get. It also proves that I've never believed that she'd abandoned us. I'm sure she's on a mission. And now they'll be closer to finding her. All because I couldn't bear not knowing if she was okay."

She did stop then. She twisted round so fast that he nearly

cannoned into her. "Oh and for their cherry on top they'll be able to use all the dodgy sites I visited as extra smears on Mr Mac. Got it now, have you?"

"But … you didn't even go on that computer at school."

"Try telling them." She was stamping furiously away again. "I've been in with Ms Spinks all afternoon – she's one of the deputy heads. Hag! She gave me official notification of the SS complaint and told me they're bringing Wendy and Gerald in tomorrow. She was trying to persuade me to say that I looked on Mr Mac as a sort of father figure in what she called 'my difficult circumstances'."

He could see one of those red danger spots burning in her pale cheek. Didn't dare interrupt.

"I'm surprised she didn't start pulling out male dollies and asking me to name the sex parts. She kept promising me it was safe to confide in her. Liar! As if I don't know the regulations. *No-one's* allowed to keep your secrets if you're an At Risk child."

They were at the buses now.

"I told her that 'father figures' represented a patriarchal view of society that should have been scuttled with the Ark. I said Mr McMullen was useful because he knew more than I did about electronics and that was that. So then she turned snotty and said that there's some sort of computer expert coming in this evening to check all the machines in the DT department for evidence of improper use."

"They won't find any."

"That's because there isn't any. Unless they fake it … They could do that if they've got someone with half a brain cell. Depends how seriously they're trying to fit him up. They can't simply copy all my searches across to the DT machines because the school screening system will stop them. That's why I hooked it up to the phone line at the vicarage."

"Gerald and Wendy aren't going to like that."

"No, they're not." Anna climbed onto the bus and pushed her way through to an inaccessible seat.

Before Donny had met Anna he'd have thought that people who were really logical wouldn't get so upset about things. He wished he was getting on the bus with her, even if she was heading into a vicarage mega-row. It seemed as if there was nothing useful he could do – except cycle in and out of school and hand his homework in on time.

He needed to take action.

There was the regular afternoon queue of buses and cars in the turning circle: people walking, texting, mucking about, shouting to one another. A few teachers stood around making sure everyone got off the site safely. Donny spotted Ms Spinks over by the admin entrance leaning towards another woman who, he was pretty sure, was Anna's form tutor. They went inside together. He considered running after them, grabbing their arms, shouting, forcing them to understand.

He knew he'd only mess up.

Xanthe was in orchestra and Maggi'd got a hospital appointment. There were notices all over school to say DT open nights were cancelled. Plenty of people were going to be annoyed about that. He hoped they wouldn't blame Anna but he guessed that most of them would.

Donny started walking towards the technology block. Must

stop thinking about his blisters. The cycle racks were that way. He could at least take a look round Mr Mac's room before he set off home. It would be so good if there'd been a mistake. Anna's computer might have been moved in some tidy-up. He could find it for her. Take it back to *Strong Winds*. Keep it safe as she'd always hoped he would.

There was no-one there except the cover teacher. "They've told me to wait," she complained. "Apparently there's been some problem with the network and someone's coming to take a look. They don't want this room left unattended. But I've got my own children at home. It's not my job."

"I'm waiting for my mum." Donny could lie like a pro now. "She didn't know that the after school session had been cancelled. She won't get here for ages. I've only got homework and reading. I could sit in here if it would help? It is my form room."

The teacher obviously knew that she shouldn't say yes but she did anyway.

As soon as she'd gone, Donny took his shoes off, dumped them on a bench near the door and began to search.

Anna's computer had been inside one of the big walk-in cupboards where all the DT projects were stored. There were clocks and CD racks, self-propelling karts and carousels. Each school year group had a different section in the cupboard and Mr McMullen had labelled every student's shelf-space. That way no-one had any excuse to touch anyone else's work.

There was no computer in the Anna Livesey space. Just a grubby music folder that Donny recognised as being the type issued to all Year Eight students. He was surprised that it was such a mess. She must have dropped it somewhere in the department and someone must have handed it in. He'd tell her, if he remembered. It didn't seem to matter much. She was Year Nine now.

Adult voices. He looked out. Ms Spinks was marching down the path with a small man in a suit. And Toxic, in an acid-green coat and high-heeled shoes with red soles!

He'd bump straight into them if he left now.

The two doors through to the textile rooms and the main corridor were closed. Almost certainly locked. Donny couldn't risk moving right across to check. He mustn't be caught near the project cupboard either. Toxic knew that he was Anna's friend. Mustn't do anything to get her in more trouble.

There was another DT storage cupboard, much smaller. Books and stationery. No need for anyone to look in there. Donny pulled the door shut. There wasn't a handle on the inside, so he grabbed a thick bit of card and slipped it over the latch. That way it stuck out both sides and held the door closed, but not fastened.

"I thought my colleague said she'd left a student here." He recognised the deputy head's irritating accent from assemblies. "I do apologise, Ms Tune. It was probably the parent to blame. They're always in such a rush."

Donny heard Toxic sneer something about lack of Professionalism.

"What a place to leave shoes!" Ms Spinks tutted. Then she read one of Granny's neat labels. "John Walker. I don't know him. I'll put them in Lost Property – though whether they'll ever be claimed. Some of these children behave as if they were made of money!"

Toxic probably leered and nodded but she didn't answer. Surprising because she would have known this was his form-room. She issued a few technical-sounding instructions and then the two women went away.

No shoes! All the way home in his socks. Unless he could get back to his locker and find some plimsolls.

How soon could he come out? That small bloke must be the IT expert. Once he was working he surely wouldn't be that bothered by some unknown boy slipping past? The latch on the cupboard door wouldn't click because he'd got that card tucked over it.

Donny needed to be starting home. Skye would soon be looking out for him. It was about all that she did in the day – except sleep at odd times and keep folding their few clothes. She hadn't even made any dream-catchers.

He blamed the happy pills.

The new doctor didn't understand sign language so Donny had to interpret for Skye when she went for her appointments. People kept telling him that he must be sure to include everything his mother said. No editing. So when Skye had asked the doctor if he could give her any of the brave sleep drink, Donny had done his best to explain what she'd meant. He told the doctor that he thought Skye was finding it hard to settle and needed help with her bad dreams but all he'd got was disapproval and lots more notes in the file.

He knew she'd begin worrying. He'd got to go. Even if he was risking an awkward conversation with the small man in the suit.

He couldn't hear any movement outside the cupboard door. Most of the computers were at the other end of the room. The expert must be busy by now. There was no point looking at what he was doing or trying to ask an intelligent question because he wouldn't understand the answer.

Donny wriggled his rucksack onto his back so it didn't swing about. Then he began inching his fingers round the edge of the door to muffle any possible noise.

The attacker moved with an expert's speed. The moment that the door began to shift, it was grabbed by its external handle and heaved open.

Donny tumbled out. The attacker kicked him hard between the legs then dived forward, both hands to Donny's chest and sent him reeling in again.

The cupboard was shallow. Donny hit the back of his head on a shelf and slumped down.

The door slammed shut.

As this was a DT room, the attacker had no problem finding some quick-setting glue to squirt into the latch. He didn't waste time checking any of the computers. Simply wiped the hard drive of the network server and left.

CHAPTER ELEVEN

Don't Joke with the Tiger

Thursday 5 October

He couldn't tell how long he'd been unconscious. His right shoulder was stuck under one of the bottom shelves, while his left shoulder and head were crammed between the corner of the wall and the door.

It took him some time to work this out as it was pitch-black inside the cupboard. It didn't help that the throbbing pain in the back of his head was having an ouch-factor competition with the pounding ache in his balls.

When he had finally discovered which way up he was, and had levered his head away from the cold surface of the wall, he accidentally shifted his weight onto his bum. The pain that cascaded upwards was so intense he almost passed out again. He started to shake and wanted to be sick. So for a while he just lay there panting quietly in the darkness.

Then he pushed the door. It wouldn't budge. He began to wonder how much oxygen there was in an average school stationery cupboard? The atmosphere felt thick and oppressive. He had dreamt of drowning: of fighting for survival beneath tons of crushing, suffocating seawater. But there was no surface here. No blessed air to swim for. Donny's lungs heaved. He opened his mouth to shout.

Shut it again quick.

To shout might bring back the attacker. He'd got to think. Not shout.

He wasn't underwater. He hadn't been torpedoed. Wouldn't drown. There was a school DT department on the other side of that door and he surely had enough oxygen for a long time yet. There might even be a ventilator.

You're not going to die, he told himself. Not here anyway. Not now.

Donny forced himself to count to ten. Slowly. As if he was coming up in some sort of decompression chamber. Then he got carefully to his feet.

Silently, shakily, he felt around the different surfaces until he was certain he'd identified the door. He ran his fingers round its frame then put his ear against it.

He couldn't tell whether it was light or dark in the room outside. He didn't know whether there was anyone still waiting there.

But. There would be NO MORE PANIC.

His rucksack was still on his back. Inside, underneath the homework folders and the cycle helmet, the waterproof jacket, puncture repair kit and ridiculous trouser clips, were his few best things. Not the books but his map, a small torch from Xanthe and a knife from Joshua Ribiero's bosun's bag. Donny knew that there'd be a huge row if this was ever found in school but he kept it anyway.

Silent movement by silent movement, Donny shrugged the bag off his back, undid the straps, and extracted the knife and the torch. He prised the flat blade underneath the latch but discovered that he couldn't shift it.

Didn't understand why. Had to stop for a moment to gulp back the fear.

Used the torch to investigate the hinges inside the cupboard door. Another big disappointment – there was nothing that could be unscrewed.

If his knife couldn't be a tool, it might have to be a weapon. Donny put his rucksack back on; switched off the torch to save the battery and waited in the darkness clutching his knife in one hand and trying to ignore the bits of him that hurt. If the air didn't last until school reopened in the morning he'd try kicking a hole in the door. And if there was someone waiting out there, he'd be ready for them.

Donny leaned himself against the hard edges of the shelves. Constant vigilance. That's what was needed.

The cleaner, whose duties this evening included letting Donny out, had been delivered to the school at eight p.m. She had been provided with a suitable industrial solvent to remove the glue in the latch and told to leave the opening of the cupboard until the end of her three-hour shift. If freed boy didn't run, he could be collected and dumped when the van came back.

She didn't do as she'd been ordered. She knew what it felt like to be sealed in dark places and this was a child. She hurried to him straight away. She hoped he'd have a mother waiting.

Donny had been in the cupboard almost four hours. He was still standing but he wasn't quite awake. He'd lost track of time. When he heard her first quiet movements he fumbled to flick his torch on.

The light of the DT room made him blink. Instead of the attacker he saw an unknown woman whose soft face was creased with concern. He didn't even try to rush her.

She knew she mustn't speak but he looked so pale, and moved so sore. Her son back in Fujian province would be about this age. She brushed his soft cheek with the backs of her fingers. "Go home quick," she said. "You're too young to joke with the Tiger."

Donny left without saying anything. His bike was the only one in the sheds. He undid the lock and began pushing it back towards Pin Mill. His blistered feet weren't bothering him any more but the saddle really hurt and when he first tried to ride he felt so wobbly it was dangerous.

After a while he began to feel better and he cycled some of the last bit of the journey.

His mother was asleep in the bus shelter with an empty bottle beside her. It wasn't Rev. Wendy's raffle wine and it wasn't even the ship's brandy. One last colourless drop came trickling out and dripped to the concrete like a tear.

This wasn't water: it was vodka.

And there was Inspector Jake Flint, blue, white and orange lights flashing on his big black car. He'd arrived just a couple of hours after the time Donny would normally get home. Skye hadn't totally passed out then. She was wandering, desperate, incoherent. She wouldn't go back to *Strong Winds*. She wanted her child. She kept asking people, especially any young ones, but they didn't understand. Or said they didn't.

Flint had acted like all his birthdays had come at once. He whipped out a camera and a breathalyser kit and made note after note on his palm pad. He showed no interest at all in helping search for Donny or even putting through a call to the school or local accident services. Didn't even take the bottle away. He simply asked Gold Dragon loud, repetitive, questions about Skye's drinking. At one point he accused her of keeping alcohol on board *Strong Winds* deliberately to control her disabled niece. If he provoked her into attacking him he could arrest her for breach of the peace.

Flint couldn't really do subtle. Gold Dragon ground her teeth and held her hook behind her back and concentrated on her worries, not her rage.

The fat policeman's only other disappointment came when Donny showed up with properly working front and back bicycle lights of the correct luminescence as well as a kite-marked helmet and industrial quality fluorescent strips. There were no regulations to forbid cycling in socks and Donny was able to confirm that he'd passed his proficiency test when he was at primary school in Leeds.

But by that time Flint had a list of Community Representative Action Points and was reading them out to the world in his most pompous tones. His points were mostly to do with finding any trouble in the area and trying to pin it on Skye. Plus advising the local pub to hire extra security and alerting neighbourhood watch groups to the Hazard in their Midst. All stuff to make them really welcome in their new home.

"How could she have bought vodka?" Donny asked Gold Dragon, once they'd finally managed to lug his wasted mother back on board.

"Ask the fishes. Of course I've seen the way she's been behaving but I'd put most of it down to those pills."

"Her happy pills …?"

His great-aunt snorted. "Happy pills! If she were under my command I'd sink the lot of 'em. Her life's hard enough without the sawbones messing up her head."

"You don't think her head's messed up already?"

"No." She didn't hesitate for a moment. "No, I most definitely do not. She's Eirene and Henry's daughter and she's steering to a different star. I haven't got a fix on her yet but I will. If those blithering bureau-rats stop taking my wind."

Donny loved her for this but he knew more about the ways of the welfare than she did. "They will, though. They'll be round all the time doing assessments."

"Then we may yet have to take the tide out of here." Gold Dragon sounded grim. "And what in tarnation happened to you?"

Donny told her that he'd lost his shoes and had an accident. He said he'd been knocked out but not that he'd been locked up. He sort of slid past explaining the computer stuff. That was Anna's business. He did tell his great-aunt about Mr Mac not being at school and Anna thinking that he was probably being persecuted because he'd stuck up for them at the SS meeting.

"That's a smudge on the horizon," she agreed. "Now take a piece of pie and some hot chocolate and cut along to your bunk. Dizzy or sick? Not any more? Good. Help yourself to some pain-killers if you want 'em. I'm going to watch the stars a while. I'll put my head round your door before I turn in."

A whiff of tobacco rolled down through the hatchway as Donny clambered exhaustedly into his sleeping bag. It was a good smell. It meant that Gold Dragon was sitting in the cockpit of her ship, thinking over the happenings of the day and puffing meditatively on her short black pipe.

Friday 6 October

The bike ride next morning was a real struggle and Donny was late for registration. That earned them a Visit from Toxic in the afternoon. At first Donny thought it was quite funny to see the Welfare Officer picking her way distastefully to the beginning of the Hard in her fancy footwear but after that it was as infuriating and humiliating as usual.

She had two big Year Tens with her – on work experience she said. Donny recognised them from the bus. And other places.

She also had a trainee SS worker who she sent to check *Strong Winds* for Suitability. The worker was ultra-picky and quite nervous and didn't know anything about boats so it took a long time. One of the boys accompanied the trainee and the other stood sniggering as Toxic sneered at Donny.

Gold Dragon had walked to the village to buy bread and Skye was asleep in her cabin. Donny was therefore unsupervised. More evidence of Neglect.

Things weren't going well for Anna either. The blank hard drive in the IT department caused outrage – and panic among the students whose exam coursework had been deleted. Anna was a handy target for everyone's anger even when it was discovered that Mr Mac had a full set of back-up files at home. Which, however, he was only prepared to reinstall once he was back in school teaching and running his clubs as usual – with a full public apology for unfair suspicion.

Maggi managed pretty well protecting Anna from most of the other students but Gerald and Wendy were predictably horrified to discover that she hadn't been using her old computer to write essays. The ingenuity of her system for linking to the Internet failed to impress them and the single word 'chatroom' sent shivers through their souls.

It wasn't totally their fault. Toxic's Research Findings would have convinced even the calmest foster-carer that 'social network' and 'den of iniquity' were twenty-first-century synonyms. Anna, naturally, refused to explain what she had been doing or apologise for plugging into their phone system so Rev. Wendy withdrew her right to use the diocesan laptop.

When the foster-carers came into school to meet with Ms Spinks she supported their action by blocking Anna's password and taking away her library user card. Anna was denied all unsupervised access to the school IT network for the rest of term.

"What about my homework? All the teachers assume we can look stuff up whenever they tell us to."

"Books?" suggested Gerald.

"Were quite good enough in my day," snapped Wendy, whose experiment with trust seemed to have skidded to an emergency stop.

"You may request all printed material via the librarian and I'll put a note on the staff bulletin board alerting all teachers to the fact you have no Internet access for the rest of term. I will also explain why. While I'm naturally relieved that my colleague has been discovered not to have acted improperly, I'm afraid that your conduct represents an abuse of his goodwill. And of your guardians' hospitality." Ms Spinks looked smug. Then she remembered her responsibility to be caring as well. "The web can be a dangerous place, Anna, and we all have a responsibility to ensure your safety."

"Too right," said Xanthe, when Anna reported back to the Allies. "I'm definitely gonna approach nerds with a lot more respect. Look at the way that computer geek took out Donny! He must spend all his free time playing Jackie Chan games."

"It felt more like Mortal Kombat than Jackie Chan," Donny muttered. But he didn't really want Xanthe to know how scared he'd been as he'd waited there in the dark, clutching a folding penknife and wondering whether the person who'd locked him in truly intended him to suffocate.

"Any ideas about the identity of this 'Tiger'?"

"Small, dark hair, Asian, wore a suit, carried a briefcase. Either paranoid or psychopathic. Might possibly have been at that SS meeting? Definitely not someone I'm planning to add to my Christmas card list. Let's forget him. I think we ought to concentrate on helping Anna get back on-line. None of us like the sound of this Oboe character but it seems he's the only lead she's got."

"You'll have to come round ours, Anna," suggested Maggi. "One time soon when we can say we need the net for homework. You can tell them we have books as well."

"Stacked thicker than the gold in Ben Gunn's cave," agreed Xanthe.

"Thanks."

Although the sisters were eager to help, their parents seemed preoccupied. June and Joshua agreed that they'd be delighted for Anna to visit after school or at weekends, but they kept putting off ringing the vicarage to arrange a date. There'd been a outbreak of infection at the hospital that appeared to come from poor hygiene standards in Joshua Ribiero's department. He'd been plummeted into a round of emergency meetings with the hospital authorities, as well as trying to rearrange his normal work and run a full investigation so patients could honestly be reassured that they were not at any additional risk.

This left June trying to manage Xanthe and Maggi's complicated schedule of activities, plus Maggi's broken collarbone and her own committee work and commitments as a magistrate.

"You would not believe some of the trouble that we're seeing at the moment," she sighed, on one of the rare occasions that she found to time to drink a cup of tea on board *Strong Winds*. "When we came to Suffolk I expected this to be a tranquil place. I had thought I would be bored. I am sorry that I was wrong."

Gold Dragon laughed. "I could have used a gale warning or two before fetching up here myself."

"What concerns me most – and my colleagues – is our feeling that the cases we actually see in court represent only the tip of something that is happening deep down. Violence, exploitation, intimidation. Organised crime."

"When we visited Lowestoft I delivered some messages to the owner of a Chinese restaurant. She would say that you are right. But she would not say that directly to you."

"I don't see any great number of Chinese in court."

"And she offered me no names. But we had a saying in the Three Islands: 'A hungry pirate never lets the seaweed grow.' If you have members of a triad here they'll snap up anyone who's vulnerable, whatever their nationality."

"Xanthe's a hungry pirate," remarked Maggi who hadn't really been listening. "It's why she's so hard to beat when she's racing. Seaweed doesn't stand a chance."

Gold Dragon stroked her hook. "Shivers a few timbers as well, I hope. But there are pirates ... and pirates. Where I've been living the pirates are like tiger-sharks; they sink their teeth in your softest places and keep tugging till they've had your lifeblood. We call them snakeheads. You wouldn't want to find them in these waters."

June stood up to take her daughters home. She looked thoughtful. "Triads ... snakeheads ... I do hope not. Do you speak Cantonese, Miss Walker?"

"Yes, although I'm more comfortable in Mandarin."

"And were *you* once a pirate?" Maggi couldn't stop herself from asking.

"Only when I lived in the Three Islands. And even then I was more a timber-shiverer than a tiger-shark. Remember Miss Lee?"

"We've read about her," said Maggi. "She was *wicked!*"

"I considered her my pirate godmother."

"Where are the Three Islands anyway?" asked Donny. It wasn't intended as his million pound question. But from their reaction you'd think he'd requested the precise co-ordinates of the Queen's knicker drawer and was planning to pass the information instantly to Al-Qaeda.

Xanthe rolled her eyes. "What kinda hermit-shell have you crawled out from, Donny-man? Everyone knows that nobody knows the answer to that question. If they do know, they don't tell you that they know. And if by the remotest chance someone – like our legendary hostess – might actually have *lived* there, any sailor with any savvy would be sent to sea in a lobster-pot before he'd ask that question."

"Sorry I spoke." Donny felt cross and stupid. The others all knew about Miss Lee yet he hadn't even opened that book they'd bought in Colchester. He was so tired every night that he fell asleep as soon as he climbed into his bunk.

He stomped off on deck to sit with his mum. Skye hadn't been part of the tea-drinking party. When June and the girls had arrived she'd posted herself inside *Strong Winds* sturdy bows. He'd assumed that she was keeping out of the Ribieros' way because she was still ashamed of damaging their boat. Now, looking at her as she sat there, he thought she was possibly on guard.

"What is a sachem?" he asked Great Aunt Ellen later.

"Eh? Oh, you mean Henry? A sachem is a word for chief. He might also have been a mide. That's more spiritual. It would explain his dreams and the idea of the healing journey. But I'm not sure. We had so little time together. Then they sailed west and I went east – towards the Islands, though I didn't know that when I left home."

He'd shove her book in his rucksack tomorrow and try and find some time to read in registration or English lessons. He hoped things would have been more straightforward in those pre-historic, timber-shivering days.

The signaller's strength was fading now. The equinox had passed; he wouldn't see another solstice. His last hope of contact, dying.

Perhaps … the child?

CHAPTER TWELVE

Planning an Expedition

October, a fortnight later

Even getting to school wasn't straightforward any more. Donny's bruises healed, slowly, but every morning seemed to bring some new small problem. Delivery vans were left blocking the single-track road from the Hard or his bike tyres would be flat or the padlock combination mysteriously stuck. He'd had to hacksaw it twice already.

Donny had asked the people at the pub if he could keep the bike in their car park but it kept being moved so he couldn't find it in the mornings and once it even got chucked onto the community skip. He didn't think it was the pub's fault and he didn't like to say anything because his family was getting pretty unpopular anyway.

He got up earlier and earlier but he kept on being late. Almost the first job Mr McMullen had to do when he finally returned to school was to put Donny in lunchtime detention for a week. "This won't look good on the SS report," he warned. "But I haven't any choice. No-one's going to accept all these excuses as bad luck."

"Exactly," said Anna, sipping her coffee thoughtfully as Donny munched a pasty and grumbled about his tutor. "It makes so much more sense once you see it as persecution. Why not try leaving the bike at ours? There's a shed and you could get the kids to guard it. They'd like that."

When Anna got banned from the school ICT network Donny'd

tried to squash his disloyal relief that she'd be so much easier to talk to during the day. Now that he was going to be stuck in the sin bin every lunch hour, it'd be break-times only. Just twenty minutes, max. It was so unfair they wouldn't let him on the bus without charging Great Aunt Ellen all that money. He wasn't in the mood for good ideas.

"That's a load of extra walking. It must be a mile from the Hard to the Vicarage. I'm knackered all the time as it is."

"Suit yourself." She snapped the lid back on her polystyrene cup and turned away.

"No, no. You're right. Of course you are." Quick change of subject needed. "Er, picked up anything from Oboe lately?" The school couldn't ban her from ICT lessons as they were core curriculum and, supposedly, supervised. No-one had realised that she'd already completed all her coursework for the year and was up-loading it selectively so the teacher didn't notice what she was actually doing.

"Since you ask, I'm meeting him this weekend. On Saturday."

"You're *what?* You can't do that – it's dangerous!"

Anna could get furious faster than a world water-speed champion going nought to sixty. "Fine! If that's your attitude. Ask no questions and you'll be told no lies. I said the same to Maggi." She stood white and glaring. "Though I seem to remember covering for you when you weren't exactly five star health and safety."

"Huh?"

"I was worried sick all the time you were down the river in the dark in that silly little boat. But I shut up about it. I even helped."

"Okay, okay, calm down. Can we go back to the beginning

please? Where and when are you meeting this bloke? And just exactly *why*? Can't you keep it virtual?"

"When I've so much net time to spend chatting? Like in school lessons twice a week? No, I can't."

"Ribieros?"

"Not a lot. They've signed me on at the local library. Wendy and Gerald think it's for books. And I've learned some neat ways to get round firewalls. But it's hardly ever open. And it needs money."

"Thought libraries were supposed to be free?"

"Not when it's Internet. And now I need bus fares as well. He wants me to meet him in Ipswich. I think I'm going to have to find a job."

Depression set in as they both thought about money and how much harder everything was when you didn't even have enough to catch a bus. At least she'd stopped being cross.

Donny finished his pasty and licked his fingers and wondered what sort of job Anna might get and whether Rev. Wendy would allow her. He sort of wished he could get one too. Were there lots of jobs for fourteen year olds? What could he do that anyone would pay him for?

"Sail!! I can sail! Anna, I can *sail* you to Ipswich. I mean I'm not exactly sure where we'd land but I know we can do it. It's free and it'd be fun."

"Sail?"

"In a silly little boat, yes! You've done it before – remember? You even liked it until Flint tried to ram you."

"Ye-*es* …"

"Deal!" He rolled the cling-film into a ball and flicked it into the nearest bin. Score! "I'm going to do your suggestion about locking up the bike at the vicarage; you do mine about using *Lively Lady* to get to Ipswich. Let's check the tides for Saturday. What time do we have to be there? And where exactly are we going to meet him?"

"What's with this 'we'? This is my business, not yours."

Donny stared. "You can't seriously think that I'm going to let you go to meet this pervy guy in Ipswich all by yourself, do you? If you try, I'll … I'll dob you in – as you'd say yourself!"

Anna froze. Then she laughed. "That's quite funny. It's almost exactly word for word what Maggi said!"

"What did you expect? We're your Allies – remember? But Maggi can't sail at the moment. Not until her collarbone's mended."

"Which is why she's not going racing this Saturday and Xanthe is. So we've asked her parents if we can spend the day together. They were quite pleased. They think she's coming round to the vicarage. Which she will – to start with."

"Wendy and Gerald?"

"Are sorted. Gerald because it's prison-visiting day so he's going to Highpoint with Luke and Liam. And Wendy because – oh, because she's always got something amazingly important to do. She'll be relieved that she doesn't have to worry about me. She won't even have to worry that she ought to be worrying about me."

"Vicky?"

Anna gasped as if she'd spotted a scorpion in her coffee dregs. "I am such a lead-head. No-one's said anything about Vicky. Which must mean they're assuming that me and Maggi'll automatically look after her. Er … Donny?"

"Would I have her? Course I would, normally. But I'm sailing you up the river. So you don't have to do bus fares."

"Maggi'll lend me some. Until I get a job and pay her back."

"Well, couldn't we … ?" Donny was racking his brains. He didn't dare say to Anna that she and Maggi had to have a male to go with them, for protection. Or that the more he'd been thinking about sailing her to Ipswich, the more desperately he wanted to do it. He was land-sick. He knew that.

"Couldn't we ask my mum? She loves Vicky. And she's really good with her."

Anna looked awkward. "Mmmm, not entirely sure. Vicky's my sister and, I mean, what if … ?"

"You mean what if Mum got drunk? Even if she did, she'd never hurt Vicky."

"Of course she wouldn't hurt her! But she might doze off or forget to look out for her and … you know what Vicky's like. She could pull herself up and topple over the side and … "

"And there'd be no-one there to scoop her out of the briny like we scooped Hawkins. Er, is he okay, by the way?" Donny didn't want to talk about his mum's alcohol problem. Not even to Anna.

Skye hadn't got drunk since the night that he'd been late home. But then he hadn't been late home since that night. He hadn't been anywhere – except to school. That was why he hadn't even been sailing.

He and Great Aunt Ellen were watching Skye almost all the time. Not to stop her untying things – she'd been fine about that ever since their voyage to Lowestoft – but to try to make sure she couldn't get any alcohol. She'd stopped asking people for the brave sleep drink but neither of them could believe that she didn't want it. When Donny'd tried to explain that it wasn't good for her, her eyes had sort of glazed.

Skye wasn't her proper self. Not the mum he'd always known. Her hands were slow and clumsy when she was signing and she slept at all the wrong times. There was a faint smell about her clothes that Donny wasn't used to and which didn't fit with the river smells of salt and mud – or even the diesel that fuelled the generator Gold Dragon was using to provide *Strong Winds*' electricity.

These days Skye looked … empty. She didn't tell him much but he knew her dreams were bad.

"Is *he* okay? You are such a sexist! I keep telling you, you don't know he's not a she. Answering your question, however. Sings a lot. Does a few somersaults off the perch. Kids love it and the Rev. still lets it have a fly around the main landing when she gets chirpy in the evenings."

"Who gets chirpy in the evenings – Rev. Wendy?"

"Hawkins, of course! But you've made your point. It does seem worse to call her it – even if she might be a him."

"Your apology accepted. So, if you don't have to look after Vicky on Saturday, would you let me sail you and Maggi up the river? We'd go under the Orwell Bridge. It'd be well fun!"

"Don't you usually look after Skye when you're not at school? To give your great-aunt a break?"

You couldn't keep anything private round here.

He needed to go sailing this weekend.

"Oh, why can't everybody look after themselves for once!" he said grumpily and stomped off to his class music lesson five minutes early.

The teacher looked up. Looked puzzled. "Hi," he said to Donny. Year Nine students weren't usually early. Even the ones who really liked music trailed in chatting to their mates and pretending to treat the subject as a waste of time.

"Hmmmm." Donny had dumped himself and his bag at a table at the back of the room. There must be a way that he could sort out looking after Skye, and looking after Vicky, and seeing that Anna and Maggi were safe with this strange Oboe bloke. Plus doing what *he* wanted to do this Saturday, which was to take *Lively Lady* into the unknown waters of Ipswich docks. He definitely didn't have time to talk to music teachers.

"Hi," said the teacher again. "You're in 9MM aren't you? You wouldn't happen to know," he looked down at the folder he'd just been marking, "Anna Livesey in 9FT, would you?"

"Might do … Except she's a girl. So probably not. What's she done wrong?"

"Nothing wrong! Consistently excellent work. Outstanding, in fact. But I can't at this moment put a face to her. Still, if you don't know her either, I'll have to wait until their next lesson." And he returned to the clean, white, well-filled folder in front of him, leaving Donny to tussle with his own version of the 'how to get a fox, a chicken, and a sack of corn across the river in one small boat' brain-teaser.

"Got it!" he told her, when he called at the vicarage that evening to put his bike in their shed. "We'll *all* go to Ipswich on Saturday! Maggi, Skye and Vicky can go on the bus 'cos Maggi's got money, Sandra gave Skye a pass so she can get to the doctor's and Vicky doesn't have to pay anyway. You and I haven't got any money and nobody's given us a pass. So we can sail. Then we'll all meet up somewhere and you can have your dodgy assignation while the rest of us'll lurk about. Good or what?"

Anna began to giggle. "You're saying that I've spent sleepless nights psyching myself up to do what everyone knows you shouldn't – ie meet a chatroom stranger and drag my best girlfriend along while deceiving our parents and guardians – and you want to turn it into a Family Outing that even Gerald would approve?"

"Well," said Donny, "since you put it that way, I did think that it was a pity we don't have a bigger boat so we could pack some grub and all go up the river together."

This made Anna laugh even more.

Luke and Liam were already back from school and keen to be instructed in their new duties as bike security guards. Luke insisted that they had to bury the key.

"Maybe bury it at weekends," said Donny. "The whole point is I mustn't be late on school days."

Then they showed him the improvements they'd made to Hawkins's cage. They'd added extra perches all the way round which Luke said were gunwales. He'd got keen on nautical words even when he wasn't quite sure what they meant. Now he was planning ratlines and halliards and a crow's nest. "Except it'll be a canary nest. Crows are sometimes bullies."

"There's a football team called the Canaries. One of the boys in my class supports them. He's a loser," said Liam.

Luke turned on him. "When we lived in Low'stoft lots of people supported the Canaries. They're only Norwich. It's not the end of the world."

"How would I know?" said Liam, looking uncharacteristically upset. "I don't never go nowhere. Except to five-a-side and in the car to see Dad."

Donny'd been so hung up on his own problems that he'd almost forgotten about the younger boys. Gerald and Wendy were much easier than they used to be but life at the vicarage was still mega-dull. Okay he was tired, he'd had a long day, but he could surely get over it for once.

"Do you two want to come down to the Hard with me? See Mum and Great Aunt Ellen and like muck about for a while?"

The late autumn afternoon was warm and sunny so they took Vicky with them in her pushchair and went scrumping near the boatyards for canary-friendly pieces of wood. There was no sign of the Year Tens and the day was suddenly fun. Gold Dragon found them some twine and Skye sat with Luke, knotting together a length of bird-sized rope ladder. Mrs Everson, the old lady with the green leprechaun hat, stopped to ask about work on Hawkins's cage. Then Vicky and Donny floated sticks under the bridge while Liam and Gold Dragon rigged *Lively Lady* and went for a sail.

This was what it should have been like. Living at Pin Mill.

Hours passed. They were all amazed when a sharp toot-toot from Rev. Wendy's car informed them that the vicarage supper had long gone cold.

"I've made a decision," said Gold Dragon later. "There's been a film crew circling ever since this old lady arrived in Shotley." She beamed at *Strong Winds*. "They want to spend time on board and they're offering a location fee. The modern equivalent to doubloons. If I accept, we can stock up on provisions for the rest of the winter and there'll be enough left over to buy a cheap sixteen- or seventeen-foot day boat. Something that would take all those young scallywags out for a sail. It'd suit Nimblefingers too. Not to mention that I'm going stir-crazy cooped up here."

Donny was signing to Skye. He didn't know what she'd say. She seemed really well this afternoon – the kids always did her good – but had their stormy entry into Lowestoft scared her off sailing? She hadn't even tried to use *Lively Lady* since they'd been here. Admittedly she was too big to do much more than row.

"We seek adventure on the rushing waters," she signed back.

"I wish," thought Donny.

"Hmmph," muttered Great Aunt Ellen when he passed this on. "If only …"

"Good," she said. "Now, Sinbad, you tell your mother she's got to stay off the grog and learn to swim."

CHAPTER THIRTEEN

Parting Friends

Next day

"I love it," said Anna. "It's the perfect cover story. We're going shopping in Ipswich to buy your mum a cossie. How much more girly can we get?"

"That's so totally cool," said Maggi. "It means I won't have to lie to the parentals."

"Yes – but you're still not telling them anything about Oboe."

"No. But that's okay-ish 'cos it's not me meeting him. I'm just hanging round to make sure he doesn't whisk you off to the white slave trade."

"That's such a dumb expression," said Xanthe disgustedly. "Assumes all other slaves are black."

"Sorr-*ee*," replied Maggi. "Where are we meeting him Anna?"

"Er, McDonald's. I couldn't think of anywhere else. I've hardly been to Ipswich and he said it needed to be near the railway station. Even though he says he'll get a taxi."

"Then I'm definitely going to have to keep Mum and Dad out of the loop – they might not be that bothered about the sealed compartment he's got ready-booked on the Orient Express but they'd have a utter sense-of-humour failure about us going to Maccy-D's."

"I reckon I'm gonna change my ring-tone. Get something in-your-face imperialist."

"Huh?"

"Ironic, little sis. Making a statement."

"Whatever." Maggi shrugged.

Donny didn't get it either. Xanthe had this big thing about being a world citizen. She'd already announced that she wasn't going to do A-levels next year, she wanted to do the IB. And then she planned to study International Politics. He supposed she'd be leaving Gallister High.

He didn't want to think about that. He'd stick to now.

Anna's plan seemed good. McDonald's might leave adults gibbering but it was a handy spot to meet. He'd printed off a map of Ipswich docks and found what looked like a side arm of the river that would take them almost all the way there.

"How are you supposed to know it's him?" he asked.

"I'm not sure," confessed Anna. "He says he'll be wearing his tie pin and I'll recognise it as a souvenir from Happier Times. He still thinks he's meeting Mum. I'm not worried. In the real world how many Saturday afternoon Maccy-D customers are going to be wearing a tie? Let alone a tie pin!"

Gold Dragon signed her location contract from the film people and suggested Donny should buy a couple of pairs of larger trousers and some new school shoes as well as the swimming costume and a waterproof jacket for Skye. There could have been bus fares all round except Donny pleaded that sailing would turn a chore into an adventure.

"Setting off by boat to buy school shoes sort of brightens up the prospect."

She grinned her wrinkly grin. "A raid on the unsuspecting burghers and you sail home laden with their finest produce. It almost makes me want to stow away with you."

"Your Great Aunt Ellen in McDonald's – I don't *think* so!" said Anna when he told her later. "Not her sort of burgers at all."

"She's such a star," said Donny affectionately. "I've never met anyone else like her. I must read that book that she's so keen about."

"Now your bike problems aren't so bad maybe you could. You're surely up to date with work after all those detentions."

"Certainly am! And did the music teacher ever catch up with you? He was marking your work as if you were some young Mozart and kicking himself into next week because he'd never noticed you."

"That's the way I like it."

"Well, there's a really scruffy old folder of yours in the DT cupboard if you want to let him down a bit."

She looked surprised. "Can't be. I've got all my books. Last year's as well. Thanks anyway."

If it hadn't been for the weather, Donny might have settled down to read *Missee Lee* at that point. Or *Swallowdale* or *Winter Holiday*. But these days were gorgeous: it seemed as if summer couldn't bear to end. The trees along both sides of the Orwell were changing colour with such reluctance that they were a mass of orange, red, and green – nature's traffic systems gone totally asynchronic.

The late afternoon light slanted low across the water when Donny got home from school each day, colouring the river a deeper, more intense metallic blue. Actually *blue* – not grey or green or latte-brown. Skye seemed steadier, Gold Dragon was spit-and-polishing *Strong Winds* for the camera crew and, now that he'd got fitter, Donny wanted to be out of doors all the time.

Even the sullen surveillance of Toxic's Year Ten thugs couldn't spoil his pleasure. They hung around the Hard a lot, drinking from cans labelled 'Vommitt' or 'Killer!' which they chucked empty into the mud, lurching and swearing. One of them had a black, half-grown bullterrier in an outsize spiked collar which was so cartoon-ish it could almost have been funny – except for the way they were winding it up, which wasn't.

Friday 20 October
On the evening before the expedition, Luke, Liam and Vicky came down with Donny to the Hard. They called for Skye and set out along an up-river path, meandering through the trees towards the Royal Orwell & Ancient Yacht Club. They didn't go any nearer than the edge of its smooth green lawn. They weren't sure that they were allowed to be there and anyway they didn't have long. These late-October afternoons finished a lot sooner than in real summertime.

Skye had brought some water and a survival mix of nuts and raisins and they stood eating these and gazing at the view. The masts of moored boats made a mat of prickles along the left bank of the river but it was the smooth concrete curve of the Orwell Bridge that dominated the skyline. The setting sun seemed to strike it full on as it towered above the surface of the water on its eight solid legs.

"We're going to sail under that tomorrow."

"You're well lucky. You might discover it's a magic doorway." Luke was yearning to be part of *Lively Lady*'s crew. "You might get eaten by aliens."

"Maybe you and Liam can come next time," said Donny, though he knew that it was the first time that mattered.

"Eff orf, won't yer?"

" 'Ere Gnash, get 'em!"

"Friggin' mutt's round me legs!"

"Let 'im go then!"

"Nah, 'e'll bleedin' eff orf, won't ee?"

"Let 'im 'av it then, useless crittur!"

"Kill 'em, Gnash!"

The Year Tens and their dog were there. Standing among the trees behind them, blocking their way home. Four of them and a girl wearing hoodies and ripped jeans. Tattooed, razor-headed, and wired for a fight. Especially a fight with a deaf woman, a baby, two primary school kids and a skinny boy in the year below them.

"You asked for aliens?" said Donny aside to Luke. He wasn't sure how to cope with this situation. He'd seen off a couple of them when he'd been completely furious and armed with a hefty wooden oar. This was different. He was unarmed, relaxed and all the kids were here.

"They look well hard. Reckon we can take 'em on?" Luke asked.

Should they run? Through the dinghy-park or across the lawn? Seek shelter in the yacht club? Even as he began thinking this, he spotted a black Range Rover parked near the flag-staff above the moorings. The fat policeman must be there, probably checking his foul shark-boat – or in the bar, slurping.

Skye picked up Vicky and turned for Pin Mill. Began walking towards the well-hards and their dog. They bunched together blocking her way.

She paused and felt in her bag with her one free hand. Pulled out the remainder of the nut and raisin mix. Offered them to the young thugs as if some sort of payment for safe passage.

They were accepted, passed round, shoved into mouths, chewed.

And then in a hail of spit and fragments they all came flying back again, splattering Skye, Vicky and the boys.

The well-hards wiped the last smears of gob from their mouths and fell about laughing. Their dog looked confused but pulled against its chain and growled obediently.

Skye put Vicky down again and took the water bottle and a muslin from her bag to wipe the child's face and hair, softly comforting. She cleaned Liam too as his mother … might have done. Smiled at Luke, shook her head at Donny, signalling that he should stay calm, not retaliate.

When the last of the water had been used, she screwed the lid back onto the plastic bottle, scooped Vicky back up on her hip again and walked across to the gang holding out the bottle for them to take.

Astonishingly, they did.

The girl began screeching at Skye to 'stick-it' but one of the boys told her something that Donny couldn't hear. Probably that Skye couldn't hear.

The girl quit screeching, cackled with unkind laughter and began putting on an act of herself glugging from the empty bottle. The well-hards loved it.

Then they stood aside and motioned to Skye and her group to pass. Followed them back along the narrow path, relishing their mumbled private jokes and lobbing the occasional beechnut, insult or hard brown acorn at the backs of retreating heads.

The woods were growing darker. Birds were hunched along the river's edge and there were sudden flappings in the trees as pigeons and pheasants tried to settle for the night, then were disturbed by this strange procession.

Donny was seething with rage. But what could he do? Vicky had fallen asleep against Skye: Luke and Liam were walking in silence, shoulders hunched, enduring. The evening had turned sour. All the younger boys had to think of now was tomorrow's car journey to the prison.

He wondered what visiting a prison was like. He wondered what their dad was like. The boys never said much about him.

There were lights through the trees ahead of them. Car-lights. Gerald was waiting where the path turned into road. The thugs vanished into the gloom, dragging the dog along and tossing Skye's plastic bottle into the air as if it were a trophy.

Gerald was looking agitated. "Miss Walker's had bad news. A friend has died. Wendy's waiting with her till you get back. Come along, children. Strap into your booster seats. Anna can supervise baths. I've set the thermostatic control."

Skye and Donny hurried home to *Strong Winds*. Donny noticed that his mum had begun shaking again. She'd been so calm. Had dealt with the thugs, so confidently.

He supposed it was a reaction. Or the shock of the news he'd just signed to her. She probably saw Gerald's car-lights as the eyes of Pauguk, the death-spirit, gleaming through the darkness.

"A particular friend has died," explained Wendy who was waiting at the end of the gangplank. "A friend from childhood. If she'd known he was alive, she'd have made contact as soon as she returned to England. She heard it on the evening news. I didn't want to leave her until you came back. God's ways can take some getting used to."

"I'll say!" muttered Donny as he watched Wendy's sensibly-clad figure disappearing into the twilight. "Poor Gold Dragon. She thought that all her friends were gone and now she knows they are."

He cooked a noodle stir-fry but couldn't persuade Great Aunt Ellen to do more than pick at it in silence. Skye didn't want anything at all.

No-one lit the cabin lamps.

Donny went early to his bunk, retrieved *Missee Lee* from his bag, and was soon absorbed in the adventure. Several chapters in, he fell asleep.

Skye couldn't sleep and was afraid to dream. Very late that night she gave up trying and went ashore.

Saturday 21 October

Next morning the cabin smelled sour and Donny couldn't wake her. Certainly not in time to walk up to the vicarage, meet Maggi, collect Vicky, and catch the bus for Ipswich.

"She's been on the grog again," said Gold Dragon grimly. "I don't know where she's getting her supplies. She's got no money unless I dole it out and they won't have her inside the pub. Someone's putting it her way and I can't figure out who or why." She looked old this morning: old and haggard and angry.

"I should have kept a better look-out. I knew she was upset. It was totally my fault. I'll catch the bus and help look after Vicky. It doesn't matter if we don't sail."

His great-aunt stared at him. "Doesn't matter if you don't sail? Eh? Chin up, Sinbad. Sleeping Beauty's out for the count. She won't miss us. Let's cut along to the vicarage and I'll step up for sprog-minding."

"Er, wicked … Er, would you want to come to Ipswich then?"

"Certainly not," a gleam of amusement lifted her expression for a moment. "Rest at ease, Able Seaman. If the Reverend accepts my services, I'll bring young Vicky back and stand a watch on Sleeping Beauty too. You youngsters don't need me cluttering your decks."

Donny was incredibly grateful but he felt really bad. He wanted to say that they did want her on their expedition; he wanted to urge her to come with them. But this was Anna's adventure: Oboe was her secret and probably a dodgy one. Skye would have been okay hanging about McDonald's but Gold Dragon was far too shrewd.

"We do really," he said weakly. "Will you come next time?"

"Wait till I get my sixteen-foot skiff: then there'll be no escaping me."

As it turned out, she wasn't needed for baby-minding either. Vicky was going to the prison with her brothers and so was Rev. Wendy. No-one had wanted to mention this to Anna.

"We put in an application some weeks ago. Luke and Liam convinced us it wasn't right that we should always leave Vicky behind. She is his child too. But because she's so young the checking procedure is much more complex. And he's not seen her since the first weeks after she was born."

"When he tried to snatch her!"

Anna was so furious she'd hardly bothered to say good morning to him and Gold Dragon.

"Anna, I understand your hostile feelings." Rev. Wendy was using her especially calm voice – the one that only ever made Anna angrier. "And I don't want to upset you further but in fairness I have to say that it's quite likely that your mother condoned the abduction attempt. Mr Whiting was still on bail then. He hadn't been convicted."

"You think my mother knew that he was trying to grab Vicky and do a runner with her? He'd never have coped. She … she was a *baby*!"

"Possibly your mother was planning to go with them?"

"And leave me! And the boys! With you? I don't *think* so!" Anna sounded almost hysterical.

Gerald tried to help. "We don't know, Anna. None of us know. One day we may find out … "

"Too right we will!" she interrupted, but for once Gerald didn't let himself be stopped. "Until that time we have to do the best we can. You have recently started to display a much more mature and caring attitude to the younger children. Perhaps your example has encouraged Luke and Liam? They asked for Vicky to come with them. It wasn't our suggestion. We agreed, however, and so did their father. And so, belatedly, have the authorities."

"Oh suit yourselves. I don't give a stuff. Come on Maggi, come on Donny, let's go sailing."

She'd turned round and was flinging out of the house when Gold Dragon stepped in her way. "Avast there, Anna. You're bound east and they're bound west but it's important that you part in friendship. They might sink with all hands before the day's out. Or so might you. Never let the sun go down on your anger. My father used to tell us that."

Anna stared at her. Suddenly she began to tremble as if she were freezing cold. "Never … let the sun go down on your anger," she whispered. "It's what *my* father used to tell me too. But parents don't always do what they tell you. He and my mother quarrelled that night. Before he was called out. It was why the music in our house had gone wrong. They didn't make up and he never came back. The plane had crashed. The sun went down into the sea that night and never came up again, for me."

Everyone stood still, staring.

Great Aunt Ellen was the first to recover. "Oh my darling child!" she said, quite out of character, and put her old arms round her. Anna began to cry as if she'd never cried before – big, gulpy sobs that ran through her thin body like waves.

Gold Dragon stood still, held her.

Eventually Anna regained control. She kissed Vicky, sniffed a lot, said good-bye to Luke and Liam and wished everyone a nice day. Maggi helped gather up their jackets, bags and purses, then walked with her out of the door. Donny and Great Aunt Ellen followed.

Gold Dragon returned to *Strong Winds*. The three children headed for *Lively Lady*.

No-one said much.

CHAPTER FOURTEEN

Oboe

Saturday 21 October

The only person wearing a tie in the Ipswich branch of McDonald's that Saturday afternoon was Inspector Flint. And he had no tie pin. Nor anything else that could conceivably remind Anna of Happier Times.

Normally the sight of Flint hogging an entire corner of a café would have filled them all with apprehension but they were feeling too emotionally windswept to care. It even seemed funny.

"Fat spluffer! I'll bet he was born here, cramming fries into his baby gob and slurping diet Pepsi instead of mother's milk."

"Are you seriously suggesting that Flint had a mother? You mean he might once have been human?"

"I don't *think* so."

Thy waited in the small McDonald's for over two hours and so did Flint. There was no Oboe. Had he ever existed, they began to wonder? Was there some mistake in Anna's arrangements? Or had it all been a set-up, one more malign happening that they didn't understand?

Their single comfort was that this time Flint was suffering too. He'd been eating a brunch muffin when they arrived: then they watched him work his way through several cups of tea, a giant ½lb burger tower, double-fries, extra-large coke and two McSpecials with side orders of onion rings. He had his briefcase with him and made a few ostentatious jottings on his palm pad but, as he wasn't using his radio or mobile phone in the restaurant, he had nothing else to do and no-one to bully.

Customers came in, stared. Then sat as far away from him as they could.

He tried walking up to the couple of non-white workers behind the counter and asking to see their residence permits.

"You'll want me birth certificate then, mate. Born here in Ipswich 'Ospital. And me mum and dad. How about you?" was one offended answer: a flood of angry Portuguese and an obviously perfect piece of EU paper was the other.

Flint was driven back into his corner and sat there, glaring and making notes whenever either worker came to the counter. But this was a sideshow: Flint's way of passing the few moments between meals.

He was there because Anna, Donny and Maggi were there: because someone cleverer than him had used the information from Anna's old computer to hack in to her messages. He was lying in wait for Anna's mother or Anna's mother's friend.

They had to be glad that Oboe never showed.

Unless Oboe had been Flint all along? Unless it was some other kind of trap?

Their worst moment came when the fat policeman waddled over and offered Anna a special McFlurry in a glass with pink sugar frostings.

Anna was so disgusted she couldn't speak.

"Ooooh I'll have it!" said Maggi, testing the theory that Flint considered her sub-human because of her colour.

"That's not fair!" Donny backed her up. "What about me?

Don't I get offered one? Just because I'm a boy? I like pink. I think it's really gay!"

"How was your Mummy this morning?" snarled the policeman, plonking the ice cream in front of Anna and stomping back to his seat.

They left the restaurant then. There was no way they could sit there any longer, waiting for a man in a tie pin who wasn't coming – or didn't exist. Not with that creamy-white and acid pink mound of embellished air and sugar beginning to drip away in front of them.

Flint followed, waddling in their wake.

Did he think they were going to lead him somewhere? Was he playing them like small hooked fish – or could they play him?

Donny knew they definitely had to lose him before they went back to their dinghy. He really hated the way the fat man had begun smiling at Anna.

"Don't worry," said Maggi. "He's never seen me shop! Dad says he'd rather be an emperor penguin doing incubation duty through the Antarctic winter than buy a single bar of soap with me when I'm programmed to selective mode."

Her pickiness was amazing. Donny had never realised that anyone could make such a fuss about the length of lace and number of eyelet holes on a pair of trainers. Nor that it could be so completely crucial that school trousers should have waistband buttons instead of hooks or that the large, plain, swimsuit they were choosing for Skye should not be black but an exact shade of navy blue.

Anna stayed quiet. She was going along with the tease but her heart wasn't in it. She'd hoped so desperately that meeting Oboe was going to lead her to her mother.

The sooner they ditched Flint, the sooner they could get back to the river and try to think what she could possibly do next.

Maggi and Donny began moving even more slowly, stopping between shops to wait for the policeman and ask for his advice. Always within earshot of other members of the public – as if he was some sort of favourite uniformed uncle, doing special school liaison duty. Did he think turn-ups on boys' trousers should be made illegal? Mightn't they offer an unsuspected hiding place for a weapon? What were his views on trainers with flashing lights? Had the emergency services ever been mis-directed by them? Could he tell them which shops had the best range of outsize clothes? He must surely be an expert!

Flint's retail stamina turned out to be in the mayfly league, not the emperor penguin.

"I'd need a little more privacy if I were advising *you* on sizes," he said to Anna, completely blanking the others. And he sent his fingers trailing across her skinny chest as casual and as deadly as the tentacles of a lion's-mane jellyfish.

He'd already got a caller set up on his mobile phone. Proving he'd been on official business all the time. He strode off down the busy street, giving orders, a solid figure, authoritative and reassuring.

Anna looked ill. Donny felt as furious with himself as with Flint. He already knew how dangerous the fat man could be. How could he have let her get in that situation? He had come along to protect her.

Maggi was as big-eyed as if she needed extra optical capacity to believe what she'd just seen.

"Can we buy everything and go now please?" said Anna.

"You're not …"

"Going to lodge a complaint? You still haven't understood, have you? How people like me can be treated. What 'vulnerable' means. Think what you like about Wendy and Gerald but at least they're totally straight."

They'd left *Lively Lady* moored alongside a pontoon in a branch of the river called the New Cut. There was a boatyard there, heavily protected against vandalism. A survivor from a different world.

A disused railway track ran further along the quay then was blocked by a high fence with spiked grey metal palings and razor wire. Someone had bent away a corner of the fence to make a hole through which trespassers, dog walkers, litter throwers and other people with private business could easily pass.

REDEVELOPMENT AREA
DANGEROUS
KEEP OUT

The railway line stretched on into a wasteland. It didn't look dangerous. All that was there – apart from litter, shrubs, dog mess and rubble – was a pile of cream-painted metal containers, the same type as were constantly being loaded and unloaded from the huge ships in the Port of Felixstowe.

Except they were older and rustier. Rejects probably. Their corners were buckled, joints and rivets weeping with corrosion. They were stacked two-high behind a huge screen which had a colourful impression of the offices and executive apartments that were going to be built on the site. Not a cloud in the painted-blue sky.

The children hung around for a moment staring vacantly. The containers had single doors and occasional windows and instructions pasted onto them: assembly point, drying area, overall storage. A flesh-pink flower logo curled over the words *Pura-Lilly Services*. There was a TV aerial and a washing line with t-shirts, underclothes and pillow-cases, which looked as though they'd been recently pegged out.

"No-one could be living there," said Maggi. "They must be for workmen to change their clothes and stuff."

"But they aren't doing any work. It says completion 2012. That's years away."

"I think they are … houses," said Donny. "I think I saw a face like peeking out. From that top one with the wire-mesh over it. That wouldn't be workman, not on a Saturday afternoon. Anyway that's someone's personal washing."

"Do you want to go through the hole in the fence so we can check them out?" Their disappointing day and her broken collarbone hadn't slaked Maggi's appetite for adventure.

"No I don't," said Anna. "If there are people who have to live in boxes like that I don't even want to know. It's totally creepy. I'd rather be down in that smelly mud. Can I have another go at helming? The rest of today's been such a total write-off."

"We went shopping," said Maggi. "We got the trousers and the cossie and the shoes."

"Yeah," said Donny "Shopping. That's what people do on Saturdays."

It was almost teatime and the water level in the New Cut had fallen to a thin, brown stream. High walls blocked any breeze and *Lively Lady*'s sails hung slack as Donny rowed her out into the main river. Anna was at the helm and Maggi sat snugly at the foot of the mainmast. She said she was ship's cargo.

The breeze caught them as they exited the Cut and the dinghy heeled sharply. Donny worried that Anna might panic or even capsize. They'd had an easy trip on the way up. But she wasn't caught out. She loosened the mainsheet and shifted her weight onto the dinghy's gunwale as they went flying down the river.

"You're good!" he said, clicking the jib sheet back into its cleat.

"I've been reading," she called back. "And I keep looking at those red and green strips of ribbon to check which way the wind's coming."

"They're tell-tales," explained Maggi. "Gold Dragon was probably using them for Liam."

"Couldn't *Lively Lady* have a proper flag? On top of her mast, with maybe some special symbol on it?"

"Huh? Who was it said that flags were stupid? Who wished she'd never made one?"

"If it was me, I blame you. You were probably stressing me out at the time." Her face was pink, her hair whipping untidily in the wind. For the first time that day she looked almost cheerful.

"Break it up, you two," said Maggi. "We'll have an Allies' meeting and ask Xanthe."

They had passed the commercial area at Cliff Quay and were heading towards the centre of the Orwell Bridge. The cars above them were invisible but a constant flow of lorry tops indicated that this was the major connection between the Port of Felixstowe and the rest of the UK. The view beneath the bridge looked like a framed old master painting.

"Luke said this might be a magic doorway. I can see what he meant."

"That boy's got quite a mind," replied Anna dryly.

"I think Luke and Liam are cute," said Maggi. "And Vicky. Maybe we should let them be Allies too?"

"Nope," said Anna, leaning forward and gazing ahead. "They can't keep secrets – except for Vicky 'cos she can't talk properly. She and Donny's mum are good like that."

"Confederates then," said Donny. "They'd like to be confederates and they are guarding my bike for me."

"You mean they're burying the woodshed key and digging it up six times a day like puppies with a bone … but, okay, Luke and Liam can be confederates. If Xanthe agrees."

"She will, she thinks they're cute too," said Maggi. "Hey! Look behind you, Anna!" An East European grain ship had pulled away from Cliff Quay and was overtaking them rapidly as they headed for the bridge. Two yachts were approaching from the other side. Suddenly the wide central space looked much narrower, a potential disaster area, not a tranquil canvas.

"Help! Donny! Maggi! Tell me what to do – quick!"

Donny glanced astern. The grain ship was already crossing their wake and the yachts were hanging back to let it through. It was no big deal.

"No probs," he said. "Helm down, sheet in, bring her closer to the wind. Go about even. Head for those two old rust-buckets moored over there. Never mind the stink. The ship'll be past in a few minutes. You could let the yachts through as well. Then straight down river for *Strong Winds*. I want my tea."

❉

Skye retreated back to her cabin when she saw them come alongside. That was Donny's worst bit – even worse than seeing Flint put his pudgy hand on Anna. That his mum should want to avoid him. He'd been so proud of her, only yesterday.

Maggi and Anna pretended not to notice and Great Aunt Ellen was ready with bread and paste, ginger biscuits and a pile of newspapers.

"I want to tell you about the man who died," she said. "I told the Reverend he was a childhood friend but that was … the smaller half. I want to tell you, Sinbad, because we're family and you, Anna, because of what happened earlier. You probably didn't know but … you broke down a barrier."

Anna looked a bit uncertain.

"Should I leave?" asked Maggi. "I'm okay – if you need the space."

Great Aunt Ellen closed her eyes a moment, then shook her head.

"You're … ship's company," she said and launched straight in. "Towards the end of the war, September 1944, to be exact, I was finally old enough to be doing my bit. I was working in a radar station – Bawdsey – and my job was to plot shipping and also air traffic. That was the year of the flying bombs, V1s, doodlebugs. More and more were coming our way as the Germans retreated up the North Sea coast. They came in so fast. Crossed the North Sea in minutes. When we operators were changing shifts we had to leap out of our seats to let the next girl take over without missing a single cross on the plot. A matter of honour – and important. It happened one night that the bomb I'd been tracking was coming direct for Bawdsey. They very often came close – we were so near Harwich. But this was straight for us. My shift ended. I jumped up: my relief carried on. Then I ran outside to watch. I was young. Even if we were going to die I wanted to see. It was dark. The sound of waves against the shingle was always there but I could hear that V1 engine. It was heading for our array – those pylons that they've demolished. There were wires between them: one and two, three and four. If it hit – and I couldn't see how it was going to miss – we would all be gone – and the main radar defence system for eastern England would be gone with us. There was someone beside me. The engine cut. That was the moment everyone dreaded. The moment you knew that the bomb was coming down. It was him and I was in his arms."

Utter silence in the cabin.

"It was the Boff. He didn't work there then. He was inspecting or something. Must have thought he was about to see everything destroyed. But the bomb missed. It found the only gap between the pylons and came down in the marshes behind. Didn't even kill a sheep. It was a double miracle. I had found him and we didn't die."

"The Boff?" asked Anna.

"It was what the others called him. I expect there's one in every group of friends."

"What happened then?" Maggi was looking at Gold Dragon as if she was seeing her in a completely new way.

"Nothing. We jumped apart, laughed, exclaimed, chatted. We were alive. We were happy. We probably kissed a bit more but that was it. No more than an extraordinary coincidence. He had to leave the next day and I went back on duty. It was only a few months later that the torpedo killed my brothers. He wrote, of course, he and his sister. Letters of condolence and deepest grief."

"Sister?" It was Anna again.

"Theodora. They were close friends with the older ones. They'd often holidayed together, before the war. She worked in one of the Ministries. Cal was a specialist in digital encoding. I've been reading his obituaries all day."

Her voice was soft and tired. Donny had never known Gold Dragon like this. She pushed a selection of papers towards them.

He took a big swig of his tea and started to read. 'Professor Callum Reif: distinguished scientist, telecommunications pioneer, ornithologist, spiritualist …' After a while he looked up. "This guy sounds okay," he said. "He had a dinghy …"

"On the Norfolk Broads …" added Maggi. "They're sort of behind Lowestoft. We've never been there. Don't know why. They sound well cool. We've sailed past Bawdsey Manor though, loads of times. That's where he worked, it says. Not during the war, afterwards."

"Objective Bombing of the Enemy," Anna's voice was so faint that they had to stare to hear her, "was his greatest single contribution to the war effort."

"All those lives saved on D-day," agreed Great Aunt Ellen. "And there was so much more. He was part of that brilliant group of scientists, linguists, mathematicians. The code-breakers at Bletchley Park – you'll have heard of them but there were so many more great minds. The importance of what they were doing … it made my school-girl crush seem pitiful."

"Objective Bombing of the Enemy," said Anna in the same flat tone. "O.B.O.E."

Donny and Maggi looked at her: they were beginning to get it.

But she was looking at Great Aunt Ellen. "Ellen," she asked. "Do you know who you're talking about?"

"I'm talking about the man I loved and never married," said Gold Dragon with just a fleck of asperity in her voice. "The man who's just died without me knowing he was still alive."

"Yes, I'm sorry about that," said Anna. "It's … that you're also talking about the great-uncle I never met. The man who didn't show up in Ipswich today. His screen name was Oboe. He must have expected me to guess." She shook her head at her own stupidity. "You can use a screen to hide things or to see them differently. I thought Oboe was a musician. Like my mother was – is! In fact he was the uncle she'd told me about. The one who made a bomb-aiming system even though he was a pacifist. She was completely horrified by him."

"But …"

"Oh I'm not horrified. I love my mother but I don't agree with everything she thinks. She told me once about the quarrel." She was quiet a bit longer then she added, "That would have been what was on his tie pin. He must have meant the double meaning. They'd been very close when she was young." She saw that Great Aunt Ellen still hadn't quite understood. "I called myself 'Thea', you see, in my messages to him, because that's my mother's middle name. *Her* mother was called Theodora. She was his sister."

"Yes," agreed Gold Dragon, sounding even more depressed, "She was."

"You could have been *my* Great Aunt Ellen as well …"

"I wish …" said Gold Dragon, trying to smile but not succeeding.

"Well, it says here," interrupted Maggi, who'd been reading as well as listening, "'Professor Reif's last weeks were brightened by the hope that he'd finally made contact with his estranged niece, the singer Lottie Livesey. She was the only child of his beloved sister, the late Theodora Thorrington. Professor Reif himself never married. He died without issue.' Maggi looked up from her paper. "You might have got your signals mixed, Anna, but at least you made that old guy happy."

CHAPTER FIFTEEN
Out of the Nettles

October half-term

Anna and Great Aunt Ellen went to Oboe's funeral together. It was in the senior common room of a college in Cambridge. It was during half-term week so Anna didn't even need permission to have the day off school. Rev. Wendy made sure she was working from home in the vicarage all day and Gerald drove them there.

It wasn't a religious funeral, just a sort of gathering, Anna explained afterwards. There'd be a box of ashes to follow in a few months time. They'd met a lawyer who had explained that Professor Reif had left his body to science. When science had the bits it wanted, everything else would be cremated. She said that the lawyer had been quite bothered about this.

"I'd assumed he'd want the ashes interred near his sister. She's buried in one of those pretty Cotswold churchyards. But in his final Letter of Instruction the professor said that wouldn't do. It would be illogical, he said, for him to take space in a churchyard when he'd no belief in God. He was a stickler for logic."

Anna had nodded approvingly but Great Aunt Ellen had objected. "That makes him sound chilly. Callum had imagination."

At this point some elderly professor had almost patted Gold Dragon on the head, Anna reported with a giggle.

"Very good indeed, my dear. Of course he did. That's what made him such an outstanding scientist – demonstrating those astonishing connections between the migration patterns of birds and their perception of frequencies. Then expressing the formations digitally. Now in my own research …"

He'd looked as if he were about to launch into a lecture.

"Quite so," the lawyer had interrupted. "No lack of imagination, certainly. Imagination *and* logic. His Instruction states that, as he'd spent so many years of his life on the edge of the North Sea – that that was where his final ashes should *logically* be scattered. Out at sea on a windy day. Anywhere between Woodbridge Haven, Orfordness and Lowestoft."

"I'll do it," said Gold Dragon.

The lawyer had looked tremendously relieved, Anna told them. But not all that surprised. "He was such an admirer, Miss Walker. He used to follow your voyages. Often spoke of you to me. He never expected that you would return to England. A tragedy of timing."

The lawyer pursed his lips and shook his head. This was when Anna had decided that he was quite a decent sort.

"Thank you," he'd said again. "I'll be in touch when the ashes are available. It won't be for a few months. As Professor Reif's Executor, my main problem is discovering the whereabouts of Ms Lottie Livesey."

"I'll help you. Does she get money from his Will?" Anna was so direct that it must have sounded a bit rude.

"No, my dear, not as such. There are issues of Trust and Conveyance and … it's all rather complex for someone your age."

"I'm fourteen and I'm not stupid," said Anna. "And I have my sister to think of as well as my mother."

This had definitely come as a shock. "You have a sister? Oh

dear, oh dear. I don't think the professor knew there had been another child. I may have to revisit the Final Instruction. Er, how old is the second young lady?"

"Eleven months."

Anna reported that the lawyer had looked oddly relieved at this. She simply felt annoyed that neither Vicky nor Lottie had been left anything in Oboe's Will.

"But I was," she told them.

The Allies stopped eating and stared. They were back in school after half-term and having lunch together in the dining-hall. It was crowded and noisy but they didn't have any other choice. The weather had turned wet and windy so no-one was allowed to take trays of food outside any more.

Donny didn't like it. People had mainly stopped getting at Anna, now that everything was sorted again in the DT department but the well-hards were back in school. They'd been excluded or out on work experience or something in the weeks before half-term but now they were back and mean and looking for people to bully. He planned to keep out of their way but it wasn't so easy when everyone was stuck indoors like this.

"Sacks of priceless treasure?" asked Xanthe keenly. They knew Anna never had as much as twenty pence that she could call her own.

"No. It's a torn diagram and a binary string. The lawyer said that the string's time-limited and he'd been Instructed to hand it over as soon as he met me. That was apparently okay, legally. Since it isn't Goods or Chattels. Or money."

The others said nothing. Money would have been a lot more use.

"I don't mind," said Anna. "About the money, I mean. Wendy says she might allow me to do a weekend paper round if I prove my commitment by helping with the parish mag until Christmas. So I'll be earning after that. Actually I feel quite fond of Oboe for guessing that I might like a challenge. I get his dinghy as well but that's somewhere in Norfolk and needs a lot of work done. So I can't afford it yet and anyway it's a Chattel."

"Have you got it with you?" asked Donny. "The puzzle, I mean."

"Mmmm," said Anna pulling a single transparent punch-pocket from her bag and placing it carefully between the lunch-trays.

```
Insert symbols 1111111101001100100-.
[0]11100011010010. <[0]1100001110111011 to
estimate numeric value of crumbs. Repair
diagram only if you feel understanding.
```

Xanthe, Maggi and Donny stared.

"Er … what are you supposed to do with that lot?"

"I've sellotaped his diagram for starters." She turned the punch-pocket over. Showed them a complicated diagram with intersecting lines. It had been ripped and then repaired.

"This was the invention that upset Mum." She faltered a minute and carried on. "She'd been on at him to tell her what he did in the war. She was a pacifist and he was too, normally. But not in 1940. So when he had to tell her that he'd developed a bomb-aiming system, she totally freaked. Tore his diagram in half and said she'd never speak to him again. They'd really liked each other before that. That was why he was trying to message her when he knew he was going to die. Wanted to part friends …"

"Ooh," said Maggi. "That's so sad! "

"It's all been a mess. One of the younger profs gave me a book that he'd written about telecoms pioneers and it had loads about Oboe. I wish we'd met. Some of his ideas were amazing. I mean, like this diagram – it's such a simple concept, it's completely brilliant."

Donny had another look. The curving lines went out from the East Coast and across the North Sea. To Germany he supposed. He wasn't sure the concept was that simple.

"It's a cat-and-mouse principle. Two radar base stations transmitting at pre-determined ranges. They intersect at the spot where the aircraft should drop its load."

"Of bombs? Eugh!"

"It was a *war*," said Anna. "And his system was so amazingly accurate they used it to drop equipment to resistance fighters too."

He could see trouble coming. The sisters were both strong on World Peace.

"Tell us about the other bit – the puzzle? "

"A last minute idea, the lawyer said. When he wasn't getting any response from the person he thought was Mum. That was when Gerald and Wendy had taken my computer and before you got me the laptop access."

"Precise as that?"

"Yeah. Apparently Oboe really wanted there to be someone who'd remember him personally. Except for other scientists, where he's famous. He didn't think it would be quite right for him to try to contact me directly. 'Cos of my age and he didn't think Mum would want him to – ironic when you think it was me in the chatrooms all the time – so he thought he'd leave me a puzzle. The lawyer explained that Oboe had known my dad ages ago and thought that if I was anything like him … I'd enjoy it. "

"Are you anything like your dad?" asked Xanthe.

"I … hope so." She turned the punch-pocket puzzle-side up. "It's binary, which makes sense. Oboe liked digitalising things. And there was something about crumbs in one of his messages. I think it was a quote but I didn't get it. I'll put the binary back into decimal. Take out those redundant zeros first. I could find a converter but I thought I'd work it out by hand. While I'm still officially off-line."

The Allies looked at one another and shook their heads.

"You can have my new notepad," said Maggi. "It's a Moleskine, It's well classy."

Money. What a pain.

Polly Lee was earning theirs but it came at a cost. Maybe they should have guessed that the film-makers would be more interested in her than in *Strong Winds*. Every day they asked her to haul up one or other of the junk's wide-battened sails. Then they made her sit in her cockpit, good hand on the helm, reminiscing about the hundreds of solitary miles she'd travelled under the wide skies of two hemispheres. They kept pleading for a trip down the Orwell, which she had to keep refusing. She used the tides as her excuse: didn't tell them the real reason – that she had been grounded by the SS as a potential child abductor.

Great Aunt Ellen had been brought up never to complain. She'd taken the film-makers' doubloons, now she was earning them.

The money had made it possible for them to eat better, for Skye to begin attending swimming lessons, and for the camper-van finally to be released from the car pound and towed to the vicarage driveway. Donny and Skye could get access to all their old possessions.

Donny couldn't think of anything he wanted. Not at this price.

Every day, after the film-makers had gone home, Great Aunt Ellen linked her hook into the 360 degree swivel joint she'd attached to *Lively Lady*'s tiller, hauled in the dinghy's mainsheet with her good hand and bashed off into the failing light. She went sailing in all weathers with only the briefest words to Skye and Donny. Her soft mood had vanished. When she came back they'd hear her pacing *Strong Winds*' deck until late at night, or see her sitting on the cabin roof, puffing her pipe into an angry red glow instead of its usual thin blue trail of falling smoke.

Donny dreaded her bad temper but he sort of understood. He wondered whether he could get up a petition to try to convince Tony that it was cruel and inhuman to insist that his great-aunt had to keep *Strong Winds* stuck on the Pin Mill mud. They hadn't heard anything about another meeting and, apart from Toxic's visit, no-one had come to check on them. Not a single assessment.

When Flint had snarled at him in Ipswich Donny had been sure that the fat policeman knew that Skye had been drunk the night before. But no-one had come round. Not even Sandra. He'd almost forgotten what a clip-board looked like.

Which was actually quite spooky.

He asked Rev. Wendy whether she'd received any SS letters or been to any meetings that he didn't know about. She said she hadn't and he believed her. She wasn't his official foster-carer any more so they probably wouldn't invite her anyway

– especially after the last time. So, if the SS weren't that bothered about checking up on them, why did they have to stay grounded? Even *Strong Winds* being out on a mooring would be so much better.

He went with his mum to the doctor's every couple of weeks but he'd given up hoping that would do her any good. The doctor didn't want to hear about Skye's dreams or her feelings. Just kept on dishing out the pills.

The swimming lessons were okay but the rest of the time his mum drifted around keeping out of sight, except when the younger children were allowed to visit. She had tried making friends with the half-grown dog but its owner jerked its chain and hit it so it snarled when she came near.

Donny went up into the Pin Mill woods and collected her a whole pile of stuff to make into dream-catchers. She thanked him with her usual sweetness then sat there stripping everything to its veins and dropping it despondently. She didn't get drunk but never quite lost that faint sour-sweet smell he'd come to associate with 'grog'.

One Monday, when Donny returned his bike to the vicarage woodshed to be guarded by the young confederates, Luke met him round the back, his finger dramatically to his lips. "There's a Viking ship in the nettles behind Duke's yard!" he whispered, almost bursting with excitement.

"A Viking ship?" It was getting dark much earlier now and it had been raining all afternoon. His tormentors had been giving him a hard time at school – they did a great line in deaf-mute impressions – and he was cold and wet from where a white van had driven dangerously close and soaked him with muddy water on his way home.

"Yeah! Me and Liam found it yesterday afternoon when we snuck off. It's right far behind those sheds. Must have been there ages!"

"Um, great," said Donny. "You must show me sometime."

"Reckon we could go right now! You could tell Gerald after. We could say we'd been having a jog. That's fitness, see, and I'm meant to be writing it down for a project."

Donny tried to say he was tired and wet and that he'd got homework to do but the expression on the younger boy's face got to him almost as effectively as one of Anna's tense pale shrugs would have done.

They met Gold Dragon on their way to the yard. She'd spent the afternoon in the cabin with a media publicist. Things couldn't get much worse for her.

"Luke reckons he's found a Viking ship. It's in the nettles behind the boat yard. If you come, we could walk straight in."

"What does the expedition leader think? Have you a berth for an old, beached pirate?"

Luke considered her seriously. "Li an' I sometimes thinks it's a pity it was only your hand that got cut off, not your leg. It'd be better still if you had a patch over one eye and your parrot hadn't died."

The end-of-the-day look vanished. "Sure you don't want me slashed to the bone with a cutlass blade's cold steel? That settles it, I'm signing on!"

Reaching Luke and Liam's Viking ship was rather like scrambling towards the Sutton Hoo burial mounds when even the grave robbers had abandoned them. As they stepped over rusty anchors, abandoned trailers and half-hidden heaps of mooring chain, Donny wondered what Gerald would say if he'd known that Luke and Liam had 'snuck off' here. Health and Safety hadn't checked this place out for a millennium or two.

The boys had beaten down the tallest of the nettles surrounding their find but the light was fading too fast for Donny to make out much more than the broad gracefulness of the boat's shape. She was maybe four or five metres long, tapered at both ends and reassuringly beamy in the middle. Donny guessed that the feature that had excited Luke and Liam was the broad strake of wood that ran along either side. It curved upwards to a beaky prow at the front and a high rudder-fitting astern.

"Made for hanging shields, you reckon?"

"Yeah! An' look, me and Liam think this here's her mast."

Sure enough, close under the forgotten boat, they could make out spars, long oars and a rudder. Everything had been left carefully chocked up away from the damp earth and a hand-daubed notice proclaimed that the boat had at some time been FOR SALE. Looking at the height of the surviving nettles, that had to have been a while ago.

"You know I think your Vikings must already have discovered fibreglass," Great Aunt Ellen had worked herself round, and underneath, and was tapping the boat's hull.

"Oh," said Donny. He felt a bit disappointed.

"Count your blessings, Sinbad. You'll be begging me to trade in *Strong Winds* when I get you slaving on her spring refit. Cut along home now, young Luke. Your tea'll be waiting and I'm not at all sure that you've been showing your navigation lights correctly. Donny, pass my respects to the Reverend. I'll see whether I can't find someone in the office to tell me the history of this raider."

"Don't let on we was here though," said Luke, suddenly alarmed. "One of them blokes shouted at us."

"They can hoist me bones in Execution Dock before I'll say a word." She looked at Donny. "Don't get your hopes up, Sinbad, but this might be the saving of your mother and myself. Anyway, time spent on reconnaissance …"

"Is seldom wasted." It had been one of Granny Edith's main mottoes.

He saw Gold Dragon smile through the dark. "All naval families know that one," she said. "Learned it from the Vikings, probably. Reconnaissance is exactly what I need to do. And this could be the boat to do it in. Steady enough to take Nimblefingers and a whole tribe of Scallywags. I'll offer them a fistful of doubloons if she's still on the market."

CHAPTER SIXTEEN

Vexilla

Mid-November

He was learning to hate roads. And tracks, lanes, paths and corridors. All the closed-in places that you had to go down even if you saw your enemies waiting at the other end, or guessed they were going to step out in front of you or come up quickly and jump you from behind.

When the white van drove too close and soaked him the first time he had assumed it was an accident, like the time he'd been walking home with Anna. When it seemed to be coming straight at him, fast and menacing, in the growing darkness of the next three evenings, he began checking his map for alternative routes.

Many of the back roads between Gallister High and Erewhon Parva were twisty, single-track lanes, sunk deep between high banks and hedges. Donny dreaded meeting the van round any of these corners. Each night he chose different turnings so he never made the same journey two evenings running. He pushed his bike down footpaths and round fields. It took longer and he was more and more tired and he was ashamed of himself for avoiding the confrontations.

But what chance did a boy on a bike have against a speeding van? And who could he ask for help? The police? Police meant Flint as far as Donny was concerned. He'd rather end up in casualty than go anywhere near Flint.

So he wore his cycle helmet and florescent strips almost

willingly and pedalled around the unlit lanes at the end of each day feeling apprehensive and humiliated.

He knew he'd seen the van before. As if this could be its regular route – a journey to work maybe? It had a logo and some writing but it was always coming so fast that Donny couldn't read what it said. Otherwise he could maybe have rung up the driver's employers and reported him for dangerous driving.

Who'd listen? He was only fourteen and there were white vans everywhere. Even the company who cleaned the pub had a white van.

Corridors were bad too. The Year Ten well-hards didn't seem to spend much time in lessons and it felt as if someone had handed them his exact time-table. By now he should have been settling in and making more friends. He'd got his Allies for break and lunch-times but walking between lessons was normally an easy way to get chatting with people you didn't know who were in the same sets as you. You could maybe mess around a bit.

No chance of that, when every time he came out of a classroom, there'd be a couple of drop-outs waiting to call him a girl or a pee-doh or do their grotesque impressions of Skye.

Most students avoided them. They were certainly expert at swinging their school bags to knock other people over. And their bags were so heavy you'd think they'd been specially weighted with encyclopaedias.

Spitting was one of their favourite weapons. Anyone who walked with Donny would soon get a slimy yellow gobbet in his or her face. He didn't now what they chewed but their spit was disgusting. And there were endless glugging-from-plastic-bottle routines which he didn't understand but which were somehow the most infuriating of all.

He finally lost his temper and went at two of them with his fists. A crowd quickly gathered and a few people cheered him on. He got put in isolation by the student managers and had to admit that it had been him who hit out first.

The student managers made him sign a letter, which they were going to send home to his parent or guardian. Any more offences and he would automatically be suspended. That would be the end of his 100 percent attendance record.

Gold Dragon wouldn't be too pleased. She was keeping her part of the Care Plan. So was Skye. Well, at least she was going to the doctor and taking the pills. He would be the one who'd messed up.

But the letter never arrived.

They never got letters now, except a few for Polly Lee.

Donny realised that the bullies would have won if they provoked him into another fight. But he couldn't help feeling a bit pleased when he remembered the moment that his knuckles had connected with the first well-hard face. Its owner had looked so shocked.

He thought about cycling the direct route home again. And being ready to take the white van's number.

He'd left the bike in the vicarage woodshed as usual and was walking the final mile down the narrow lane to the Hard when he was mugged. Someone jumped him from behind, pulled his rucksack off, kicked him in the small of the back and ran swiftly away into the darkness.

Donny was flung forwards and saw nothing. By the time he'd picked himself up and had chased back up the lane, there was nothing much to see.

Except for his rucksack which had been chucked onto the verge immediately before the main road and Inspector Flint, twenty metres further on, chatting to some resident who Donny recognised as being part of the local Neighbourhood Watch.

He wasn't sure what he should do. He picked up the rucksack then hesitated. Should he say something to the resident? Surely he and Flint would have seen the attacker?

He didn't want to. He wanted to go straight home. There was the Flint factor for one thing – and also he thought the man had been one of a group of people who'd come to see them after the first time Skye got so drunk. They said that they would be keeping an eye on her. Maybe it had been meant kindly; it hadn't sounded that way.

But what if somebody else got mugged in the same place? Got hurt even? Some nice old lady – like their friend, Mrs Everson?

He should have saved his breath. Neither man had seen or heard anything. Made it sound like his fantasy. Apparently there'd had been an SS worker with them but he'd just left.

Flint said he'd be sure to let Education Welfare know that Donny'd been in trouble, again. Then he went on about Problem Families and Some People's misdirected charity. The resident agreed sourly and nodded towards Erewhon Parva vicarage.

Donny had to force himself to go down the lane the following night. He kept in the middle of the road, stopping and staring right round, then running as hard as a salmon in spate. The next night he went round via the footpath through the woods. It had been raining and he couldn't see the boggy bits because he didn't want to use his torch. That meant that he got black leaf mould on his socks and up his trouser legs as well. Skye tried asking him what had happened but he wouldn't tell her.

The only good thing was that Great Aunt Ellen had bought the Viking boat. They were all going to spend the weekend helping to fit her out.

He'd asked the boatyard a few times whether there was anything he could do to help with *Snow Goose* but they'd always said no. Now that Gold Dragon was a Customer it was different. She'd rented space in their shed where everything was dry and there was light if they wanted to work late. It was a pleasant place, with sawdust and shavings on the floor, and plenty of trestles on which to rest the boat and her equipment.

The new boat was white inside and out. She looked okay after a pressure wash, but dull. The white was slightly yellowing and stained in a few places. Skye ran her fingers over some tiny cracks.

Luke had come to help with the first day's work. He and Skye stood together and frowned.

"They sells paint here," he said.

Skye chose a rich deep red and used it to gloss the top strake all the way round. Luke fetched a pencil and paper from *Strong Winds* and drew two fierce unblinking eyes, which he said that they should paint on either side of the new boat's bow when the red had dried.

"Eagle-eyes. So's she can see her enemies."

Donny had noticed that several of the Thames barges and the older fishing smacks that visited Pin Mill Hard had beautiful scroll work either side of their bows. None of them had eagle-eyes though.

"Maybe they ain't too quick to spot trouble coming. Us lot …
we've gotta be well sharp."

"What do we do?" Donny asked. "When we've spotted trouble?"

Luke looked at him in surprise. "Fight 'em if we can. But there's
too many or too big, then we dodge off. Like being a little 'un at
school."

He spoke matter-of-factly, as one who knew. Fight or dodge:
a practical, everyday decision, not something to make you feel
ashamed and sick.

Gold Dragon chuckled. She said that if her simple scouting
skiff was turning into a fully-fledged man-of-war, then they
should re-paint the rest of the hull as well. A dull grey undercoat
first, but tomorrow a gleaming navy blue. And now the new boat
had grown so grand, she supposed they'd want to raid her stock
of gold leaf when they came to inscribe her name.

"Did the man in the office tell you what she's called?"

"There's no record. It's over to us."

Donny'd been wondering about *Wild Cat*, which was the name
of the yacht that the Swallows and Amazons were sailing at
the beginning of *Missee Lee*. Unfortunately she'd blown up and
sunk. Also *Wild Cat* had been a bright green schooner with space
for about nine or ten people to sleep on board. Not an open,
fibreglass day boat with a single lugsail, one pair of oars and
fittings for an outboard motor if required.

Luke suggested the *Black Pearl*, but only half-heartedly because
their boat was going to be almost every colour except black.
Then he said that Gold Dragon should choose because she'd was
so old she must have seen every boat there ever was. She set him
wire-brushing the anchor for that.

It was late evening before Donny took Luke back to the vicarage. He called in to see Anna who was in the sitting room covering pages of Maggi's notebook with calculations. Work on her great-uncle's puzzle seemed temporarily to have taken the place of her search for her mother. Perhaps she didn't think there was much she could do with no Internet access.

Or was she hoping that there might be some connection?

"Anna … when Oboe was trying to get your mother's attention by sending out those messages, why did he say he was signalling from Mars?"

"I asked Gold Dragon that one when we were coming home from Cambridge. She said it was more Arthur Ransome stuff. She said that Cal and his sister were almost as obsessed with the *Swallows and Amazons* stories as her brothers and sisters were."

"Makes sense, I suppose. If they were all such friends."

"Might be infectious, you think? I'd better get myself vaccinated. So I'm assuming that he might have read Mum some of the stories or taken her sailing when she was a child – though she didn't ever mention it."

"Seems that there's a lot in our families that never gets mentioned."

"Yeah." Anna put a pair of brackets round a set of numbers and started some complex multiplication sum. She didn't sound all that interested.

Donny got his bike out of the shed and hurtled home down the narrow lane. Great Aunt Ellen had ordered takeaway fish and chips and by the time he'd parked in the pub yard and knocked on the serving hatch, they were ready to collect.

There was a big pot of workman's tea on the cabin table and Skye and Great Aunt Ellen were waiting hungrily.

Those fish and chips were the best ever. No-one said much for a while but then they began on the name question again.

"Maggi and Xanthe always call their dinghies after famous round-the-world boats. But I think this boat needs a name that's completely her own."

"Next you'll be demanding her own flag. What happened to that handsome dragon your friends Anna and Maggi made?"

Donny's heart gave a lurch. He'd been signing the conversation to Skye, in between swigging tea and scooping up the last flakes of fish from the crumpled, salty paper. Now he'd have to tell them how he'd found the black and gold flag slashed into tatters on board the *Hispaniola*. And explain why he hadn't said anything about it at the time.

He fetched his bosun's bag and pulled out the remnants.

Skye hadn't ever seen the Allies' dragon flag. She'd been in hospital on its day of glory. She told him to wash the grease off his hands while she cleared the table, then she made him spread it out for her, fragment by fraying fragment, until she could guess at Anna's dramatic design. She smoothed each individual piece, slowly, as if she were thinking through her fingertips.

Gold Dragon sat ominously quiet.

He told them that he'd found the signal halliards cut, two of the flags bundled together and the third slashed. He mentioned the TRESPASSERS WILL BE PROSECUTED notices, the over-painted windows and the padlocks on the doors. Nothing else.

When he'd finished Skye gave Donny's cheek one brief, loving caress – just as that Chinese cleaner had done, he remembered, weirdly – gathered up the remains and took them to her cabin.

Gold Dragon looked hard at Donny. "Was that it, Sinbad? No other messages?"

The message was in the viciousness of the cutting and the way the *Hispaniola* had made him feel that day. The sense of fear and wrongness. He couldn't explain all that.

"There was a sign that said GO HOME LONG, with a sort of splash over the O. I didn't get it."

"That'll be meant for me – LÓNG means dragon."

"Oh."

"Nothing in character writing?"

"Nope." (Except what I did, he didn't say.)

"You did a quick recce, collected the spoil and left."

"Yeah, pretty much."

She frowned. "There's something going on here that I don't like. I wonder whether I did the right thing coming back. I could have shipped you out to me. But I needed to cut cables …" She was almost talking to herself.

"Don't let it get to you. That was mainly why I didn't say anything."

"We weren't acquainted then. I think your mother's guessed that you've been holding out on her. She's quick, you know, when it comes to picking up other people's feelings."

"Do you think it makes her drink?" asked Donny suddenly.

"Blunting the pain? No idea … and I don't see that there's a lot we can do about it. She's addicted and she's found a supplier and we don't know who or why. Still, you've come clean on this one and she's stood down happy. We can but hope."

Skye's cabin was empty when they called her for breakfast the following morning.

Without saying anything to one another Donny and Great Aunt Ellen hurried ashore and begun checking the bus shelter, the seats by the pub, the nearest stretch of foreshore – wherever she might be sprawled unconscious, cradling a vodka bottle.

This thing was so random. They didn't get it at all.

There was Skye fully dressed and alert, walking down the lane with her dark hair plaited, and a thin, tissue-wrapped package in one hand. She smiled as if she were pleased to find them there, and gestured that they should follow her into the work-shed. With one proud look at the new boat, she opened her parcel.

It was a swallow flag.

Eirene had made it, more than seventy years ago: a triangular white flag cut from remnants of canvas and with a blue serge swallow let in to the fabric so that it looked the same from both sides. It had a little wire flagstaff so it could be hoisted to the top of a mast.

Skye had found it in the back of one of Granny's drawers and had stowed it in the camper van when she packed for their journey south.

"But I thought you gave everything away," Donny objected. "Or you burned it in the garden before we left. You said that Granny's spirit should travel without burden on the long road westwards."

"The flag was different," his mother answered. "The flag did not belong to Nokomis."

"No," said Gold Dragon, "That flag was left for me. Eirene should have taken it with her in the *Houdalinqua* but … she hoped

I'd have a special use for it."

"Special use?"

"She'd guessed how I felt about Cal. I don't know how she worked it out because I certainly never said anything. He thought dinghies should have bird names and she hoped that we might hoist our flags together one day. I was still a girl then. Not a dragon."

Another relic tucked away, thought Donny. Something else I didn't know.

"I've set my sights upon a name," she said abruptly, when they were all three back at work, slicking on the dark blue gloss.

"You're going to call her *Swallow*?"

"Certainly not! I'll take a small bet that there's already a *Hirundo* or a *Hirondelle* waiting on the Norfolk Broads for your friend Anna. I'm going to name our boat *Vexilla*. It means flag – but a battle standard rather than a signal flag. We may yet need one."

"*Vexilla* … so that's Latin?" It wasn't a language he'd ever learned but …

"Aha!" she said. "You've made a start on *Missee Lee*. Consider it History!"

She went suddenly silent and painted with extreme concentration. When she next spoke it was as if she'd been talking all the while to herself.

" … Anyway we'll need hard evidence. Once *Vexilla*'s launched, Nimblefingers can sail me down river. Take a closer look at that *Hispaniola* of theirs."

"You won't go on board, will you?"

She sort of shook herself and laughed. "No, no, my days of

bobstay-scrambling are past. And I don't expect her owner'll be rolling out the welcome mat for me."

Donny's stomach lurched as he remembered the silly classroom poster message he'd left outside this unknown person's wheelhouse. But he didn't say anything more that day and neither did Gold Dragon.

CHAPTER SEVENTEEN

Stormy Weather

Early December

The beginning of December was seriously windy. Gales from the south-west tore across the country and, as the tides rose towards spring levels, most of the boat owners who'd been tempted to extend their sailing season hurried to take their yachts out of the water. Migrating birds began to arrive in great numbers. Exhausted and storm-tossed, they colonised the mudflats and salt marshes, calling to each other as they settled into their winter quarters.

Vexilla moved in too. As soon as the paint on her eagle-eyes was dry and her name had been engraved and gold-leafed onto her rubbing strake, the men from the boatyard took time off to help Skye and Great Aunt Ellen lift her onto a trailer and pull her to the water's edge. They offered a launch to tow her out but Gold Dragon said that she and her niece would manage.

The Orwell was dotted with unused moorings. It looked bigger and wilder with the summer sailors gone and flocks of Brent geese, widgeon, turnstone and grey plover blowing in to take their place. Gold Dragon hitched *Lively Lady* behind *Vexilla* then set Skye to row both of them out to the nearest available buoy. When Donny got home he found his mother as tired, dishevelled and triumphant as if she'd recently returned from the tundra.

But there, on the mooring, *Vexilla* had to stay while the waves came racing white-flecked up the river. The trees on the top of

Pin Mill's low cliff bent and howled but gave some shelter to the anchorage. The open water off Shotley would be much worse.

"I remember the Stour from years ago. When the wind's in this direction and it's battling the tide, those waves come down like walls. *Vexilla*'d be swamped in minutes. Nimblefingers would never ship with me again."

Donny had finished reading *Missee Lee*. He wished he'd been a bit quicker.

"Do you think it's the Taicoon Chang on board the *Hispaniola*?" he asked Gold Dragon. "The one who had a tiger flag? The one who liked caged birds?"

"Don't be so ridiculous," she snapped. "He's a character in a storybook."

Donny gaped. "Huh? You said yourself that *Missee Lee* was History! Anyway, I've been there – in one of my dreams. We were escaping in the dark, through a gorge with whirlpools. It was well scary."

She shoved her hook into her pocket. "I don't pay attention to dreams."

"Well, Mum does and I do too, a bit." Then he remembered something else. "That Chinese cleaner. When she let me out of the stationery cupboard … She warned me not to joke with the Tiger. I thought it was, you know, like some sort of Chinese saying or something … "

"I absolutely do not know! What stationery cupboard? What cleaner? What else have you not been telling your mother and me?" The dark plait down the centre of her spine hung ramrod straight as she stiffened to her full height. "From the beginning with *nothing* left out."

Donny was taller now than she was but it didn't feel like it.

So he took a breath and told her everything: the attack in the DT room, the problems with the bike, the van, the bullies, the mugging, his fear.

He was glad Skye wasn't there. She'd gone ashore to check the communal mailbox. Even though she couldn't read she'd learned the word-shape of *Strong Winds'* address and so had made the job her own. There were hardly ever any letters – except fan mail for Polly Lee. Nothing official – nothing from the school or the health service; none of the brown SS envelopes he'd been dreading.

"And how much have you told your friends?" Gold Dragon didn't look calmer when he'd finished. If anything she looked crosser.

"Well, bits … to Anna. About the bike but otherwise … not a lot."

"I trusted your Alliance! Of course we didn't tell our parents everything when we were your age. But not to tell your friends! I hope they'll roast you. It'll save me the bother of a proper keel-hauling."

Her language told Donny that the squall was blowing out. "Um, not so easy with *Strong Winds* in all this mud – keel-hauling, I mean … "

"You wait till I get us away from here," she threatened. "Seriously Sinbad, if you keep people in the dark they can't look out for rocks. And if the ship gets holed we all go down. Where are we now? Thursday. Good. Weekend ahoy and the forecast's improving. I'm going to invite First Mate Anna and those two Amazons, to take you and *Vexilla* for a good long sail. Saturday.

On the tide. You're to tell them everything that you've just told me. Everything! And that's an order."

Donny sighed. "I was probably about to tell them anyway. Are you planning to tell anyone?"

"That we might be afraid of a storybook wolf? No. Not quite. But I am going to talk to the Reverend and Mrs Ribiero about your school journeys. And I'll be giving them the lat and the long as to why I'm worried. It must surely soon be the end of term?"

"Six more days, including tomorrow."

"Attendance 100 percent. Not that anyone's noticed. Rotten apples, the lot of them."

"Sandra was okay."

"She's been lying pretty low. Sinbad, we're making leeway. You must tell your mother what's been happening. Don't keep trying to protect her. She can spot a set of villains when they heave over the skyline almost as quick as I can. I'm not surprised she's been hitting the bottle with you holding out on her like this."

"Huh?"

But Gold Dragon wasn't talking any more. She'd said what she had to say and there were jobs to be done. There were always jobs to be done with three boats to look after.

So Donny talked to his Allies and Great Aunt Ellen talked to hers. He got yelled at of course but they didn't seem to think he'd been a total wimp.

A transport rota was soon arranged to cover the final week of term – though Rev. Wendy said that if she were collecting he'd have to tag along to some of her carol services or help deliver cards.

Christmas was something else he'd shoved into his mental nettle patch. He'd never had so little money or so many people for whom he wanted to buy presents. DT open nights had been re-started so he could probably finish the Jacob's ladder he was making for Vicky as well as the weaving frame for his mum. Luke and Liam might like a couple of little Viking ships. Anna? Gold Dragon? The Ribieros? He hadn't a clue.

No more bike journeys until the New Year! That was worth any number of carol services. He'd have dressed up in full Santa kit if Rev. Wendy had asked him.

Somehow, though, he forgot to have the heart to heart with Skye.

There was still a fuzziness about her late at night and that smell lingered. The weather had improved, though, and Gold Dragon was taking her sailing in *Vexilla* almost every day. She'd get healthier, then they'd talk.

They'd sailed round the *Hispaniola*. Polly Lee was scathing. "She's no more a schooner than I am. Those masts have been added and the more you look at them the less convincing they seem. That ship was never built to sail. Knock off the masts; paint her battleship grey and you get a remarkable resemblance to an ex-Royal Navy gunboat."

"So does she belong to the Taicoon Chang from *Missee Lee*?"

"Once and for all Donny, he is fiction and I am your great-aunt who has returned from the East. End of story."

"Okay, okay. Where else have you andMum been sailing?"

"Prospecting up the Stour. I thought we might have earned a change of scene over the Christmas holidays – if the bureau-rats remember we exist."

Thursday 14 December

"A word in your shell-like, Donny."

It was the last DT session of term and Donny was assembling the various bits and pieces he needed to finish at home. Vicky's Jacob's ladder clattered down in a most satisfactory manner. He'd have to convince Gerald that the varnish he'd used was 100 percent non-toxic. If Vicky liked his present she'd want to chew it.

There were several students hanging around so the teacher beckoned him into the storage room. That old music folder of Anna's was still there, he noticed.

"Would you mind telling me why none of your family showed up at this morning's Review Meeting? I had to request cover for two of my Year Eleven GCSE groups so I could get to Colchester to present your report. Then I found myself the only non-SS person there! Wherever were your mother and your great-aunt? They hadn't even sent apologies. These things do matter, you know."

"Huh?" said Donny. "No-one's invited us to anything. We haven't seen Sandra for ages."

"Sandra's been taken off your case. Months ago. You have an agency worker. A Mr Wang. He turned up all right. With his report. Finds you all very evasive, he says. Reluctant to Engage."

"Never seen him. We haven't had a single letter or a visit or anything. It's been quite good actually."

"So it may have been but no-one's going to believe that. Denise Tune assured us that she'd had everything hand-delivered to Pin Mill. Mr Wang has been passing all official correspondence directly to your mother. He's recorded everything – times, dates, mileage. Most transactions have also been witnessed – by some of your fellow-students."

Donny understood now why there had been no letters. As Great Aunt Ellen had said, Skye could spot a set of villains as fast as anyone.

"I did the best I could. I told them that you'd achieved your attendance target; that your reasons for lateness were genuine and that you were fully up to date with your assignments."

This missed meeting was serious bad news.

"What's going to happen? We've done all the things they told us. And Great Aunt Ellen got someone at the Citizen's Advice to check that her paperwork's in order. What more do they want?"

"I think you're going to need a lawyer. I'm afraid there was some rather negative discussion of your mother's … health."

"You mean her drinking," said Donny.

"One of the many things I dislike about those SS meetings is that I come out speaking their language. Yes, that is what I mean. The doctor's report was damning. And there were photographs."

"She never drank before she came down here."

"I've not met your mother and I don't know what's been happening to her – I'm not sure I know what's been happening to you either. I do know that alcoholism's a serious illness. If that's her problem, she will need help."

"Well, I'm not asking my mum to spend any more time at that stupid doctor's," said Donny, suddenly angry at his tutor too. "If that's the System, you're dead right we're not Engaging."

He seized Anna's old folder from the shelf, marched back into the classroom and pushed it into his bag. Then he shoved all his work in as well and headed for the exit.

Mr McMullen let him go. He'd been a boy that age.

Donny turned back just before he left. "Sorry," he said. "It's not your fault."

"No it isn't," agreed the tutor, "You and I had better have a proper talk after Christmas. Perhaps the holiday will do your mother good."

"Possibly," said Donny. "Um, Happy Christmas then."

Right now all he wanted to do was go home and spend the evening working on his presents or reading something that simply meant what it said – like a tide table or his Great Uncle Greg's *Sailing* handbook. He'd had it with conversations.

Friday 15 December
The boatyard manager came to talk to Great Aunt Ellen next day. Several of his customers had complained that the cords tying down their winter covers had been cut. They hadn't worked loose; they'd been severed.

It had started happening about the time that Donny, Skye and Gold Dragon had been working on *Vexilla* in the shed.

The manager was a fair-minded man and he agreed that the timing could have been coincidental. Lots of people hadn't covered their boats until they knew bad weather was on the way. So there hadn't been much opportunity before, perhaps.

He'd no evidence, he said, to connect the damage to anyone in particular. All the same he couldn't deny that people had heard about the accident at Shotley. *Snow Goose* was in the yard. Her hull repair had been completed and the new mizzenmast was shaping up nicely in the shed. People knew *Snow Goose* and they knew what had happened to her and who had been responsible so they might quite likely put two and two together. And it wouldn't be difficult to guess what answer they were coming up with.

He'd done what he could to improve security but he couldn't keep watch 24/7. It seemed only reasonable to give some warning.

School holidays. Time to lie in bed and doze – or read. Time to put on Xanthe's old wind-proofs and go sailing. Time to finish making presents for the kids, help Anna decorate a tree, play noisy games with Vicky or simply hang out with his friends.

Three nights into Donny's school holidays there was a violent outbreak of rope-slashing. This time it wasn't only boat covers; it was mooring ropes as well. All along the line of houseboats and out into the river as well – except for *Strong Winds* and *Vexilla*.

Skye was discovered the next morning, helplessly drunk, with Gold Dragon's rigging knife sticking out of her anorak pocket.

Miss Walker and her family were told to leave the Hard by the next possible high tide.

CHAPTER EIGHTEEN

A Winter Holiday

They only had forty-eight hours to wait until the spring tide would be sufficient for *Strong Winds* to float off.

They were among the most miserable of Donny's life. Not only was everyone angry and accusing but Skye was really ill. She had passed out during some brutal public questioning by Inspector Flint, who just happened to be on duty when the damage was discovered. He seemed to have forgotten that Skye's deafness was not something that could be overcome by him shouting at her.

Gold Dragon put herself between Flint and her niece. Then hooked Donny firmly by his waistband to prevent him from launching in.

A bystander suggested that an ambulance should be called.

Flint squashed that idea straight away.

"Our National Health Service doesn't need cluttering up by drunks," he growled contemptuously. "I've always thought it was a mistake to do away with traditional village lock-ups."

"Perhaps you would like to reintroduce the stocks, officer?"

Joshua Ribiero had arrived.

"Alcohol in this quantity is a poison: it is not to be treated lightly. I am a doctor. If I were a lawyer – or a policeman – I would like to prosecute the person who supplied the vodka. Hospitalisation may yet be necessary but the first thing we can do is to return Ms

Walker to her boat. She will require constant monitoring – for her own safety. I believe her family are the best people to provide this."

That night Donny learned what the expression 'blind drunk' actually meant. Skye wasn't sick when she woke up: she was blind, she couldn't see.

That, added to her deafness and her virtual inability to speak, was truly terrifying. She couldn't see Donny's signing. She couldn't understand what had happened. She wailed in the dark, fighting for escape. Only Donny could hold her quiet, though Joshua Ribiero and Great Aunt Ellen stayed with him, offering what help they could.

Wendy and June stayed too.

So, when Tony arrived with a duty SS worker, ready to remove Donny into the Safety of Residential Care, they were able to insist that he was already being supervised. By a vicar and a doctor and a magistrate – as well as his own great-aunt.

When a crisis health team turned up, offering sedatives and restraints, they too were sent away.

Skye slept at last – and Donny slept alongside her.

Her sight returned, blurrily, in the morning and she managed to understand some simple questions. She couldn't offer any answers though. She had no memory at all of whatever had happened the previous evening.

Later that day she began to shake and to beg, mutely, for something to steady her. Donny thought that perhaps she should be given her happy pills but Gold Dragon said no. "They do her no good. They're in the same league as the grog. I should have heaved them overboard weeks ago."

Perhaps surprisingly, Joshua agreed. "In the long term," he said, "many of us have begun to question the repeated use of anti-depressant drugs. I do not believe that this treatment has been helpful to Skye. I can offer some short-term medication that may help her through the next few days, but after that I recommend nothing. Except reassurance, vigilance – and possibly chocolate."

"I'll lay in supplies before we leave. Thursday night's tide may be high enough to do it."

"It'll be tight. You'll need a crew. Both June and I are ready to volunteer. The girls can bed down at the vicarage again. How far do you intend to go?"

"I'll be glad to drop a mile or two down river. Enough to get us out of sight. It'll be almost midnight before we get her off. If we do. After that we'll take the next flood tide into the Stour. I have to stay near Donny's school and we discovered a spot last week that gave Nimblefingers a good feel."

Donny'd been listening. "How do you know it did?" he asked her. "You can't talk to my mum. You can't sign."

"We've been sailing together," said Great Aunt Ellen. "It's different between us now."

Thursday 21 December
Ice was forming on the deck, and the stars glittered in a cold clear sky when they warped *Strong Winds* away from Pin Mill Hard.

Using the engine would have made the junk's stern drop a few crucial inches deeper so Joshua and Donny put a spare anchor and a long length of cable into *Vexilla* and rowed out as far as they could towards the main channel.

June kept watch over Skye.

They dropped the anchor and returned to *Strong Winds*. Then they loosed the forrard mooring warps and Polly Lee began to winch the cable in. For a few tense moments nothing happened: the junk stayed stuck, the anchor line strained.

"Into the skiff, all of you," she hissed. "Take your weight off."

Joshua and Donny clambered obediently into *Vexilla*. They waited in the cold blackness while Polly Lee kept working the winch with her good hand and the hook. How much longer before she would admit defeat?

"You too," she ordered June. "Nimblefingers won't wake now."

June joined them in the skiff.

No-one spoke. The cold and the quiet were absolute. Except for the working of the winch.

Then they felt a first slight sliding movement.

"*Yes!*" Polly Lee's beloved boat was free again.

"Back on deck everyone. Donny, up with her foresail. Quick as you like. Mr Ribiero, hand over hand with that anchor – if you'd be so good. We won't need much sail to take us out of the anchorage. Tide's already on the turn."

They dropped anchor in the next reach and had slept a few hours before they moved *Strong Winds* and her two tenders round to the River Stour.

Donny saw nothing of their journey. Skye had woken and was being repeatedly sick as the anti-depressants as well as the alcohol drained out of her system. He needed to stay with her.

Joshua was able to give her something to soothe the pain of continual vomiting but he warned Donny that she might even have a fit if they did not manage the withdrawal process carefully.

He arranged with Gold Dragon that she would use her VHF to call for help in an emergency.

None of this was orthodox but Joshua was convinced Skye needed to be in a familiar place. She needed her family and she needed to stay far away from whoever had been supplying the alcohol. He blamed himself, he said, for not having understood the situation earlier.

Donny didn't know when he'd see any of his friends again. He bundled up the wooden toys and asked June if she would drop them at the vicarage. He'd drawn a card for Wendy and Gerald but nothing for anyone else.

They'd never exactly had riotous festivities when he and Skye had lived with Granny Edith but this Christmas was going to break all records for a non-event.

Great Aunt Ellen wrote a note to the SS. It announced that they had changed their address but that Donny would continue to attend school as before when the new term started. Official visitors could call by previous appointment. She didn't precisely spell out how such appointments could be made.

The stretch of river that was now their home was almost completely deserted. After Shotley there were no marinas or extensive anchorages and only a few small ships used the dredged channel that led to the quiet Essex port of Mistley.

Gold Dragon had anchored on the Suffolk side of the Stour, off a long curved bay which was bounded by a sandy cliff and a fringe of beach. A small creek twisted inland through the mudflats offering access to a former barge dock and a track to Gallister village and Donny's school.

"I haven't asked anyone for a mooring and I'm not going to. There's precious little shelter out here if it comes on to blow but I've laid two anchors and the holding ground's good. We'll have to tough it out. When your mother's better she'll want to walk along that beach. It's prehistoric." She gave *Vexilla's* stern painter an unnecessarily fierce twist. "The Tiger may think he's bested the Dragon this time but we'll batten down our hatches and trust that it won't long before he discovers his mistake."

It was an admission.

"So you do think there's someone out to get us. You believe all that … knife stuff at Pin Mill was a set-up? You don't think that it could possibly have been Mum?"

Gold Dragon stared at him. "Nimblefingers? Setting about those mooring ropes with my old rigging knife? No! That knife's blunt as a spoonbill's beak. I'd already ordered a replacement before the Pufferfish swiped it. If they take her to court we'll call the shopkeeper in Lowestoft as our expert witness. That knife couldn't have possibly done so much damage. Neither could Nimblefingers."

"It's someone from your past?"

"That's … possible."

This made Donny feel so much better that he settled down immediately with a heap of old cod line. Great Aunt Ellen had said she'd like some samples of ornamental splicing as her Christmas present – and a pledge for future boy labour. Then there'd be time for him to finish Skye's weaving frame.

Their new home was the most beautiful place Donny had ever lived. The river was so wide: the sky so big. Every time he came up on deck the view seemed different: either the boat had shifted her position or some change in the light seemed to alter all the distances as well as drenching everything with an unbelievable range of colours.

Strong Winds chuckled and tossed as the waves ran by and she swung to the turning tides. She felt like an island, separate and safe. Their enemies would surely forget about them here. The boatyard had almost done them a favour, telling them to move. He couldn't think how they'd put up with being stuck at Pin Mill for so long. He'd still be able to get to school. Still manage that 100 percent attendance.

On Christmas Day all of them found something to give each other and when the tide was right, they rowed across the shallow bay for a first short walk along the deserted beach. It was cold and lonely and Skye was very shaky so they didn't stay long.

The kids at the vicarage, Donny remembered, would only have Wendy and Gerald. No relations at all, except each other – unless they were allowed an extra prison visit.

Tuesday 26 December

"Okay, Mum," Donny signed to Skye on the day after Christmas. "What did you do with all those letters that the SS sent us? And where exactly were you getting your … brave sleep drink?"

She looked evasive and ashamed and as if she was about to go shut herself into her cabin.

"Sorry but we've got to know. Great Aunt Ellen says that if you keep people in the dark they can't look out for rocks. And if the ship gets holed we all go down."

There were no rocks on the beautiful muddy Stour but Skye understood what he meant.

214

"There is a place from which everything is taken but some returns again," she explained.

Eh?

"Many things, glass and paper and cans. The young braves showed me. They drink from the cans that do not rust. Sometimes they are wild and hurl the cans where they may cause harm but when the small man is there they crush them beneath their feet and use the given takeaways. We used them, Doh, you and I, and the other boat-dwellers. It is a system. For all that is not wanted but can be made new."

Got it – she meant waste disposal and recycling. The bins were sited at the back of the car park, beyond the communal post box and the public toilets. They were so obvious you didn't even notice them.

That was the official system. The well-hards and the small man had introduced Skye to an unofficial system – two extra open boxes behind the public bins: one was for paper that wasn't newspaper, and the other was for plastic bottles. You could take items out of this part of the system as well as put them in.

If you were given paper that you didn't want – such as an SS brown envelope – you could put it straight into the paper crate, once you had made your mark on the small man's list, and it would be gone before you returned. If you noticed that someone had left a couple of inches of water in the bottom of a plastic bottle, you could take that bottle out of the recycling box, drink the contents and put it back again. The young braves often helped to sort the bottles.

"That water is cold fire. They like it too, though not as much as the drink from the cans. The young braves are often frightened deep inside. Cold fire water helps to make them bold."

"But why would *you* be frightened Mum? We're here with Great Aunt Ellen. We're a family. We look out for each other. We can … do things."

Skye looked desperately sad. "Gold Dragon is old as Nokomis was. Soon she will take the longest road. Pauguk is greedy, he comes for all. He took her friend without farewell. And in my dreams I see my father, standing lonely at his doorway, beckoning to me from his wigwam in the land of the Dacotahs. And the beautiful Wenonah, dead of famine and of fever."

She'd slipped into *Hiawatha*-land again but he understood. Once you started to think of all the people in the world who'd died, it did get you down. Especially if two of them were your parents who'd left you as a baby and sailed away never to return.

"But Mum, you've always known this. Most of it. So you use your dream-catchers and your worry beads and you watch the birds and make things and cook for us. Why can't you do that now?"

"Since Nokomis took the long road and we left our home in the North I have lost myself. And the Woman who makes Bad Worse told me I would lose you too if we did not leave. The other women who come with the small man. They are also frightened."

"The woman who makes bad worse … ?"

"She treads in blood," his mother added helpfully.

Donny's head was swimming and he could see that Skye was getting tired too. He mustn't stress her – but he really needed to understand who'd been supplying her with the brave sleep drink – otherwise known as the cold fire water.

"I make her call it vodka now. Make her use the proper word," said Donny bitterly to Anna, Luke, Maggi and Xanthe when they came to visit the next day. "Even one whiff of it makes me want to puke. This small man, from what Mum calls the flower company, showed her a bottle with a picture she could recognise. They – whoever they were – I'm certain it was Toxic's goons, but of course I can't prove it – made sure that there was always some vodka in one of those bottles. Pretty much every day. That kept her hooked. When any official letter arrived and she was hiding – sorry, *recycling* it – they'd maybe supply an extra couple of inches. She didn't like the letters, she didn't like the man who delivered them but she did like the drink. Until this last time. She might not hate it quite as much as I do but she's definitely getting there."

The others were shocked.

"Poor Skye," said Maggi. "Shall I go knock on her cabin? See if she'll come out? "

"We had to watch her all the time at the beginning because Great Aunt Ellen thought she might, well, try to harm herself or something. She knows she's been completely stupid. She made it so easy for them. They could pop a full bottle in whenever they wanted: stress her out a bit more and she'd drink it. They'd just reel her in. Reeling."

"What a Christmas!" said Anna. "Ours was bad because of our mum not being there; yours was bad because you've had to be sitting with yours almost every single minute."

"And my dad, Anna, he wasn't there neither."

"Even our dad wasn't there," said Xanthe. "He got called into the hospital first thing. Father Christmas's sleigh bells were still tinkling away into the sunrise. Mum got majorly stressed. She's certain that there's something going wrong in his department. So we all went and Mags and I goofed about with some of the patients who didn't have any visitors of their own. Poor old buzzards," she added reflectively.

The older ones looked at each other. Then laughed.

"Maybe loads of people have rubbish Christmases," said Maggi.

"Maybe," said Anna.

Luke didn't say anything. He looked depressed.

"What we need, fellow Allies and esteemed visiting Confederate," said Xanthe, "is a bit of fun. We need excitement!"

"No thanks!" said Donny. "I had quite enough excitement at Pin Mill."

"Come on, Donny-man," Xanthe urged. "I don't mean we're going to play dodge-the-van or family lynchings, I mean we need a challenge, an expedition. Something to get the old heart pumping."

"Xanth hasn't sailed *Spray* for almost a week," said Maggi. "She's getting withdrawal symptoms ... oops, wrong words – sorry!"

"It's okay. You're right. We need to stop sitting about. I've read those other two books that Great Aunt Ellen bought in Colchester."

They looked at him in surprise.

"Yeah, straight up! Nearly two books in five days – and signing bits of them to Mum as well. Those kids were always doing something. You know, like climbing mountains or discovering the North Pole. And there's a real boff in *Winter Holiday*, Anna. Exactly Oboe's type. Or yours."

"Could we?" said Luke eagerly. "Could we climb a mountain?"

"Mountains not exactly thick on the ground around here and they had to have a frozen lake for that North Pole stuff," said

Xanthe, who'd read the whole series. "Tell you what we could do, though, we could make a set or two of snowshoes, so you could mud-skate. There's acres of mud here when the tide goes out. It'd be extreme!"

She hurried them all into *Vexilla* to go prospecting for materials. The tide was ebbing so they didn't have long.

They collected what looked like properly bendy twigs and reeds but turning them into mud-shoes wasn't as easy as they'd expected. In the end they had to resort to gaffer tape all around the edges to stop the twigs from splitting, and twisted plastic bags for the bits that fastened to your feet.

Great Aunt Ellen opened tins of soup and Skye emerged from her cabin to help. Work went better once she joined in and by low water, they had one completed pair for Luke to try.

"'S like walking in gi-normous dream-catchers," he puffed.

"Just be careful," fretted Anna. "It's really cold and I don't want you falling over."

"Windy *Wen*-dy!" Luke shouted. At which point he trod one wide mud-shoe on top of the other and toppled sideways, ripping a plastic bag fastening.

Back on board *Strong Winds*, cleaning him up and effecting repairs, they began to plan other expeditions.

"When the weather's better we could definitely go camping," said Xanthe. "Though personally I wish the weather would get worse. Then we could build an igloo. Like we did when we lived in Canada. It never snows properly here."

Donny looked at her. "Sorry, Xanthe, but are you saying you actually *made* an igloo? One that didn't fall down – because, on the evidence of this morning …"

"… I couldn't roll a snowball in the Arctic! Thanks a *lot*. And how pathetic were you – letting Luke go first across the sucking mud?"

Luke looked surprised. "Didn't reckon I had no choice."

"Er …"

"What about the code, Anna?" asked Maggi quickly. "How are you getting on with it?"

"Not too good. I've turned it back into decimal but the numbers don't make any sense. Not yet anyway. It's here in your notebook. Pages of it!"

"You'd need canoes if you wanted to reach the source of the Stour," Great Aunt Ellen was still considering expeditions. "You'd have to carry them round the locks and the weirs. You'd be against the flow in the upper reaches. It'd take days. Character-building, I suppose."

"Dash-dot is N and the single dot is E," offered Xanthe, looking at the first line of Anna's pages of workings. "It's Morse."

"So now when I turn binary to decimal and put back the noughts it reads 522852N 014546E < 050107"

"And if you add degrees and minutes to the first two numbers, he's given you a lat and long," Donny added. "You know, they're sort of like a grid reference."

"I know what latitude and longitude mean," she snapped. "I'm not a complete moron! And I'm sure now that the last number's a date. The lawyer said the puzzle was time-limited. Fifth of January 2007 – that's the first day of term. That's what he meant by insert symbols! And to think I've been wasting my time thinking of algebraic formulae and trying to use BODMASS."

"Oboe didn't leave you a puzzle – he left you a place."

"The co-ordinates of a place." They were all talking at once now.

"Digitalised co-ordinates."

"Yeah, but you can digitalise pretty much anything."

"You know what," said Donny, opening *Strong Winds*' chart drawer and spreading a sheet out on the cabin table. "That's almost where we went."

"Not quite an East Pole, more an Easternmost Point," agreed his great-aunt, laying a parallel ruler across. "We had a Native Guide, if I recall."

"Oboe must have been to this Easternmost Point. He must mean me to go there. How soon can I set off? Let's not wait another minute!"

Anna'd jumped up in her excitement and started struggling back into her jacket. The rest of them were sitting there open-mouthed. This was so uncharacteristic.

She paused and sat down again. "Okay," she said. "So where, exactly, is it? In words this time – I'm backing off numbers for a while. "

CHAPTER NINETEEN

Journey to the Easternmost Point

Thursday 28 December

"Anna," said Luke. "It's only Low'stoft. Near where we was in that caravan park. You remember. Before we came down Ipswich."

"Well, more fool me for not noticing." Her eyes were bright, red spots burned in her pale cheeks. "I didn't want to be there so I must have blanked it out. Don't fret, Luke, you can still be our Native Guide but how soon can we go?"

Suddenly they all felt that this was serious. It was more than an outing to fill the days between Christmas and New Year, or to give them something to talk about when they went back to school. This was going to matter somehow.

"If time presses," said Great Aunt Ellen. "I'd suggest you sail up the river to Manningtree on the tide, leave the dinghies as far as you can go, then cross the fields and take a train. I don't know how many trains there are and you might have to change at Ipswich. But … whoever wants to go has to get permission first – if you want to have your expedition without oldies."

Xanthe looked approvingly at her. "It's not as good as invading from the sea," she said. "But you've already done that, and – I know this sounds like we're complete muppets – Mags and I have never actually been on a train without Mum and Dad. I mean, Mum and Dad … obviously they're great but, if you always do everything as a family, you never do much alone, do you? And I'm going to be sixteen! So we're well up for it – if Anna doesn't mind us tagging along."

But Anna was looking stricken. "Train fares. They're really expensive. And I've only got my tips from the parish mag. And I spent most of that on presents for the kids."

"Xanth," said Maggi. "We're not just over-protected muppets, we're airheads. We forgot to give Donny and Anna their envelopes! We're really sorry," she said, digging deep into her and Xanthe's backpack. "We messed up at Christmas so Mum and Dad thought you might like money as your better-late-than-never presents. There's some books at home as well, and things for Luke and Liam and Vicky, but we left all them behind. I know I brought the money though …"

"There's a boat coming," said Luke who had drifted back out onto *Strong Winds'* deck, bored by their talk of money and train journeys. "It's that mean man's boat with the pointy nose."

"The shark-boat?"

"Flint?"

"It can't be!"

It was, of course. With his genius for arriving exactly when he was least wanted Inspector Jake Flint was travelling smoothly up the Stour in his expensive black powerboat.

"He must be coming to take Donny to the Unit! Rev. Wendy and the others aren't here to make a fuss and you've broken the agreement by moving from Pin Mill."

This was no time to quibble.

"Mum," signed Donny urgently. "I've got to leg it. I will be back. I promise. It's the Pufferfish. Don't let him bully you."

"We won't," said Polly Lee, who had understood. "I'm on my own ground here."

Skye didn't panic. "Take food. Keep warm. Come back safe," was all she said.

Anna was finding it hard to hold herself together. Xanthe was their quickest thinker in this crisis. "Donny, Anna, Luke," she said. "Over the side into *Vexilla*. He doesn't know you have another boat. He might not recognise you. Take my mobile. I'll use Maggi's. Head for Manningtree and the train. We'll catch you up but it might be Ipswich. We *will* ring Wendy and Gerald. I promise. That's okay isn't it, Miss Walker?"

"Clearing the decks. Best thing entirely."

Already she'd hooked Donny's rucksack out of his bunk and was stuffing it with jackets, water bottles and food. As the three children scrambled into *Vexilla,* she dropped the single completed set of mud-shoes in beside them plus a plastic bag containing her and Donny's wellingtons. "You won't get to Manningtree: you'll do well if you get as far as Baltic Wharf at this time of tide. The wind's behind you, so pull up her centreplate and skim the mud, following the channel as far as you can. If her rudder's touching, you may be able to un-ship it and steer her with an oar."

Donny looked up at his great-aunt. He bet she wished she were coming too, whatever the dangers behind and mud ahead. For a moment he thought that they should all go. Take *Lively Lady* too. But he didn't know if Skye would cope. And it'd be dangerous. Donny remembered how Flint had tried to ram him once before.

"Keep *Strong Winds* between yourselves and Pufferfish for as long as you can," Gold Dragon carried on giving instructions. "Try to make it look as if you've come out from the creek. Keep checking that phone. If the Reverend orders mission aborted, that's it."

Luke and Anna were in.

Donny was hauling up the sail. "Stand by to cast off," he said to Anna.

"If you need shelter in Lowestoft, go to the Floating Lotus," Gold Dragon called down as she stood ready to push them away. "Go anyway. Ai Qin will welcome you."

"Mags," said Xanthe. "Your arm's okay for sailing now, isn't it?" Maggi nodded. "Hop into *Lady* on the side nearest Flint. Make it look like you're Donny trying to do a runner – let's have a hat-swap, too." She pulled off her sister's red stocking cap and chucked it to Donny, who chucked his beanie back to her. "Then mess it up … lots of flapping and tangling. Let him think he's got you. That way he'll probably slow down. We know he likes to gloat."

Anna had coiled in *Vexilla*'s stern painter; Gold Dragon cast her off forrard. Xanthe leaned out to give the mast a final shove as Donny took in the main sheet and bore away. "Anna, you're chief radio officer as well as first mate. I'll text you. Heigh-ho for the Easternmost Point!"

"What about me?" asked Luke. "What'm I doing?"

"Keeping look-out, of course. Sit forrard and look sharp. You're on the fast-track for promotion."

Vexilla was already on the move; her greyish sail spreading to the cold north-easterly wind. There was plenty of room for the three of them to sit together but Luke crept carefully forward and squeezed himself into the small space before her mast. There he crouched, peering ahead at least as intently as the eagle-eyes on her bow.

There was a speed limit on the Stour and, surprisingly, Flint was observing it. Maybe the Ribieros' complaint had had some effect – or maybe there was someone else from the SS on board forcing Flint to seem more Professional in his attempt to remove Donny from his family. Or perhaps he still hoped to see *Strong Winds* and her owner escaping to the open sea – never to return.

Anyway, it was good because it gave *Vexilla* more of a chance.

Donny kept *Strong Winds* between them and the shark-boat for as long as he could. Then he altered course so it would look as if he were reaching out of the creek. He'd already pulled up *Vexilla*'s centreplate so he could stay in the shallows as much as possible. This could be their best defence. The shark-boat didn't need much water but, as long as they were running or broad reaching, they could get by with even less.

Maggi was putting on a great act. She had hauled *Lively Lady* alongside *Strong Winds* on the side nearest the approaching shark-boat so Flint and his companion couldn't miss the sight of a child getting onto a complete muddle while apparently attempting to escape. Her black curls were hidden under Donny's navy beanie and she was wearing an old-fashioned oilskin that must have belonged to Great Aunt Ellen.

At first it was hard to see exactly what she was doing. By the time that Anna got a good view and could tell Luke and Donny what was happening, Maggi had managed to haul *Lively Lady*'s mainsail up so it seemed to have stuck halfway. She'd lost control of her jib sheets and was crabbing across the river as if she'd never sailed in her life.

"I'm insulted!" said Donny, unable to resist a quick glance round. "Even Flint can't think I'd sail as badly as that."

"Why not?" said Anna. "He's so arrogant he thinks we're all some kind of sub-species."

"To be fair, I did capsize last time he was coming after me."

"It's what birds do," said Luke. "When there's some predator right near their nest. They make out they're hurt real bad an' try an' get 'im to chase after 'em so's to get 'em away from the chicks … Liam an' me did wonder whether that was what your mum was doin' Anna?"

"Oh I don't know," she said, and they all felt serious again. There was no logical reason to think that their journey to the Easternmost Point was going to help bring Lottie Livesey back but they were convinced it mattered somehow. Should he have volunteered to be captured by Flint, wondered Donny, if that would help Anna and Luke to get away?

That was stupid. Flint had his sights on Gold Dragon. Wanted her out. Donny was just bait. Probably Anna was bait too – for some reason that was probably connected with her mother. Which was probably connected with whatever trouble Luke's dad had got into when he was working at Port of Felixstowe.

Too many probablies. But they did add up to mean that he and Anna and Luke were better off sticking together for as long as they could. And right now his job was to sail all three of them as close as he could to the railway station so they could make a dash for the Easternmost Point.

The wind was fair but there was very little water outside the dredged channel. Donny focused his full attention on keeping his sail drawing steadily. He'd looked at a pilot book on board *Strong Winds* so he'd already got a few ideas how this next stretch of the river worked. He needed Luke to keep watch ahead to spot the red and green channel buoys that would mark their way to Mistley. There'd be a yellow and black north cardinal buoy warning them of a shingle patch named Ballast Hill. The channel turned and narrowed there. It also got very shallow.

Long moments passed. The water gurgled under *Vexilla's* forefoot as wind and tide helped her on her way. It would have been fun if they hadn't felt so tense.

The shark-boat finally closed on Maggi and realised, with a snarl, that she'd been tricked. She swirled round and surged towards *Strong Winds*.

How long could Great Aunt Ellen hold them off? How long before Flint realised that the boy he'd come to take was not on board? How would Skye cope through all of this?

Donny tried not to distract himself. His duty was to *Vexilla* and her crew.

They had almost reached the cardinal mark and were half a mile from Mistley Quay when a warning text pinged through from Xanthe.

They didn't need it. The river was so quiet that they could hear the howling of the shark-boat's engines before they could see her. There she was, powering up the river, white water curdling away and fanning out into rolling Vs behind her.

Vexilla was still sailing well but in comparison to the speeding powerboat it felt as if she had drifted to a halt. They had no chance of reaching Mistley before Flint reached them.

Donny looked at the tall black and yellow mark and deliberately altered course to pass it on the wrong side. He was sure they'd be okay with their weight well balanced and the centreplate up. He remembered what Gold Dragon had said about unshipping the rudder and steering with an oar. He didn't want to do that yet. Too much of a giveaway.

How well did Flint know this stretch of the river? Would he be fool enough to follow them?

Suddenly they could see the riverbed less than half a metre beneath them. Not mud but shingle. Hard … if you hit it.

The shark-boat was closing in. Flint ignored the hazard mark and swooped directly towards *Vexilla*.

There was a shriek of metal and a wild churning of water into spray as the powerboat's propellers struck the shoal. Flint battled furiously, revving his motors ahead and astern, for what seemed like ages.

Then he accepted the inevitable and switched the engines off. Donny glanced back and saw the black boat sink down from her racing position. This had the effect of lessening her draught and she floated meekly off. Donny saw Flint settle to his wheel again and point her towards the main channel.

He was still going to catch them.

Donny kept *Vexilla* sailing. It was all he could do. Mistley was a distance away. He could stay in the shallows for now but they'd have to return to the channel if they were to have any chance of getting ashore. And the shark-boat would be waiting for them.

The noise behind had changed again. Flint was revving his engines but he wasn't getting anywhere. He must have damaged his propeller blades!

The river was quiet again.

"I think he's anchoring," said Anna. "There's someone with him. Something's happening at the back of the boat. I can't make it out … "

Donny remembered what he'd seen that morning off Felixstowe: the shark-boat's stern could open hydraulically. There was a mini-shark-boat inside, high speed and shallow draught.

They'd reached the first possible landing place. Flint could see what they were doing. So he'd be transferring to his mini-shark and landing here too.

"Change of plan, Lukey. See that ring on the quayside? I need you to pass the painter through it soon as you can and give it back to me. Then you two jump ship and start running. There's a station at Mistley as well as Manningtree. Take the phone and one of the envelopes. We know this is Anna's expedition but I guess he thinks it's me he wants."

Anna and Luke were out so fast that *Vexilla* had scarcely stopped moving before Donny was able to turn her bows away, slip the painter and sail on towards Manningtree. He could hear the speedboat engine whining closer. He didn't know how much water she was going to need. More or less than *Vexilla*?

The dredged channel ended here. There was hardly any water anyway. He cleated his mainsheet while he struggled to lift out the heavy rudder. This unbalanced her. She lurched and almost gybed.

It wasn't going to work. He couldn't see anywhere to fix a steering oar and the channel ahead was no more than a twisting runnel through the steep banks of mud.

He'd lost control.

Vexilla lurched again. And stuck.

Donny released the mainsheet and dropped the sail. He bundled it out of the way, picked up an oar and began to punt. Even rowing was impossible now, the channel was so narrow.

Flint was only about ten metres behind. He stood up and bellowed. The speedboat swerved violently and the other passenger caught Flint by the arm and forced him to sit down. It was Creepy Tony and he looked sick. His suit was splattered with mud and spray and his thin dark hair had blown the wrong way revealing an expanse of balding scalp.

Donny didn't have any sympathy to spare. He carried on trying to pole *Vexilla* round the tight right-angle bends. She was too long: it was impossible. If only he'd been in *Lively Lady*!

Vexilla was hard aground and so was the speedboat.

The tide continued its steady rise. Soon they'd both be floating again and Donny would have no hope of fending off the two men in their agile craft.

A mooring buoy on a length of chain lay limply across the mud a couple of metres away. Almost automatically Donny reached out with *Vexilla*'s boat hook, pulled it closer and made her fast. Then he began stowing his sail.

The mud-shoes were under the sail. He'd forgotten. Now he gazed at them, his heart racing. The plastic bag fastenings had been mended. He'd watched Luke. He didn't have to make the same mistakes.

Donny laid both oars in the bottom of the boat and put his rucksack on his back. His money was inside with the jackets and water bottles and his maps. Then he sat on *Vexilla*'s shiny crimson gunwale and tied the big woven ovals to his feet.

The hardest part was scrambling away from the boat up the steep mud bank. Donny hung onto the mooring chain and pulled himself up like a mountaineer until he was onto the flat soft plateau of ooze. It glistened as it stretched ahead.

All the way to Manningtree? He could give it a go.

Donny ignored the shouting from behind and took his first wide circular step. And another. Then he leaned forward slightly and began swinging rhythmically away across the mud as if he was competing in some Arctic sport.

He wondered, briefly, whether Flint and Tony were still the jolly chums they'd seemed when first he'd seen them at the SS meeting. He guessed not.

The Allies met at Ipswich Station. Xanthe and Maggi just made it in time to catch the Lowestoft train. They were strained and anxious. They'd had the adults to cope with.

Once the shark-boat had gone tearing up the river they'd had to contact their own parents to explain what was happening. Then Xanthe had phoned Gerald and Wendy to tell them where Anna and Luke were headed. Great Aunt Ellen spoke to them as well. Maggi stayed close to Skye wordlessly trying to reassure her that Donny would be okay.

"Maybe we should have waited," he muttered guiltily, as the two-coach train trundled them along into the twilight. "Maybe all that escape stuff was childish."

"Didn't you hear what I was telling you?" Xanthe sounded completely fed up. "They've got their Emergency Order. They said Gold Dragon had left Pin Mill without giving proper notification to the authorities. The note Mum passed on to them didn't count, apparently. So you've broken the SS contract. And there's no effective postcode system beyond the low water mark at Gallister Creek so you're not allowed to live there anyway."

"We had to leave Pin Mill: we were chucked out," Donny protested.

"That don't cut no ice, brother," Xanthe was trying to make light of the situation but she couldn't. "Being ordered to leave Pin Mill makes everything worse because it lets them add 'persistent anti-social behaviour' to the charge sheet."

"Mum says Gold Dragon's definitely got to get herself a lawyer but she says she hasn't any money left. The insurance company made her pay a lot extra because of the accident with *Snow Goose*." Maggi's starring performance in *Lively Lady* should have left her elated but instead she looked distressed. "She even said that it had been irresponsible of her to buy *Vexilla*."

"Then she and Mum couldn't have gone prospecting and we wouldn't have escaped. Even from Pin Mill, probably," Donny objected.

"*Vexilla* makes us be like Vikings," added Luke.

"And now I'm taking us somewhere, for some reason I don't understand, to arrive in the dark with no torches. I wish Oboe had never given me the stupid challenge." Anna slumped in her seat.

The train journey seemed endless; they'd eaten all their food and there was no way they would reach the Easternmost Point in daylight.

"Vikings didn't know where they was going and they still went." Luke was nothing if not persistent. Donny was sure that in a moment he'd try to reassure his stepsister by pointing out that Vikings didn't have no torches neither.

"But I've got one," he announced quickly, rootling in his faithful rucksack. "It's not very big but it'll do."

"So've I," said Xanthe. "I never go anywhere without. And my compass and my knife. Not all in the same pocket, of course."

"We can use the backlights off our phones," said Maggi, giving Anna a quick hug. "Cheer up, Anna. This is what adventures are like. Probably."

CHAPTER TWENTY

Messages from Mars

Thursday 28 December, late afternoon
The traffic outside Lowestoft station was being diverted every which way. It seemed as if half the streets were being dug up and the other half blocked off. Several times Luke led them down roads that he was sure he remembered, only to run up against wire fences with forbidding notices from private security firms.

"Reminds me of that time we went to Ipswich," Donny remarked to Anna. He knew she was feeling tense. He thought maybe conversation might be good. "They were digging up places there as well. Do you remember that railway line that ran under that fence and those containers that looked like they'd been dumped but probably had people living in them?"

"They were minging. And I mostly hated this place too when we lived here."

Luke was taking them round the empty trawler basin that they'd seen when they were here on *Strong Winds*. Not many lights. Very few people.

They were almost to the sea. The wind was blowing directly on shore and it was cold. They could hear the waves. Couldn't see them yet. Suddenly they were startled by a completely new noise somewhere above their heads. It was an intense hissing, whirring noise that none of them could recognise.

A huge wind turbine towered over them, its three pale arms whirling in the rushing air. Donny'd seen it from a distance last time, but he'd sort of got the scale all wrong. It was so much bigger from underneath and more dramatic. It looked stark and white and lonely. As if it might at any moment come to life.

"There's a whole gang of 'em off shore," Luke told Xanthe. "We saw 'em from the boat. I reckon this one got split off and it's wavin' to get back to its mates."

"Could be," Xanthe agreed. "Or it's calling the others to come marching inland and take over the town – like in some weird horror movie."

"Cut it, Xanth," Maggi's voice was sharp. "Just now I don't need your horror stories."

They were almost there. Occasional municipal lights revealed a rusting gasometer, another fenced-off industrial unit and a small car park. They saw a gap in the seawall, with heavy metal floodgates ready to close it off. The finger post said 'Ness Point'.

Donny and Xanthe switched on their torches and the five of them walked cautiously down the access slope onto a lower promenade. There were railings round the outer edge of the promenade. Beyond that, a breakwater of rocks, splattered with 'No Climbing' and 'Danger' notices. Defences in the on-going battle between land and sea.

It was littered like a battleground too. Because of the way the tides ran round the east coast of England, high water Lowestoft was about two and a half hours earlier than on the River Stour. The water had flooded right over the promenade and dumped a sodden mess of seaweed and dead crabs, which it was leaving behind as it was sucked reluctantly away.

The Easternmost Point wasn't a spectacular natural feature

or anything. It was a snub nose shoved stubbornly into the sea: a jut of coastline sticking out against erosion.

The onshore wind was Arctic-cold. Dark waves erupted in crests of angry foam and wild gusts of water were blown back across the promenade.

"What did we come here for?" worried Anna. "What did Oboe want me to see?"

"You'd have thought there'd be some sort of monument," said Xanthe. "An obelisk or something."

"The chart showed two cardinal marks about twenty metres off shore," offered Donny. "That must be what we can see flashing straight ahead."

"I'm definitely not volunteering to check them out," said Maggi, jumping backwards from an unexpected spurt of water.

The place was completely deserted. Apart from the hazard warnings, and some graffiti on the seawall, they couldn't see any notices either.

"There's a sort of round pavement thing," Luke remembered. "They brought us down from school to do tracings on it."

Donny and Xanthe pointed their torches downwards and searched around the point of the ness. Once they were looking in the right direction it wasn't too hard to see the large flat compass rose set into the promenade. West, North, East, South, they read as they walked around it clockwise.

East was the scariest because it was closest to the sea. You couldn't really look down at the words because you had to be ready to dodge the spray. After only a few moments everyone retreated westwards and clustered round the torches. There was a lot more writing round the edge and it wasn't particularly easy to read.

Donny's torch was going yellow so he switched it off. At first they tried not to kneel or lie on the stone surface – it was so damp and so cold – but they soon found they had to. Most of the writing was embossed on metal so you could feel it as well as read.

Luke's 'round pavement thing' was a Euroscope. All the way round its perimeter it gave the direction and distance to capital cities: Lisbon 1086, Madrid 873, Helsinki 1038, Moscow 1468, Brussels 158, Berlin 490. In daylight they might have run from one name to another, calling out the information. This evening, huddled round Xanthe's torch in the biting wind, it was hard to get excited.

"It's just Europe, isn't it?" said Xanthe. "Nothing beyond."

"Yeah," said her sister. "That's all it's meant to be. But if you stood here long enough it could make you think of everything else that's out there, all round the world – if you carried straight on, as the crow flies."

"Except it wouldn't be crows, would it?" said Anna. "I mean I don't think crows fly all that far. I think it would be cranes or swifts or Arctic terns. Maybe that's the reason Oboe wanted me to come here. To feel the globe sort of sloping away into the distance and the air masses and the different lines of force bending round it."

"And stuff bouncing down from satellites or whatever."

"But not the sun."

They'd piled on all the clothes Gold Dragon had packed and Maggi and Xanthe had brought along some extra scarves and gloves. The wind cut straight through the layers, especially anywhere that was wet. Wherever it could find a gap it sort of chewed its way in like some busy rodent with a thrusting wet nose and icicle teeth.

They stood on the stone circle in the dark and felt the cold, each one wondering how long they could bear it. Behind them the giant turbine whirred ecstatically.

"You have to sort of think outwards from yourself and try to guess where the wind was last," said Donny, suddenly remembering the day he'd stood by the reservoir, the day his life had changed. "What it might have touched before it touched you."

"Dogger Bank Fishing Grounds," said Maggi after a while. She'd crouched down again and was using the backlight of her phone to read another inscription.

"That'd be where my Grandpa was born," said Luke. "An' where he died. I s'pose my dad'd have gone there too if the fishin' hadn't finished."

"Sole Pit Gas Field … Leman Gas Field … Indefatigable Gas Field …" Anna was tracing her way further round towards the East. "That's where my father was killed. There were other people killed as well. I don't like this place. I don't want to stand here any more. Come on, Lukey, let's go home. Forget all the dead people in the past. Forget Oboe too."

She put her arm round him, probably for the first time in her life, and walked back towards the seawall. There was an overhanging parapet that offered some almost imperceptible shelter.

"Can we stop here just a couple more moments, Anna?" Donny asked. "Great Aunt Ellen gave me a watch for Christmas. I want to try measuring the flashes off those navigation buoys. I'll be really quick."

"Suit yourself."

There was a scene in *Winter Holiday* where some of the children had been playing some game called Signalling to Mars. Donny had just read the book: Oboe must have read it as well. It had been in one of the email messages he'd been sending out to Anna's mother. Those books were the link between their families. They had mattered to Great Aunt Ellen's older brothers and sisters and they had mattered to Anna's great-uncle and her grandmother too. They were the centre of their friendship.

"I remember what the crumbs were. In the book, not in your message. It was something in an imaginary story. The brother and sister were outcasts on some lonely shore, sharing their last few crumbs."

"That's nice, I suppose," she said bleakly. She still had her arm round Luke.

Donny was thinking desperately hard. As Anna's Oboe was such a boff – and she was too when she wasn't freezing cold – was there anything in the flashing navigation lights that he'd expected Anna to pick up? Morse code or something?

He pulled out a notepad and started trying to jot down the different timings.

The spray soaked into the paper; the lights seemed totally random and he sensed that the others were getting seriously fed up with him.

Xanthe had already turned away and was using her torch to examine the concrete wall. "Classy graffiti in your part of the world," she commented to Luke. "I mean, get an eyeful of these stick people with their flags … *we* know they're only scribbles but get an art critic onto them … " Her voice trailed off.

"Yeah," said Maggi. She'd switched her phone's backlight on

and was trying to support her sister. "Significance and all that."

"I j…j…just like the b-bird," said Luke. His whole body was shaking now with cold but he was on Xanthe's fast-track list. "It's … well g-good."

"Significance?" Anna's mind was coming back to them. "You mean … like hidden meanings? Where?"

"There's another bird here," said Xanthe. "He's flying in. Sort of marking off the people. Avast your flash-counting, Donny-man. I'm having an Ornithological Moment! You hold the torch; I'll draw."

Xanthe grabbed Donny's pad and pencil, tore off the wet top sheet and started copying the row of little stick figures that extended from Luke's bird to her own.

He watched her in dawning amazement. "I know what this is," he said. "It's not Morse."

"It is *so* not Morse," she agreed. "It's semaphore – like in the books – and I know what it says! At least I thought I did. I got the first two words straight off, I've read them before – like I might even have written them, I know them so well. They say THREE MILLION. But, according to me, the next word should be CHEERS … and it's not. I gotta think, Donny-man." She'd finished copying now and they gathered round staring at the line of flag-wavers dancing merrily across the notepad in the torchlight.

"Xanthe," said Anna. "Could you write the letters of the words you do know directly underneath the figures you got them from? T H R E E M I L L I O N . Yes, I see. So the last word's something O, something N, something S. God, I sound like Gerald trying to do the crossword! But there aren't any clues. Please, Xanth, *try* to remember!"

"Okay, okay, don't hassle me." Xanthe stood up and began whirling her arms as if she were some sort of amateur wind turbine. "Mags," she said, "You've learned this too. Watch me. Use all the torches and the phones. I'll do the alphabet, you check against the drawings … A … B … C … D."

"Stop!" shouted Maggi and Anna. "D! The last but one letter's a D!"

"Write it down then!" said Xanthe, still signalling manically. "If I stop, I'll forget."

They were breathless with excitement.

"P!" Everyone shouted together. "The first letter's P and … the letter before last is … U! So the whole word is … POUNDS! THREE MILLION POUNDS!! Stuff three million CHEERS – this message spells Money!"

They all stopped and stared again.

"So we still don't know what it means," said Anna.

"No," said Xanthe, "we don't. But, dunk me if I'm wrong, I think we've got what we came for. This must be what Oboe meant you to find?"

"Yup," said Anna. "It's another mystery. Can we go now? Luke's completely frozen and so am I. Don't suppose anyone looked at the train times for getting home?"

"Well, actually, no," said Maggi. "But, luckily, the parentals seemed to think that that it would be easier to get here than get back."

Xanthe shoved the notebook deep into her pocket.

"So – no offence to the Native Guide, obviously – but we've got directions to the Floating Lotus. They've booked a table and the vicarage lot are coming as well – Rev. Wendy and Gerald and

Liam and Vicky. Lifts home afterwards. Dad thought we might have had enough of independent travel. And Mum said we'd be needing an Oriental Banquet if we'd ventured this far East."

"I *love* your Mum," said Donny. "Is Skye coming too?"

"Everyone's coming."

And the code-breakers vacated their Easternmost Point without a backward glance.

CHAPTER TWENTY-ONE

Room at the Floating Lotus

Thursday 28 December, evening
How totally over-the-top luscious could it be – a Chinese eat-as-much-as-you-like banquet?

They found fourteen places, including a high chair, already laid in a side room away from the main restaurant. It was a colourful room including a tank of exotic fish, holographic silk pictures of flying duck that shimmered as you looked at them from different angles and a vase of tall striped lilies with their strong, sweet, scent.

Donny wasn't that bothered about the décor – it was the sight of food that made the room look lovely. The centre of the large table was already covered with warming trays and, as soon as everyone was sitting down, the younger Chinese girls began bringing in dish after dish of steamy noodles and rice, sweet and tangy fish, meat, fruit and vegetables, crispy prawn crackers, spring rolls and a basin of chicken satay which Liam said was the best thing he'd tasted in his whole life, ever.

"Then I hope you live very much longer and enjoy much more." Ai Qin Pai was dressed in her black satin trousers and starched white shirt, with an even more ornately embroidered waistcoat than Donny remembered from before. Her make-up was immaculate, her round face radiating goodwill and she seemed to be treating this meal as some sort of special occasion.

The other adults also seemed quietly festive. You'd think that the code-breakers had been trekking for months in survival conditions instead of being on their own for eight hours (not much longer than a school day) and journeying about fifty miles on two trains. June embraced everyone; Rev. Wendy beamed and Skye … well, the fact that Skye was there said enough. Joshua's deep voice sounded somehow delighted and Donny even saw Gerald give Anna an awkward hug.

"Why fourteen places?" asked Anna. "Do Chinese people think thirteen's an unlucky number as well?"

"No, that is not a problem" replied Ai Qin. "The fourteenth place is for a guest who has had further to travel. Perhaps he is here now?"

Donny flinched. He guessed Anna had felt a pang of hope that the place had been left for her mother.

A tall man in a dark overcoat and homburg hat sidled in. He carried a briefcase and a rolled umbrella and looked round awkwardly. Donny watched Anna swallow her disappointment as if it was the tail-fin of a tiger prawn. She took a single deep breath, then stood up and walked across the room to shake hands. This was the lawyer she and Gold Dragon had met at Oboe's funeral in Cambridge.

She helped him with his hat and coat, couldn't quite manage a smile but changed her place politely so that he could sit beside her.

The lawyer looked pleased. His name, it turned out, was Edward.

No-one was drinking alcohol because of Skye but Edward obviously didn't know about that. He asked Ai Qin for a glass of house champagne and raised it to Anna.

"Congratulations, Miss Livesey. You de-coded your great-uncle's directions."

Anna looked surprised. "It was mainly my friends and I don't understand why it mattered. How did you know anyway? You've only just arrived."

"Ah well," Edward sipped his champagne. "Much as I'd like to claim omniscience … Some weeks ago I asked your carers to contact me as soon as you expressed any desire to visit Lowestoft Ness. I didn't offer any explanation and they didn't ask for one. I've been holding myself in readiness ever since. I wanted to be the first person to congratulate you."

"Um, thanks."

"You did find the message, the graffiti on the wall behind the Euroscope? We assumed you'd recognise semaphore even if you didn't know it. Perhaps it was too dark for you to read? The Euroscope shows three distinct positions for dawn at different times of the year, you know."

"We didn't see that," said Anna. "They must be on the far side. The East side. We couldn't see that side very well because the waves kept breaking over the wall."

Edward looked slightly disappointed. "Callum knew that he wouldn't live until the solstice. He donated a substantial sum to the Friends of Ness Point when I made the arrangements. They'll be able to do considerably more than clean up our graffitti. Of course it was a sentimental idea. But rather fun. I drove him up here very early one morning, fairly rattling with aerosols … Our last lark!"

Donny tried to imagine this dry lawyer and Anna's dying great-uncle arriving on the deserted promenade to have a go at street art.

Edward carried on explaining to Anna. "He regretted that he'd not been allowed to get to know you. He'd attended your parents' wedding and met you when you were a baby. But time had passed too quickly and then your father's death and your mother – so distressed and also … angry. He'd held your inheritance in trust and hoped, when the time came to hand it on – when he would himself be dead – that you might sometimes look eastwards out to sea and think of him."

"Of course I will." Anna's answer got a bit muffled because she'd hidden her face in her napkin. "I'm … sorry. I somehow thought that I was going to find … my mother. I knew I wasn't being … logical."

June Ribiero put her arm round Anna's shoulders as her own dark eyes filled up. Gerald stood up and sat down again while Rev. Wendy clasped her hands tight together as if sending off prayers by express delivery.

For one bad moment it seemed as if Vicky was going to pick up on her sister's emotion and begin howling in sympathy. Skye quickly offered her a knuckle to chew.

Edward looked incredibly uncomfortable. "Oh dear me, yes," he muttered. "What wouldn't we all give to have Ms Lottie Livesey present. Three million pounds and now the patent residues and the apartment as well. It's too great a responsibility. I can't see how it's to be managed."

"What do you mean, 'three million pounds'?" asked Xanthe.

Edward looked surprised. "The legacy, my dear. Miss Anna Livesey's legacy – though it will now be shared with her sister, Miss Victoria Whiting." He seemed to have worked out who Vicky was and nodded across the table to her, raising his champagne glass a second time. "Their grandmother, Theodora, was a highly successful novelist. You won't remember … but that film they made of *The Castaways!*" He sighed. "Charlotte – Charlotte Livesey as she became – was Theodora's only child and she made it clear that she would not accept a single penny of her mother's money. So it was all put in trust for her daughter … daughters, I should say. The income has been mounting up and it must be spent for their benefit. Yet how are we to interpret this without the advice of the children's mother? Professor Reif made every effort to find his niece. But there had been a rift. On political grounds. And now he too has died, there is the additional question of his residual patents and his home. The entire top floor of Bawdsey Manor was his personal property. He has left it to Miss Anna Livesey."

Anna was sitting up, white as her napkin, staring at Edward. "You are saying that, because I did a completely straightforward binary/decimal conversion, I get all that? Because I didn't do anything else. It was Donny and Maggi and Xanthe and Luke who got us to the Easternmost Point."

The lawyer's eyes crinkled with amusement. "No, no, my dear," he said. "The quest was Callum's last-minute attempt to create some feeling of connection between himself and the person he thought was his only surviving relation. Once he had finally despaired of making contact with your mother. He hoped to take you on an adventure with him. That's why I was somewhat taken aback to learn of Miss Whiting's existence. I wondered whether I should modify the challenge to enable her to participate. But she really is too young. I will have to rely on you to explain matters when she is able to understand. The inheritance is yours and hers whether you like it or not. As your Trustee I cannot even allow you to refuse it until you have both come of age."

"I don't want to refuse it," said Anna decidedly. "I want to use everything I've got to help my friends – and my family. I don't think you knew I have brothers. We're all in this together. I won't let anyone split us up."

Luke and Liam leaned behind Great Aunt Ellen's chair and did high fives.

"I wouldn't dream of such a thing," said Edward. "But we really *do* need your mother back, don't we?"

"I've been searching on the Internet for ages," said Anna. "But I can search better now I've got money. All those sites where you have to pay, I can go on them now."

"As your Trustees we have already disbursed considerable funding via investigation agencies and similar channels. Without the least success. Hence Professor Reif's final attempts to make direct appeal using the Internet. Fruitless, as it transpired. Troublingly so. But we must not give up. *Perseverando!* I would ask you to consider how your mother would choose to communicate – if she had something private to convey?"

There was a long silence round the table. Chopsticks lay idle; helpings congealed on plates. Edward hadn't even started. The problem was that Lottie had vanished deliberately, knowing that her children would be Looked After, and she hadn't sent Anna a single message to say she was okay. This was why they thought she might be … dead.

"Anna," asked Xanthe, at last. "If your mum had been trying to tell you something, how would she have done it? I mean, you said she never liked computers …"

"We used to talk. Quite a lot. But she does get fired up. She isn't what I'd call logical. Although, possibly I'm not as logical as I thought I was."

"Your mum liked singing best," said Liam. "She singed stuff to me an' Luke. Loads of times."

Anna looked at him, fondly. "Out of the mouths of babes! Liam's completely right. Music was Mum's real life – like I thought maths could be mine. I'm not sure how it helps us."

Donny jumped up as if an electric eel had stung him on the backside. "Oh my stars and compasses," he gabbled. "I've got it right here; she's in my bag."

He pushed his chair aside and rushed over to the corner of the room where they'd dumped their jackets. There was his rucksack. And there was the grotty old music folder he'd taken from Anna's marked space in the DT cupboard.

He shoved it at her, unable to speak with hope and excitement.

The first batch of manuscript pages was as off-putting as the cover. Someone had been practising writing out key signatures and simple scales. Their pencil was blunt and they were basically clueless so there were lots of scribblings-out and smudged erasing with a dirty rubber. Then there were time signatures that didn't add up and tunes that started on impossible notes and didn't progress any further.

No-one who knew Anna could have believed this folder was hers and no teacher would have wasted more than thirty seconds leafing through it.

Then there was a diagram of a piano keyboard. Not a very good one because the keys went up like steps instead of being in a straight line. A message in a leaking biro said "2 x 13 = 26. Remember Dr Gradus ad Parnassum."

"Oh!" said Anna and swayed as if she might be going to faint.

"*Gradus ad parnassum*," said Edward reading over her shoulder. "My oh my, that takes me back. Steps to heaven!"

"But in our house it was the staircase, a chromatic octave, thirteen steps. And Mum is telling me to go up the stairs and down again. And twenty-six is the number of letters in the alphabet!"

Edward handed her his fountain pen without her needing to ask.

"This is the sort of code I understand," she breathed ecstatically, ready to write.

"Not on the book!" Ai Qin stepped forward hastily. "You may need to send a message back … "

She handed Anna a blank order pad. Anna looked at her a moment, looked alarmed, then bent her head over the music and began spelling out her mother's message from the shapeless tunes and odd key signatures.

"I work for Pura-Lilly Cleaning. There are many of us and we are all afraid. Usually we work at night, sometimes in your schools and other places. I am held here by a debt that I cannot repay and by my fears for you if I should fail. We live in the wastelands. Tell no-one except in extreme emergency. Write me a note in this book and kiss sweet little Vicky. Be good to the boys."

No-one said anything for a moment.

"So she does care!" said Maggi, her face alight with happiness.

"That folder's been in my bag since the end of last term. And it was on the shelf for weeks before that. She must think you're never going to answer." Donny felt terrible. Why hadn't he insisted that Anna should check the book out properly? Would she start crying again, now she knew?

But Anna, who'd been so emotional before, was completely calm and collected. "Well," she said to Edward. "I hope Vicky's and my Trustee will see it as a 'benefit' to pay our mum's debts and get her out of that cleaning company. And this time she won't be able to say no because it's not her mother's money any more, it's ours!"

"Yes indeed," said Edward. "Of course we'll need to appoint a second Trustee before we can make any decisions at all. I rather hoped one of your carers might be willing?"

"That'd be nice," said Anna with a quick shy smile at Wendy and Gerald. "If it wouldn't be too much trouble for them. They have to work quite hard, looking after all of us."

"We'd be delighted," said Wendy, with an upward glance. "I take a professional interest in miracles and this one's really quite exceptional. I wonder whether Pura-Lilly's in the telephone directory. Perhaps we could ring your mother straight away?"

"No," said Donny. "No, I don't think you should. There's something not right about this. But I don't know what it is."

He hadn't been signing but Skye saw from his body language that he was worried. She asked him what his trouble was.

"The cleaning company," he signed back. "Pura-Lilly. There's something I don't like."

Skye looked puzzled. She gestured at the vase in the corner. "Is it the flower company?" she signed. Her hands were still weak. "Is their mother working for the flower company? The small man is not good. She must be careful."

Suddenly Donny saw it. "Yes, yes she is. But they don't sell flowers, they do cleaning."

"I know that!" Skye's hands expressed the exasperation she couldn't utter. "The flower is on the van. It is a picture."

Of course it was! That bath-pink lily sign. And not only on the van! It was embroidered on the pocket of the Chinese cleaner's overalls. And stamped on the sides of that horrible heap of containers in Ipswich – the place where they couldn't believe any human could be living …

"Oh my God!" he gasped.

Rev. Wendy glared at him.

"Er … sorry. But I've just sussed it out – Anna's mother's working for the Tiger!"

CHAPTER TWENTY-TWO

Ghosts

Thursday 28 December
"Tiger? Who's the Tiger?"

"The Tiger is the man who employs the Chinese cleaner who let me out of the cupboard. That bit really doesn't matter but the point is that her overalls had the Pura-Lilly logo. And she was kind. She could be a friend of Anna's mum. She could even have brought in the folder. Unless there were lots of them."

It was no good. Only Donny's Allies and Gold Dragon understood what he was saying. People like Gerald, Joshua Ribiero and Edward the lawyer were new to the idea that there was anything criminal happening at all. Wendy and June had at least begun to suspect that Flint and Toxic might be more than power-mad bullies but while June was eager to learn more from Ai Qin, Ai Qin was not yet willing to talk to anyone outside her own community.

She and Gold Dragon spoke urgently to one another in Mandarin while Donny tried to make everyone else understand that what had been happening to him and Skye was somehow connected to the plight of Lottie Livesey.

"Because she's not on a mission, is she? She's almost some sort of prisoner."

Ai Qin summoned the big, scarred chef from the Floating Lotus kitchen and seemed to be asking his opinion. He spoke Cantonese, not Mandarin, and it took ages. By the time all the explanations, translations and connections had been made,

Vicky and Liam had fallen asleep and Luke had propped his elbows on the table, his chin in his hands and was staring at the fish tank with glassy-eyed intensity.

Maggi and Xanthe were determined to get things clear. They questioned Donny even more thoroughly than they had on the afternoon of *Snow Goose*'s accident.

"So, if the Tiger is the manager of Pura-Lilly, and Lottie and these other people are controlled by him, then he's more than some sidekick who's doing Flint and Toxic's dirty work."

"Except that he *is* doing their dirty work, isn't he? They want Gold Dragon out of here and he's the person who's been trying to make her leave by getting Skye addicted and chasing after you in his white van."

"It must have been him who slashed the dragon flag and wrote those warning signs on the *Hispaniola*."

"He must want Gold Dragon out as well."

"I think," said Donny, "that he was at that meeting." He remembered the inconspicuous man in a suit who had looked so interested when someone – was it Toxic? – had asked Great Aunt Ellen where in China *Strong Winds* had been built. "I think that there's something in Gold Dragon's past that really scares them. She thought she'd come home to be a good great-aunt. But they won't let her."

Xanthe nodded at this but Maggi frowned. "Still not sure I get it. When Toxic brought him into the school, posing as a computer expert, it was Mr Mac and Anna they were after. You were just some random kid in their way. How could they have decided that that was exactly the right moment to hand your mum the vodka bottle?"

"Because I'd left my shoes on a bench by the door and my name was written in them."

"What an idiot!"

"I had blisters …"

"They'd read my computer by then anyway," said Anna. "They knew Mum hadn't sent any messages. They were just making extra trouble for Mr Mac."

"And the music folder was in his department all the time! That is so neat!"

The chef finished what he had to say, bowed politely to Gold Dragon and returned to his kitchen. Ai Qin decided to speak English and the discovery of Anna and Vicky's three million-pound fortune was almost lost in the disgust of the other things the Allies learned that evening. Things they really didn't want to know but were there in the world whether they liked them or not.

When Great Aunt Ellen had lived in Shanghai – and for many years before that –people often gave her information. About tiger-sharks. That was all she said. Once she'd made the decision to return to England, she'd agreed to deliver some private messages from the families of poor workers who had borrowed money to pay smugglers to get them into England.

"Then that would be the end for me. If I was to live with you here, in a family, I had to cut my cables from the past. You can lose more than a hand if you swim too long with tiger-sharks."

Donny thought about the Floating Lotus chef who walked in that strange way because he only had one leg …

Ai Qin explained that the people smugglers always told

the illegal workers that it would be easy to pay off their travel debt. England was a great place, full of good jobs, they said. As soon as the debt was cleared, the workers could begin sending money home to their villages to support the elderly parents and the children they had left behind. If they failed to keep up their repayments their families would suffer. Even if they were sick or died, their families would still have to pay back the journey money. But no-one really expected that that would be a problem.

The illegal workers were not offered good jobs when they arrived. The pay was low, the conditions terrible and they didn't have anyone to whom they could turn for help. Who could they trust? They were almost invisible, ghosts in the local economy, doing the jobs that nobody else wanted. They had to hand all their money to their gang-masters but the debts never seemed to go.

Ai Qin's Floating Lotus was like a refuge, especially for women and young girls. A legal way for them to work and earn money, get advice and keep safe. She had a network of contacts and could get messages to people who needed to stay hidden. She helped as many as she could. Especially when they wanted to go home.

"Since the Tiger arrived conditions for the workers have become even worse. He seems to be able to do just as he likes. We believe he has powerful friends among the ghosts."

"You've lost me, Ai Qin. Who are the ghosts?" Xanthe was puzzled. "I thought you meant the invisible workers were like ghosts but now you say ghosts are the Mr Bigs?"

"I am so sorry. This was rude of me. We Chinese often call Westeners ghosts because, well …" She giggled. "Because of the way they look! These powerful ghosts who are making a much worse situation are English not Chinese. This Tiger has crossed from Holland and his territory is growing. He brings fear and violence. He makes addicts."

"Yes," said Gold Dragon. "I think we know that."

"Flint and Toxic!" breathed Anna to Donny. "They must be the English ghosts."

It seemed completely obvious to the Allies that the bullying policeman, the poisonous Professional and the small man in the Pura-Lilly van were all one sinister gang.

"But you have no proper evidence for this," Edward interrupted firmly. "I insist that we must be cautious. Our approach to Lottie Livesey must be handled with the greatest care. Until she is safely reunited with her children and can speak more freely about her experiences, I do strongly urge everyone in this room to say or do nothing that might prejudice the situation."

"Cal Reif's niece has been cast up on a dead lee shore. She may not be easily plucked off. This is no time to look abaft the beam."

"We don't know how much money Lottie Livesey owes, nor to whom it is due," said Joshua gravely.

"It doesn't matter how much. It can't be more than Three Million Pounds!"

June smiled at Anna. "That wasn't what we meant. Of course you will pay whatever is needed to release your mother and of course your Trustees will sanction that. But we have to think how best to get the money to her. If she is in the hands of extortionists and they see that she is rich, they might demand more ... "

"Which could endanger you children – whom, it appears, she has been trying to protect all this time," said Gerald. He looked shocked. Here was another unexpected re-think to disrupt his settled life.

Luke suddenly came out of his trance. "We don't dodge 'em no more: we fight 'em!" he pronounced, then gave a most enormous yawn and fell forward on the table as sound asleep as his brother and sister.

This seemed like a good decision and everyone relaxed a bit. Edward ordered another glass of champagne and asked Ai Qin whether she could find him a room in Lowestoft for the night. Other people sipped cups of jasmine tea or spooned up the last coatings of savoury sauce from their bowls.

"It's time we took the children home," said Rev. Wendy. She was frowning and looked unhappy. "Now that we have a means of communication, we will surely be able to pass money across in a way that will seem convincing." She hesitated but carried on bravely. "I have a suggestion. If her situation is as we fear, if she is … enslaved, no loan shark or gang master will believe that she could come by large amounts of money except through dishonesty. If they think that she has stolen the money they could threaten to report her to the police. Blackmail her for more."

"Don't!" said Donny. He knew whose hairy paws would be digging in there.

"Praise God the little ones are asleep." She was speaking very fast now, gabbling her terrible suggestion. "There are areas …" She couldn't quite bring herself to spell it out. Her face went red. She looked only at June, the magistrate. " … that disgrace the Diocese! Our husbands can pose as … clients. If Lottie can be persuaded to act a part, they can pass her all the cash she needs. Then get her out with them before there are any awkward questions asked."

Had they really heard what they thought she'd said?

Then first Anna and Maggi, then Donny and Xanthe, began to giggle. The prospect of anxious, cardi-wearing Gerald and tall, grave Joshua posing as punters visiting Anna's mum disguised as a back-street hooker seemed totally bizarre.

Ai Qin did not laugh. "It happens," she said. "It's not so funny."

They were sorry at once. She was right. It wasn't funny, it was horrible.

"But wouldn't they still want more? A percentage?" asked Maggi.

"Then we give it – and we take her, swiftly, into sanctuary. To her children and to me, in the vicarage." Rev. Wendy at that moment seemed sure and powerful.

Anna looked as if she was seeing her foster-carer for the first time in a different way. Everyone else began getting up from the table, paying for their food, picking up the younger ones and collecting possessions.

"Now Vicky and I are rich," said Anna, handing Edward his wide-brimmed hat, "can we get a lawyer please to help Donny? There's an Emergency Order against Gold Dragon for moving her boat which means the SS are trying to take him away to a Unit."

"I'm sorry, my dear. Trustees can only disburse funds in the direct interests of the beneficiary. This case, however worthwhile, would not qualify. However," he continued as Anna opened her mouth to argue, "I have also been an admirer of Miss Polly Lee for many years. I will be honoured to champion her cause – *pro bono publico*, for the public good. That's Latin, you know."

"I guessed that, thank you," said Anna demurely, clutching the forged music folder close to her heart.

CHAPTER TWENTY-THREE

Ben Gunn

Sunday 31 December 2006

It was the last day of the year. A grey and charcoal day with rain most of the morning and more expected later. The River Orwell was uncompromising pewter and the bare trees on the further shore stood dark against the building clouds. The barometer was dropping fast as *Kingfisher* and *Spray* went racing up to Ipswich.

Anna had said that she could not bear not to know whether the pile of Pura-Lilly containers on the empty building site was where her mother had been living all along. She struggled to accept that she could not go herself and that they must allow the adults time to carry out their crazy plan.

"*Why* can't Edward just turn up and say that Vicky and I have inherited this money then hand it over to get Mum home?"

"Because if your mother was simply working to repay debts there'd have been no need for all this secrecy in the first place. Let alone leaving the four of you in foster-care at public expense. There's a wider picture here that we haven't got."

June wasn't to be argued with. She was making tray-loads of hors d'oeuvres for a New Year's Eve party at the Royal Orwell and Ancient Yacht Club. There would be fireworks at midnight and she'd invited Donny and Anna to come as their guests and stay with them afterwards

"In a bed? Awesome! And can I have a bath as well? With Radox or something?"

Donny loved living on board *Strong Winds*. There was nowhere better and a combination of bucket washes and school showers had so far kept him perfectly clean even through the coldest weather. But a bath – and maybe sheets!

They went upstairs to sit in Maggi's room. Xanthe's was piled with GCSE revision notes. She'd got mocks as soon as term began.

"Okay, okay," Anna carried on. "I know your mother's right. But adults are so slow. And we can't even take the music book back to the DT cupboard until school re-opens. Please, couldn't one of you just go and check it out?"

Donny and Xanthe looked at each other. The rain had stopped and there were hours before they had to get ready for the party.

"Time spent on reconnaissance … " His home was on the River Stour now but there was still so much to discover on the Orwell.

"The issue with revision is whether it gives you an unfair advantage," said Xanthe and he could almost see white sails dancing in her eyes. "I've done loads already and today's a Sunday. It's almost cheating to do more."

"Mum," she called downstairs, "you know you said you wanted to take some trays down early? Could Donny and I come too? We might mess about on the water for a bit. We'd take our clean clothes with us."

Baths were over-rated anyway. Plenty of people did without them all their lives.

He'd never sailed anything like Maggi's *Kingfisher* before. Xanthe'd looked at the conditions, checked the yacht club barometer and chosen the smallest of their range of sails. She'd lent him some

thermals and a wetsuit and demonstrated how he should adjust
the footstraps to lock himself into the boat.

"Steer with your whole body," she said.

They were on a broad reach but it was gusty and he was
fighting to keep *Kingfisher* upright. It would be worse on the way
back. Xanthe was ahead of him of course. He guessed she wasn't
pushing *Spray* yet, was giving him time to get himself in tune
with this new dinghy. Get excited, even.

He shifted his weight slightly aft and let his sheet out. Then he
took a deep breath, braced his stomach muscles and arched his
upper body backwards. *Kingfisher*'s hull flattened onto the water
and she surged forward. Donny's breathing quickened, his heart
pounded: he was going to catch Xanthe – if he could.

The sail was great: the mission disappointing. Anna had
borrowed Maggi's laptop and printed out some pictures of
Lottie taken a few years ago at a concert. In case there was some
unknown woman there whom they wanted to identify. And,
maybe, casually, speak to?

But the Pura-Lilly containers were almost abandoned. A
bonfire had been built on the wasteland, ready for lighting later
that night, the gaps in the mesh fence had been mended and new
notices put up. There was some sort of PR operation in progress.
The Mulciber Development Co was committed to enhancing
2007 for all and wished neighbouring communities a Bright
Future. Spectators at tonight's grand sponsored firework display
were All Welcome but advised to remain beyond perimeter fence
for Own Safety.

Donny and Xanthe took advantage of the fact that they were

both wearing wetsuits and avoided the fence by scrambling round via the river's edge. They climbed over the embankment and walked towards to the containers intending to take a look through the windows anyway.

They didn't see the squat black terrier tied to a metal post. But it saw them and began to bark hysterically.

The three apprentice thugs inside were slow reacting. Probably because they were already halfway off their heads on whatever it was they were sniffing or drinking. There was plenty of time for Donny and Xanthe to retreat behind the river wall again, lie down, peer over and watch.

The dog got shouted at. Was used for target practice with a few spare cans and stones. They weren't good shots, mostly.

The boys had lurched back into their den when a metallic-blue Mercedes drew up at the locked double gates. Two or three sharp bursts on the horn sent the dog manic but failed to summon the goons. The driver selected a silk headscarf patterned with leather and buckles to prevent her hair being inconvenienced by the wind. Then she swung her legs out onto the wet road, unlocked the gates with her personal key and a hideously familiar figure came mincing impatiently across the wasteland in a short Burberry mac and zebra-striped stiletto boots.

"Toxic!" Donny breathed to Xanthe, who hadn't seen much of Education Welfare in her successful school career.

"Those boots are … something … Maggi would know. Something expensive."

"Jimmy Choos?" Donny offered, remembering what Anna had said once.

"Nah. Don't think so anyway. It's the red soles."

"Oh yeah, I see them."

He was beginning to see more than the crimson soles. He was beginning to see who it was with the crooked tongue who had stressed Skye out on that first disastrous morning in Shotley marina. Who it was his mother had meant by the Woman who makes Bad Worse.

"She treads in blood," he muttered.

"Possibly bit extreme, Donny-man. It's more of a fashion statement. Plenty of people say they'd kill for a pair of those. But only metaphorically."

"Skye was talking metaphorically – but you begin to wonder. Oh, don't worry Xanth, I'll explain later."

The dog was muzzled and pushed inside the container: the door was slammed, the boys marched across to the car and driven away.

"Welfare in action – rescuing the socially excluded from illicit substance abuse?"

"Or Toxic grabbing herself a posse?"

It didn't feel like a brain-buster.

"I don't want to sound paranoid, Donny-man, when we're all going partying and that, but what does she want a posse for?"

"Must have other people to pick on. I mean, what can they do to us? Gold Dragon's got a lawyer now and Edward's already written to the SS demanding some sort of injunction to hold up their Emergency Order. So I can't get snatched."

"Even over the holiday?"

"They're full-on this time of year, apparently."

"So what are your lot doing tonight? Letting off lanterns from *Strong Winds*?"

"Nah. Chinese New Year's different anyway. Gold Dragon and Skye are at the vicarage having a pirate party with the kids. Dressing-up and treasure hunts. Rev. Wendy's on some vigil for world harmony and happiness so Gerald's invited Mrs Everson and her daughter round to make whoopee. They haven't seen Hawkins's cage since Luke and Liam finished customising it."

"Could be cool?"

"Yeah. By Erewhon Parva standards it's a total rave."

They'd started walking back to the dinghies when Xanthe stopped again. Turned back. "I'll tell you who does want rescuing. But we won't need Anna's photo ... "

"Who?"

"That dog. You read the notices. There's going to be a grand firework display here later. Poor mutt'll be terrified but it's got that thing on, that muzzle. It won't be able to bark so no-one'll know that it's in there."

"That's cruel. It's a really vicious dog, though." Donny had had several bad moments with the dog when his family was still living at Pin Mill.

"Should we ring the RSPCA or something? Police?"

"They'd have it put down. It is dangerous."

"Yeah."

They both thought of the abuse they'd seen the dog receiving.

"I don't think it's all that old, even ... "

"The goons may be planning to come right back ..." Xanthe was already halfway to the containers when she said this. She looked pretty weird padding across the wasteland in her wet-suit and buoyancy aid but there was no-one about to see. Donny knew that what she was doing was right.

There were half a dozen metal containers with the pink Pura-Lilly logo, most of them locked. They circled round peering through tiny mesh windows. An office, a chemical store, then, when Xanthe climbed up to look in the second level, she found what they'd been expecting, spaces with mattresses on the floor, a few scattered clothes and blankets and an old TV. The washing line had been pulled in and dropped.

"They'd have moved people out over the holiday, I suppose. Especially if there's going to be this PR display happening."

"Where do you reckon they'd go to?"

"Must be loads of places, empty houses, offices, empty boats. "

"Mmmm," Donny was beginning to get a bad feeling about tonight. Empty boats?

The dog was in the container where the boys had been. There were empty cans and half-smoked roll-ups and a tatty stack of porn mags. No dog bed, water or food.

The animal hurled itself at Donny but there was nothing it could do. Couldn't bark, couldn't bite. It was surprisingly heavy though, for something quite small. Donny sat down with a thump before he got knocked over. Although the dog's long, strong jaws were strapped shut, there were gaps at the corners of its mouth where its desperate efforts to snarl revealed pink gums, dribble and white teeth. It was lunging at him, tense and trembling and off its head with rage.

"Bit like Vicky throwing a tantrum."

"We're gonna have to go, Donny-man, and we'll have to take it with us. There's a van turning in the gates. Spectacular Sensations. They must be about to set up the display. Toxic's goons won't be coming back now. We gotta take the mutt."

"In our dinghies?"

"Trust me," said Xanthe. "I'll sort something."

She rejected the length of chain left by the dog's owner. Instead she pulled out a much longer piece of para-cord from one of her many zipped pockets. As she tied it, swiftly and securely, to the terrier's harness Donny felt the animal relax. Xanthe felt it too. She stroked the dusty black fur, ran her capable hands over the dog's face, around its ears and underneath its chest.

"We do need to go." Donny still didn't dare move.

"We do." She held one hand experimentally a few inches in front of the terrier. "C'mon, mutt." It moved forward cautiously to push its nose in her palm and let her stroke its head again. It made him think of Skye and Hawkins.

"Found your feminine side then," he said, knowing that she couldn't retaliate. "Could we maybe leave? Now?"

"Okay," she said, as they jogged back to the New Cut where they'd left *Kingfisher* and *Spray*. "As it happens, I know that Dad knows the owner of this yard. I'm gonna call him up and ask him for his gate entry code so we can pull the dinghies in. I'll tell him I've got a novice sailor with me and we've been caught out by the weather."

"Oh … okay," said Donny. "S'pose so." He could see that it was blowing even harder out on the river. But in a favourable direction. He'd been looking forward to the sail back. Ragged puffs of slate-grey cloud were beginning to race across the sky promising worse to follow. The wind-rain combination could have been exhilarating – given that they would be heading for the RO&A clubhouse with hot showers and clean dry clothes.

"You're not the novice sailor," she misinterpreted his reluctance. "You almost put *Spray* under pressure earlier. It's the dog – Ben Gunn, here – that I'm talking about."

"Obviously. But how will we get back to the others for tonight?" Donny's uneasy feelings were getting stronger. Gold Dragon and Skye would surely be okay in the vicarage. But what about *Strong Winds*, left at anchor and un-watched in the lonely Stour?

"I've got plastic, we'll call a cab." She was already tapping the boatyard number into her mobile phone.

"And then – I'm really sorry, Xanthe, but I need a change of plan."

Beds with sheets were probably overrated too. Plenty of people didn't have them either.

CHAPTER TWENTY-FOUR

Rule Britannia

Sunday 31 December, later

The first heavy drops of rain were beginning to fall as Donny scrabbled around in the earth near the vicarage woodshed looking for the key.

The taxi had dropped him outside the drive and Xanthe could have been under the impression that he was going straight indoors to talk to Great Aunt Ellen. She herself was taking Ben Gunn back to her house and was going to find him somewhere quiet to settle. She reckoned she'd be able to take his muzzle off okay as long as she'd got food waiting. She'd explain to her mother that Donny had got worried about not being with his family for the night.

"Except it's not directly them I'm worried about, it's *Strong Winds*. If anyone wants to get at Gold Dragon, that's her weakest spot. Not me or Skye. If they trashed her boat she'd find it really hard to stay."

"Yeah. But you're not going to fend off the rabble single-handed?"

"Course not. I don't even see how they'd get to her in these conditions. I know I'm being hyper. I can't really explain. I only want to check with Great Aunt Ellen."

"Take my mobile. It's got full battery and Maggi's number's on speed dial. I'll call her from the home phone. You gotta promise you'll keep her and Anna in the loop. Allies, remember."

Allies, great: confederates, a pain. Donny's hands were smeared with mud and his fingernails gritty by the time he'd found the key and had unlocked the shed to retrieve his bike. He'd decided not to go indoors and risk spoiling the pirate party. Gold Dragon would be shivering Luke and Liam's timbers by now and it wasn't often the kids had fun. He'd done the bike ride to Gallister so often that it'd be a total cinch to cycle to the creek and make sure everything was okay. They'd left both the dinghies there. And if there was anything wrong with *Strong Winds*, he could use Xanthe's phone to call for help.

It was good he was still wearing the wetsuit because the rain was fairly bucketing down. It had washed his hands clean before he'd gone about ten metres. Who needed showers!

The roads were quiet – he was glad about that. He was sort of haunted by the fear that he might meet the white van. Or possibly, tonight, Toxic's special edition Merc. Worst of all would be Flint's black Range Rover.

It was a relief when he reached the soggy track that led from an empty car park down to Gallister Creek. The reeds were lashing in the wind and he guessed it would be rough out on the river, though the rain might flatten the worst of it. He propped the bike against a stunted oak and used its shelter to check Xanthe's phone. There was a text.

Hi sis. Where u? Dad stuck at hosp again. Mum stressed. Hag and ogre both here. Anna wants out :(

Flint and Toxic at the party! No wonder Anna wasn't happy. It did sort of neutralise them though.

He tried to reach Xanthe on the Ribieros' home number but there wasn't any answer. He hoped that meant she was serving

Ben Gunn's supper or scratching his nose. Not trapped with his teeth in her arm. He left a message to tell her to call Maggi asap.

Another text arrived.

Walking to PM to join pirates. Wood spooky. A says not as spooky as hag and ogre. C u later xm

Donny was shocked. They shouldn't be doing that. The path though the trees would be well dark. He pressed reply.

B careful. X at home + rescue dog. Plse call her there. I have phone :) D

He wasn't much good at texting with wet fingers and was struggling with the hollow feeling that he'd messed up. Flint and Toxic were at the Club: the well-hards wouldn't be out on the river in weather like this. He ought to be with Maggi and Anna in the spooky wood. Or with Xanthe and that psychopathic dog.

He was hungry. He was tired. He'd check the junk and go straight back. Have some New Year's Eve fun. He stowed the phone in a waterproof pouch inside the zipped pocket which was inside his wet-suit and underneath the close-fitting buoyancy aid. Xanthe had made it pretty clear that she wouldn't accept any dinghy-capsize or similar accident as an excuse for wrecking her mobile.

The tide was still high and *Lively Lady* floating where he'd left her. *Vexilla* too. Donny ran to the point at the edge of the bay and looked out. The River Stour was about a mile wide here but if he focussed hard he could see occasional quick flashes from the channel buoys on the further side. The rain was easing a bit – though it didn't look as if it was going to be much of a night for fireworks. Nearer him, where the creek led towards the deeper water of anchorage, the river was completely dark.

It shouldn't have been.

He should have been able to see *Strong Winds'* anchor light, even in these conditions. He remembered Skye hoisting it this morning before they all left. Perhaps she'd forgotten to check the paraffin and it had run out. That was something he could fix. Not that there was ever much passing traffic. Let alone on a night like this.

The wind had veered west and was blowing straight down the river. The ebb could scarcely have begun. He ran back to *Lively Lady* and rummaged for her old red jib. He wanted to set something small and quiet and non-reflecting. He didn't choose to ask himself why.

Donny didn't have to worry about sticking to the line of the creek at this state of the tide. The withies and the small, unlit buoys weren't easy to spot anyway. He pointed *Lively Lady* as directly as he could for the place where *Strong Winds* should have been. The wind was on the beam and the jib pulling nicely. He peered ahead for the first sight of *Strong Winds'* solid shape amidst the blackness.

Then he began to catch the steady sound of a boat engine. He felt as if he recognised it, though it certainly wasn't the reassuring throb of *Strong Winds'* motor nor the terrifying snarl of the shark-boat. It wasn't the speedboat either.

Donny looked all around him as *Lady* rode cheerfully up and over the swell. It must have been properly rough earlier when the wind and tide were diametrically opposed. He remembered what Gold Dragon had said about 'walls of water' coming down the Stour. Neither of Flint's boats would have been able to reach *Strong Winds*. He was certain of that.

Anyway Flint was at the party. Filling his fat face with June Ribiero's food, no doubt. Not surprising that Maggi said her mum was stressed.

The only time he'd seen a boat beside the *Hispaniola* it had been Flint's black speedboat. Was there a maritime equivalent of the Pura-Lilly white van? He'd never noticed one.

There were still no lights.

And that was odd. He'd been checking the green flashes of a starboard-hand channel buoy on the far side of the river. That too had vanished. Was someone going round with a deluminator?

The engine was getting closer.

Or he was getting closer to it. The green light of the starboard-hand channel buoy hadn't been extinguished. The reason he couldn't see it any more was that *Strong Winds* was blocking it out. He'd arrived.

Much too soon.

He let his jib fly and pushed the tiller down so *Lady* turned into the wind and lay neatly alongside the junk's starboard bow. No time to feel relief. The engine noise was coming from somewhere roughly amidships on *Strong Winds'* port side. There were no anchor chains. The junk was moving. The unseen vessel on the far side was pushing her in a sharp starboard-hand curve. If he didn't get out of the dinghy in a hurry, his weight in this swell might swamp her as *Strong Winds* was forced hard against her.

Donny dropped the jib and sheeted it in almost a single movement. Made fast the halliard, grabbed his painter and was up and rolling himself over *Strong Winds'* bulwarks before he even wondered who he might be about to meet.

The deck was deserted. He flattened down instinctively, looked round, saw no-one then wriggled cautiously aft along the smooth teak deck between the bulwark and the coach-roof.

There were no lights showing, either on *Strong Winds* or on the vessel pushing from the far side, whatever it was. Something powerful but low in the water. When he raised his head to try to look across he could see the flat top of a small square wheelhouse. Nothing more.

Donny's nose was close to the deck. More and more strongly he smelled diesel.

This was really odd. Odder than the absence of the anchor light. *Strong Winds* carried diesel for her engine and diesel to power the generator they'd used when they were at Pin Mill. The cabin heater was also diesel but Gold Dragon was fierce about minimising the smell. Bilges were kept scrupulously clean and any spilled drop neutralised immediately. He'd never smelled anything like this all the time he'd lived on board.

He swarmed along more swiftly. He could check if there was a leak from the fuel tank. Though maybe it didn't have to be his first priority. It wasn't as if diesel was easily flammable, not like petrol. What he most needed to do was slip down into *Strong Winds'* engine room, get the engine ready to start, then find some way to release whatever towing ropes were binding the junk to her abductor. Then, somehow … try to get her away.

This diesel smell was making him feel sick and even a bit drowsy. The cabin doors seemed hard to open. The smell from below was almost overpowering. He'd have to get to the engine room as quick as possible then get out again. Through the forehatch maybe. The air would be fresher there.

The doors opened when he put his shoulder to them and shoved.

Gold Dragon slept in the quarter berth. It was a small self-contained berth, secluded from the main saloon but closest to the engine room and the companionway. In an emergency she could be into the cockpit taking command of Strong Winds in seconds.

She was there now, in her sleeping bag, going nowhere. There was a pad of diesel-soaked wadding covering her face. Donny snatched it off. Her mouth was half-open, her breathing heavy. She was alive but unconscious.

Why? Why wasn't she safely at Erewhon Parva shivering the timbers of the kids?

No time to wonder.

Could diesel fumes kill? The cabin seemed to have been saturated. Donny put his hands over his nose and mouth to try to protect himself as he lurched through the main cabin towards the fo'csle to open the forehatch and get a stream of cold fresh air pouring through the interior of the junk. Then he ran groggily back to get his arms underneath his great-aunt's shoulders and try to pull her from her berth and up into the night.

It was really hard. He hadn't known how heavy even a small eighty-year-old could be when they were completely inert. Maybe she'd been drugged.

He couldn't do it. Couldn't get her up the ladder. Wasn't strong enough.

So he changed his plans and heaved her through the cabin until he could prop her up underneath the open hatch. She couldn't die there, surely?

What next? He didn't think of using the VHF. Didn't think of summoning official adult help. Instead he reverted to the only plan he had. He readied *Strong Winds*' engine then scrambled gratefully out of the foul air and into the cockpit hoping that, if he loosed the after tow-rope first, whoever it was who was rushing them down the river, might not notice when he scuttled forrard to release that warp as well.

Then it would be engine on, tiller hard across and *Strong Winds* would take her only possible chance of escape.

They'd almost be down to Harwich by then. He couldn't decide if that was good or bad. A fragment of his mind was still up the River Orwell with Maggi and Anna in those lonely woods. Another was lying unconscious with Great Aunt Ellen. She mustn't die. Mustn't take the longest road, not tonight, *please*.

Maybe, when he'd freed *Strong Winds*, he could get her across to Shotley marina, phone Joshua Ribiero for medical advice? Xanthe must have her dad's number in her mobile?

Another of those crashing kicks felled him as he reached out for the first of the towing lines.

The attacker was strong, had trained hard all his life, knew how to use each individual muscle. He had no trouble bundling a fourteen-year-old down into the main cabin and laying him out on one of the berths.

He was tempted of course to tip the body straight over the side. But all of this had to look like an accident. They'd been so careful how they set it up. Everyone had their alibis established. Even the boys would have been photographed by now, attending the Ipswich Vigil for Harmony and Happiness, as arranged by their Welfare worker.

All except him. He was the shape-shifter, the man in the shadows. He did what needed to be done. Ran his businesses discreetly. His women would alibi him from here to eternity if he so much as rattled the keys to their cage. Yet he wouldn't want to risk a murder enquiry. Even here, where he had friends.

Very soon they'd reach Harwich International Port. The giant cruise liner *Imago* was scheduled to leave ten minutes after midnight on a New Year Welcome trip. By then the junk would have been pinioned beneath her jutting bow, trapped between the cruise liner's inner hawser and the harbour wall. She would be completely invisible from the liner's blazing windows. None of the revellers on board need be aware of her annihilation

It was at that moment that Xanthe's phone went off. Not with the melodious ping of another text arriving but with the gale-force rendition of 'Rule Britannia' that she'd down-loaded, so she explained later, to make an ironic, post-imperialist statement. Donny never did quite understand what she had meant by that.

The soprano thundered on and on.

The attacker would have left it. Buried so deep in the child's expensive clothes. But then the Dragon spoke.

"Satellite technology, Tiger. He also has powerful friends. Those telephones can be tracked. And will be."

She was not where he had left her. Her voice was weak yet she was awake.

He slapped the boy awake as well.

"How long?"

His voice was muffled by his stocking mask. They couldn't even see the shape of his head in the unlit cabin. He had throttled back the engine of his own vessel but they would soon be nearing the liner's departure terminal.

"How long on?"

Long? Or Lóng? Donny could think of nothing but the blows to his face. What was happening to him? What was he meant to say?

The Rule Britannia ring-tone ceased. And almost immediately began again.

The Tiger was infuriated. He ripped open the Velcro fastenings and the broad flat zips of Donny's borrowed sailing gear. He was wearing gloves. There would be no prints. Found the instrument at last and threw it hard away out through the main hatch into the black waters.

"It's been on all the time. We've been texting."

"Sheer off, Tiger. No-one's going to swallow your accident now."

The Dragon was on her feet. She was swinging a heavy leather pouch on a lanyard. She was old. He could take her easily. And the child too.

"Dad," said Xanthe. She'd been ringing to tell Donny that Maggi and Anna had arrived safely at the vicarage and her mother had left the Yacht Club party and would be picking them up at midnight. Her father was home from the hospital. "My phone's gone dead."

"Battery?" Joshua's face was tinged grey with the strain of the latest hygiene crisis in his specialist surgical ward.

"Nope. It was ringing and it cut. It's completely dead. Think about it, Dad. First Miss Walker tells the vicarage lot that she senses danger and needs to be back on board *Strong Winds*. So she leaves the pirate party. Then Donny gets the same feeling and I'm so focussed on the dog that I just flutter a metaphorical hanky at him. Now this.

There's something wrong, Dad. That phone's been dunked."

"I have *Strong Winds*' call sign. We established an emergency system when Donny's mother was so ill."

"MTRM3 … MTRM3. Are you receiving me? Over."

Donny heard Joshua Ribiero's voice loud and clear over *Strong Winds*' VHF but he was in no position to respond. He was wrapped arms and legs around the Tiger holding him back from reaching Great Aunt Ellen. She was game but shaky, whirling her rigging pouch like some sort of medieval weapon.

Something heavy bumped and scraped its way down *Strong Winds*' side. A tug hooted stridently, quite close at hand.

The only accidents they would have now would be real.

The attacker kicked himself free of Donny's koala-style clasp and ripped the radio cable from its socket. He ran on deck, freed both towing lines and leaped on board his stolen ferry, taking the junk's tiller with him. Then gave *Strong Winds* one last savage shove towards some unfinished construction workings at the eastern end of Bathgate Bay.

Donny picked himself up, glanced at his great-aunt and threw himself up the companionway. The object that had bumped its way along the junks' topsides had been a metal buoy. They were well on the wrong side of the channel now and skewing into shallow water. A hazard marker dead ahead warned boats to keep away from half-submerged concrete piles and protruding metal girders.

He pressed the ignition and *Strong Winds*' engine answered instantly. Put it gently into reverse to slow her way. Needed something to steer with. Ran forward for the boat hook.

"At ease, Sinbad. We carry a spare." Polly Lee was in her cockpit now and hooking a replacement tiller out from the aft locker. "Best bring that dinghy of yours aft and make her fast securely. That scurvy swab has lost me both my anchors so we'll have to find a mooring PDQ. Or stand by to make sail. I'm not certain how much of our diesel he's left us."

She was in control and turning the junk carefully away from the danger. She switched on *Strong Winds'* navigation lights and headed back towards the channel. As Donny went to retrieve *Lively Lady* he looked out into the night after their attacker.

No sign.

"Availed himself of the cross-harbour ferry. The black-hearted bilge-sucker. He'll be tied up alongside the Ha'penny Pier by now."

Fireworks began sizzling skywards and the Harwich church bell tolled. The pale superstructure of the cruise liner *Imago* was dappled with reflected colour as her passengers carried their wineglasses to the windows and gazed out onto the spectacular display. Two of the harbour tugs were positioning themselves to pluck the liner from the shadowed quayside.

"Um, Happy 2007 then," Donny said to Great Aunt Ellen. "Don't suppose you carry a spare radio as well do you?"

"Isn't that the youth of today," she tutted, pulling out a fully-charged portable VHF. "Always on the phone to someone. Whatever happened to good old-fashioned self-reliance?"

"Laid out in a bunk with a pad of diesel wadding over her face?"

"An accident waiting to happen. I'm obliged, Sinbad. To you and to your Allies."

CHAPTER TWENTY-FIVE

Farewell and Adieu

January-March 2007

"How sick are you of sailing?" she asked him when he'd finished apologising to Xanthe for the loss of her mobile and reassuring everyone that he was with his great-aunt and all was well. He knew not to say more over the VHF as others could be listening.

"Hardly done any to get sick of."

"I haven't put my nose out of this harbour for the last three months."

"Are you saying that you want to go to sea now?" It was past midnight and he'd assumed they'd be deciding between Shotley marina for the rest of the night or a mooring on the lower Orwell. They didn't have to. No-one was expecting them. Unless they should be taking legal advice about the accident that hadn't happened – talking to Edward maybe?

"I believe he'll say don't rock the boat," she answered as if she'd read his mind. "Do nothing until Lottie Livesey has been salvaged." She was already busy with *Strong Winds*' mizzen halliards. "He's a cautious man. Run that foresail up while you're thinking. It was your life on the line back there as well as mine. We needn't carry too much sail. Enough to take us into deeper water for a watch or two. Clear our heads and flush the bilges."

"What sticks in my gullet like a fisherman's barb," she said, when they were a couple of hours out of Harwich, north-east of the

Gunfleet Sand, "Is passing one bent farthing of the sprogs' legacy to that shoal of blood-sucking parasites. Don't look so startled, Sinbad, I know that you've been nodding. I've pumped the bilges through for a good fifteen minutes without breaking the rhythm of your snores. The cabin's fresher now. Help me bring her round and pass me my wet-weather gear then you can go and get your head down properly."

"Oh, er … yeah. I do like it, though. I really do. Out here in the dark. Getting away from the land – trying to work out the different lights, then looking up at the sails against the stars."

"I know you do. You're a lad after my own heart – more than I had ever hoped. But there's no shame in letting yourself sleep when there's someone else to take her turn. It'll be tomorrow soon enough and we'll all have some explaining to do. Then you'll be back to school and first mate Anna will be coding up a message in that folder. To think of Theodora's money being used to pay-off tiger-sharks! She was a good woman you know – if inclined to be romantic. I didn't see so much of her but she and Eirene were close. And Cal … adored her."

He had thought the sky was beginning to lighten as they gybed *Strong Winds* back towards the coast. Then the stars disappeared behind low cloud and another steady drenching rain made him glad to settle for his bunk.

He had that dream again. The one about the outcasts on the lonely shore. He thought he knew where it had come from now but it was odd how the faces of the castaways kept changing: sometimes they were children from Great Aunt Ellen's generation, either Anna's relations or characters from the pages of a story. Other times they were Skye's lost parents or even the Chinese cleaner and that dog that Xanthe had called Ben Gunn.

He slept deeply and felt thick-headed when he finally woke and found *Strong Winds* scudding up the Orwell in the wet, grey morning.

"Going to collect your mother from the vicarage."

"But … we've been banned from Pin Mill Hard."

"There's more to Pin Mill than the Hard. Mrs Everson has a mooring we can use. Off the far end of the beach. An erstwhile haunt of yours, I'm told. And I believe you know various alternative paths through the woods."

"Who?"

"Her daughter. Big woman. Rowed me out to the junk last night and bought *Vexilla* back."

So that's why there'd still been two dinghies in the creek.

"After which I think a couple of days shore leave might be in order. I may need to shop around for anchors. I imagine there'll be plenty of choice in Ipswich."

Adults could be quite shockingly untruthful. Gold Dragon had no intention of buying pricey new anchors from the various chandlers and boatyards she visited in Ipswich. She was putting herself about, demonstrating to anyone who might be interested that she neither was dead nor had been scared off.

She did buy one venerable specimen, virtually given away with forty metres of rusty chain, from a houseboat dweller in the New Cut, but as soon as they returned to Gallister Creek, on the day before the beginning of term, he discovered that she'd noted exactly the co-ordinates of their former anchorage. He and Skye were put to work, rowing *Vexilla* up and down, while Great Aunt Ellen trailed a grappling iron to snag on her sabotaged gear. Then she was back on board *Strong Winds* using her powerful winch to haul up both the anchors and re-lay them as before.

Her time in Ipswich was also time spent on reconnaissance. Semi-derelict docks, warehouses with buddleia sprouting from condemned asbestos roofs, corroding storage containers, abandoned boats – she was there, hooking around.

"Pirates," she explained, "operate on the edge of other people's territorial waters. They need a no-man's land where they can retreat. Somewhere that regular law-abiding citizens aren't too keen to visit. It doesn't have to be as scruffy as this, of course."

"You would know about operating on the edge?" he was bold enough to ask her. "Retreating into no-man's lands?"

"I might," she replied.

Then, on the first day of Donny's new school term, she left Skye contentedly on board *Strong Winds*, working on some private project, and took herself to Lowestoft by train.

Anna returned the music folder to its space in the DT cupboard. Her un-appealing new tunes were coded to reassure her mother that all the children were well. They also concealed the address of a diocesan shelter in an area of town where women stood on street corners late at night and where men drove slowly, close to the edges of the pavements.

The folder lay on the shelf. Agonising days dragged past.

What if Pura-Lilly had lost the Gallister High cleaning contract? Donny hung about the DT department long after the school day ended, looking out for anyone in overalls with that drooping flesh-pink logo. He didn't recognise anyone. He hoped for the Chinese cleaner: he'd almost have been glad to glimpse the Tiger.

Anna grew anorexic with worry.

Gold Dragon claimed that *Vexilla* needed checking for some sort of disease that only attacked glass-fibre boats. She chose a calm late-January Saturday to persuade Donny, Anna and Maggi to deliver her to the far end of the New Cut, cover her with a bird-stained tarpaulin and sail all the way back to the Stour in *Lively Lady*. It took them ages, though it was a nice enough day and seemed completely unnecessary. They checked the building site containers while they were in the area. There was no-one living there.

It was almost February half-term before the space in the cupboard emptied.

The music folder was back within twenty-four hours. Lottie's love and happiness spilled into lines of manuscript that Anna longed to sing, though all that they actually said was that her mother's work-group had been away at a meat-packing factory and she would visit the all-night shelter as soon as she was able.

Rev. Wendy had already begun volunteering there. She came home before breakfast every morning looking shocked.

As soon as Lottie's message had been de-coded Edward arrived at the vicarage carrying two black briefcases. Anna was in the hall, observing Hawkins's flight patterns. She was certain that she heard the lawyer tell Gerald that he'd brought ten thousand each and come prepared to take his turn. Then Wendy chivvied both men into her study and shut the door with a slam.

Great Aunt Ellen had decided not to tell anyone how much she hated the idea of paying Theodora's money to the tiger-sharks.

She was still trying to keep out of it: still trying not to use the knowledge that she'd learned in the Islands.

"Feed them and they grow fatter. Their stomachs distend, they grow greedier. Life becomes harsher for all the other minnows in the pond."

It was Lottie who wouldn't do it. She didn't use the same words but she told Wendy in the Shelter – and then Anna, via the folder – that every time one of the workers gave in to the pressure to earn money in ways that were wrong, the lives of all the others became harder.

"Not Mum's principles again," wailed Anna.

Gold Dragon gave in. "Ai Qin Pai has already offered help. Hoi Fung, the chef at the Floating Lotus, will leave her employment angrily and move to work in Ipswich. There is a takeaway with a bad reputation down an alley not far from the river. If we can put your mother in his way he will buy her from whoever owns her debt."

"That's … appalling," breathed Xanthe. It was half-term, it was raining and she should have been revising. Instead all of the Allies were sitting in *Strong Winds'* cabin, plotting.

"Your Trustees will give him the money to do this." Gold Dragon took no notice of anyone except Anna. "When he has your mother, Hoi Fung will renege on the deal. He will say that the goods are not as promised. Your mother will run. He will put himself in great danger and you will not see your money again. It will not be paid to the tiger-sharks, it will be taken back to the Floating Lotus to help others who are trying to break free."

"That's … awesome."

287

An evening in early March

Anna, wearing white lacy tights, an off-the-shoulder t-shirt and a skirt that Maggi had decided was too short when she was ten, stood in the harsh light of the Oriental Xpress Pizza and Kebab *fast*Food Café and giggled. Inspector Flint was there – just as she'd expected. And he'd made one of his wonderfully witty jokes. She'd known Flint would turn up once she started posting lonely heart messages on the Eager To Meet You 18+ website. But this time the minnow was hooking the shark.

Gerald, who was in the café with her, was sticking close as a traumatised limpet. They'd dressed him in hipster jeans, a leather jacket and a t-shirt with studs that spelled Old Devil and she'd spent hours trying to coach him in his new role as a sleazebag. But he couldn't get it. He'd never believed that the policeman would be there.

She could see him trying to smirk knowingly – struggling to look as if he too was out for a good time. It wasn't working. She had to keep Flint's attention focused on her and trust that his own stupid arrogance would stop him catching on. She tittered again and wriggled a little closer.

"Extraordinary what items people think suitable for the church bazaar," Rev. Wendy had commented as she had sorted through the bin-bags to select her husband's camouflage for this unlikely encounter. Her own rescue plan had very definitely not included any of the children. There had been harsh words when Great Aunt Ellen had explained why she thought it necessary to use Anna to make sure her mother would co-operate in her own rescue.

"Of course no-one will ask Lottie Livesey whether she approves the sale of her debt. Hoi Fung will offer a good price and he will say that he is expecting some agreeable company now that he has moved to this new town. They will laugh at him but they will laugh behind their hands – until they are sure they have his cash. These are dangerous people. We cannot take the risk that Anna's mother will refuse to be there when she is expected."

"If this is a matter of conscience she may feel she has no choice."

"If her finer feelings prevent her arriving at the handover the best that will happen is that Theodora's money will pass to the tiger-sharks …"

"And the worst?"

"Is that a good man will lose more than his remaining leg. The Oriental Xpress has an evil reputation."

"Yet you propose to send a child there! A child In Care!"

Gerald cleared his throat nervously and pushed both hands into his cardigan pocket, possibly to stop them shaking.

"You know dear, I could … accompany Anna."

If Rev. Wendy hadn't already spent several weeks volunteering at the all-night Shelter she would have sent him back to his kitchen at once. As it was she went completely quiet and sort of gazed at him.

"You would do that? Risk your good name … to keep her safe? Because people will think the worst, you know. And, for that night, you would have to allow them to think it …"

"But you and I would know the truth, dear."

It was really sweet, Anna told the Allies later, the way they looked at each other then. Wendy seemed to think that her husband was some sort of knight in shining armour and Gold Dragon had no more trouble persuading her to go along with the plan.

"All we need is for Anna's mother to *believe* that her daughter is in danger. No more than that. Then we'll be sure that she won't fail us at the handover."

"No-one wanted to spell out exactly what danger they had in mind for me," Anna commented. "So I asked them whether it would be worse than Death by Pink McFlurry? But they didn't get it. They still can't believe that Flint is … what he is."

"But surely if he sees Gerald there," Maggi had objected, "he'll know there's something wrong."

"Okay, so it's a risk. But I reckon he'll just assume that Gerald's as bad as he is – and he'll just note it down in for next time he needs to put the squeezers on. Flint doesn't exactly have a high opinion of anyone except himself. He won't spot decency."

"So why do you think your mum'll come?"

"Partly because it's such a bad place. Also Gold Dragon says there's a local catch-phrase that would totally upset Mum if she heard it used about me – so she was going to make quite sure that it got around."

"She didn't tell you what the catch-phrase was, I suppose?"

"Course not. Even Gold Dragon's protective, you know."

There were only a half dozen tables in the Oriental Xpress. A group of tired-looking men from boats in the New Cut were eating hungrily at one: a couple of young girls in heavy make-up were lingering over cokes at another. Most of its customers stood outside, even on winter nights, eating out of polystyrene cartons – or took their food away. Most of the litter around the area could be traced back to the café.

The Chinese chef in the stained white overalls peeled wafer-thin slices from the rotating kebab spit and shook the grease from another batch of chips. He looked sullen. A group of well-hards slouched in, ordered chips with xtra-hot curry sauce, then slouched out into the dark again, clutching their cans of Vommitt.

It was a cold night, overcast and threatening yet more rain. Rev. Wendy was parked a little way down the street, fingers hovering nervously over the ignition of her Skoda. Donny was waiting in *Vexilla*; Gold Dragon was keeping out of sight in the Buccaneers' Arms, a nearby pub.

"Safe house," she'd told him. "Best in the area. If I'd had longer I could have managed the entire run without you. As it is you're standing by to stand by and I sincerely hope you won't be needed. If Hoi Fung gets away as planned I'll be only too glad to stand you down."

They hadn't told Rev. Wendy that Donny was involved and she hadn't asked. Skye and Maggi were at the vicarage. Xanthe had a coursework deadline.

A small man in a business suit walked into the café. He didn't look at Flint: he didn't speak to the chef. The boat-dwellers took no notice of him: the two young girls moved closer together, hunching their bare skinny shoulders and looking sideways from under their mascara. One of them lit a cigarette, which they shared, inexpertly.

The Tiger sat down at a table in the corner, placed a brief case in front of him and opened it. It was empty.

He looked at the big, scarred, one-legged chef.

The chef looked back, still sullen. He pointed at the door. Shrugged. Sliced another fold of meat.

Anna got an astonishing fit of giggles. She perched herself on Flint's table top, not noticing, apparently, that this brought her skirt almost to her hip bones. Gerald harrumphed. Then he forgot his role completely and told her to sit down properly or he'd have to take her home.

"For heaven's sake!" she snapped at him. "Why don't you go talk to the other girls. I want the Inthpector to buy me one of his Xtra large ith-cweams."

She tried a melting smile and Flint leered as if she were a dish of sizzling scampi with a rosy tartare relish.

The Tiger crooked his finger at the chef. Hoi Fung looked the other way.

The Tiger crashed his rigid hand hard onto a wooden chair, which collapsed. Still Hoi Fung took no notice.

Gerald snapped back at Anna. Shocked, she got off the table and hitched down her skirt, glaring at him.

That was when her mother walked in.

With Toxic close behind her.

They'd given Lottie the outline of the plan via the music folder but when she looked at Anna she didn't look like someone who was acting.

"Get out of here, wash that stuff off your face, go home and change your clothes. At once!" she said. "And I've no idea what you think you're doing," she said to Gerald, who looked as guilty as if all of this hadn't been a set-up. "You'd better leave as well. Before someone reports you. For being criminally irresponsible and disgusting. No-one's going to make my daughter into a cage-bird."

Hoi Fung started shouting then. Shouting at the Tiger in Cantonese. Pointing at Lottie and waving his arms. He pulled a bulging folder from beside the fryer and shoved it inside his overalls. Grabbed a kitchen knife.

The Tiger was coming at him. Leaping onto the high counter.

Hoi Fung was immediately in front of the kitchen exit. Why didn't he run?

Flint snatched out his radio and pressed a red button. "Calling all units! Calling all units!"

Now the well-hards were blocking the doorway behind Toxic. She had her BlackBerry out, of course and was selecting photo-angles: the psychopathic foreign chef, the under-dressed teenager and her alleged 'carer', the noble policeman at the Heart of his Community.

"Come on, Mum," said Anna. "Come on, Gerald. We've got to leave. He won't run until he knows we're safe."

The boat-people stood up then and headed for the door. They were older men, recruited by Polly Lee from the miscellany of vessels moored along the New Cut. With Hoi Fung's food inside them they looked burly and purposeful. There would be pints waiting for them at the Buccaneers' Arms.

"Come *on*," said Anna again. "It's our walking bus."

She pushed her mother and Gerald into the midst of the group. The men bunched together, flexed their shoulders and marched towards the well-hards who fell back, looking suddenly young.

Lottie had been dressed up in a short skirt and high heels – probably to impress the possible buyer of her debt. She broke ranks as they pushed past Toxic, whipped one of her stilettos off and smashed its heel down on the BlackBerry. Then she twisted round and sent the same shoe hissing across the room to hit the Tiger sharp in the back of his head.

Hoi Fung left then.

"Time you went home as well," one of the boatmen said to the two young girls. But they sat there transfixed, watching the violence as if it was reality TV.

Donny could hear the police sirens from *Vexilla*. He already had her tarpaulin off and warps ready to slip.

There was a blue light flashing outside the Buccaneers' Arms. These were regular police with legal power to enter and search. A runaway chef with a stash of cash wouldn't want to be picked up by them.

"Passengers for you, Sinbad."

Quiet voices in the darkness and a large figure climbing awkwardly into the dinghy. No kitchen knives now. Both hands needed to grip the gunwale and steady himself against the damp pontoon. Great Aunt Ellen was beside him.

"I'm shipping with you too. The Reverend's well away. No sense me waiting there to be bothered for a witness statement. Set to your oars, I'll cast off."

There were three vertical red lights at the river exit.

This meant stop. All vessels. There was a boom across the end of the New Cut to reduce the flow of the tide after periods of heavy rainfall and it had just been raised from the river-bed.

Was this bad luck or had someone guessed they were there?

"Her centre-plate's up isn't it?"

It was.

Gold Dragon spoke rapidly in Cantonese and the chef turned to lift the rudder. At that moment Donny felt *Vexilla* slide to a halt, caught by something underneath.

There was a police car by the boatyard now. He could hear foot-steps along the pontoon: questions being asked, sleepers woken.

Gold Dragon, as the lightest, had been sitting in the bows. She grabbed one of his oars and began prodding one-handed down into the water. There was relief in her voice when she spoke next in both languages. The chef scrambled forward lightening the stern. She passed him the oar.

"Look sharp, both of you, reach back and shove her off, hard. Last time I was stuck like this I was on the back of a whale in the middle of the Indian Ocean!"

As *Vexilla* slipped smoothly over the barrier, Donny realised how much his great-aunt was enjoying herself. She'd even persuaded cautious Edward to meet Hoi Fung somewhere beyond the sewage treatment works and whisk the chef and his cash discreetly back to Lowestoft.

Some people never grew up.

25 March 2007

They scattered Oboe's ashes early on a March morning – after Science had taken the bits it wanted. The date was a few days after the equinox but as close as could be managed considering tides and work and the children still needing to get to school.

The wind was from the north-east, keen and cold, building up a long slow swell across the expanse of the North Sea. It was a melancholy wind. It reminded Donny of the night they'd stood beside the Euroscope, looking out across the globe, feeling its vastness and its grief.

The little fleet had found shelter behind a curving shingle bank topped with pines. When the mourners looked up from the decks of their ships, they could glimpse the minarets of Bawdsey Manor – the house where two people had clung together in the darkness as a flying bomb passed by.

Then had missed one other for the rest of their lives.

Edward had driven over from Cambridge a few days previously; bringing the ashes in a box that he said had once housed his old friend's first telescope. He said it was up to Ellen whether she threw the box in or kept it: he personally didn't want it back. He didn't want to come with them either. Boats always made him feel sick.

At the first hint of dawn, the ships put out to sea. Even without Edward there were fourteen people on board the two yachts. Gerald and Rev. Wendy had joined the Ribieros on board the repaired, re-launched *Snow Goose* while Lottie Livesey, her children and step-children were all crammed into *Strong Winds'* welcoming saloon. *Lively Lady* was up in davits: *Vexilla* was being towed empty behind *Snow Goose*.

The River Deben entrance was unlit and potentially dangerous. Gales and strong tides throughout the winter always caused the shingle banks to shift unpredictably and this year was no exception. Joshua Ribiero and Polly Lee had taken careful bearings as they'd entered the river on the previous afternoon and Joshua had used his GPS for position fixing. Now both skippers reversed their routes with only the faintest glimmerings of morning light relieving the darkness of sky and sea.

This Sunday morning was the first day of British Summer Time. The early hour seemed even earlier as the two yachts motored slowly towards their seamark. Eirene's swallow flag was flying at half-mast on *Strong Winds*. Polly Lee's gold dragon was at half-mast too.

They'd agreed to open the box two cables beyond the Woodbridge Haven buoy. When the first light of the rising sun touched the far side of the red and white painted safe water mark, Anna and Ellen would let the ashes go.

Donny looked up at two dipped flags fluttering against the gloomy sky. If only Anna's Internet searches had located Oboe a few weeks sooner, the two old friends who should have been lovers could have been reunited one last time.

But they hadn't. There had been no happy ending.

The wind came moaning through the rigging like an Ojibway lamentation. *Wahonowin, wahonowin!*

It hit them with its full force as they swung east towards the bar buoy. The channel was at its shallowest here and the seabed was uneven. Unexpected waves reared up and rushed past, hump-backed assassins clutching cloaks to conceal their guilty heads.

Two cables beyond the Woodbridge Haven buoy the yachts moved close together and both engines were reduced to minimum revs. Donny's job was to keep the junk steadily head-to-wind as they waited for that first ray of sun.

The moment came. Anna and Great Aunt Ellen opened the box, held it over *Strong Winds'* high stern and shook its contents out. Some of the gritty ash inside fell straight into the water, the finer particles were lifted up onto the wind and invisibly dispersed.

Flags were dipped low then raised to half-mast again. Rev. Wendy probably said a prayer. Donny blinked hard and looked away.

That was it.

Callum Reif, who he'd never met, was gone. Like Granny and her brothers; Eirene and Henry, Anna's father and Luke and Liam's mum.

Gone in a blur of dust and never coming back.

"Oh my darlings," he heard Lottie say, "I've made such terrible mistakes."

After a few moments' stillness people began to move around their boats. Xanthe and Maggi took charge of *Vexilla* and sails were hoisted on all three vessels. One after another they swung south-west to begin their journey back to Harwich.

The sisters were first away, red tasselled caps streaming in the wind, while Joshua and June struggled to persuade their nervous passengers to help them set two jibs and the mizzen in addition to *Snow Goose's* heavy gaff mainsail. Soon the yacht was in pursuit of the open boat and *Strong Winds'* three broad-battened sails were straining to keep her in touch. Donny felt the junk pull and plunge as she settled onto her new course. Steadily the distances began to close.

It was so good to be alive and sailing! Donny hugged his mum and beamed at Gold Dragon. Her leathery face beamed back at him. "I think we can let her have another few inches on the mainsheet," was all she actually said.

Vexilla reached Harwich Harbour first but only just. She had taken an audacious inshore route where the larger boats could not follow. Then *Snow Goose* changed tack and went close-hauled up the Orwell back to her berth below the Yacht Club. Donny watched her heeling like a racing yacht and wondered what on earth his former foster-carers were making of this experience.

Strong Winds headed westwards up the Stour.

They had passed the Shotley Spit buoy and were approaching the fake *Hispaniola* when Skye produced another flag. It wasn't one that you would find in any Nautical Almanac or Register of Ships and Shipping; nor within the pages of a classic children's adventure story. Not even on the Internet.

Over the past few months, while everyone had been waiting and planning for Lottie's return, Skye had collected all the fragments of the Allies' dragon flag and re-woven them into a shimmering rectangle of black and gold. She had feather-stitched each frayed edge with embroidery silk and pressed them smooth. Then she'd wired her new standard to a stout bamboo pole.

Skye didn't run her flag up the mast as her mother Eirene or anyone else would have done: she took the pole in both hands and waved it from side to side in great sweeping arcs so the black and gold silk rippled like a triumphal banner.

Luke and Liam left Lottie and came scrambling over. "Ha, ha, ha!" they shouted in defiance of everything gloomy and cruel. "HA, HA, HA!"

Anna started shouting too: so did Lottie, bouncing Vicky on her lap. Donny ran to the other two sets of signal halliards and raised the dipped flags back to the mastheads.

The sun was up; the sky was clear and the wind fresh. It was a beautiful spring day.

They were together. They were happy.

After a few moments Donny grabbed his mother's arm and made her stop her flag-waving and look upwards.

There, sharp against the bright sky, were the first two swallows of summer.

From the Ship's Log

The first draft of this story was written during the winter of 2006-2007 when *Peter Duck* was spending the winter in Shotley Marina. *Peter Duck* is a wooden ketch who I have known since I was three years old. She was built for Arthur Ransome at Pin Mill on the River Orwell and her logbooks stretch back to 1947. Looking at my entries for the mid-winter of 2006-2007 I see that the weather was just as wet and windy as my story says it was. There was certainly a day when we gave up an attempt to beat up the River Stour against wind and tide because the waves were 'like walls'. Our return journey to the River Deben in late March 2007, coming in over the shingle bar with a strong North-Easterly behind us and the dinghy threatening to leap into the cockpit, was a piece of research I'm certainly not keen to repeat in a hurry.

Grumbles aside, I enjoyed *Peter Duck*'s months in Shotley Marina. One of the unexpected pleasures was the presence of the dancer Miranda Tufnell, who was living a few miles further up the Orwell. Miranda has a deep feeling for non-verbal communication and for the importance of dreams in other cultures. She introduced me to books by Hugh Brody and Louise Erdrich which helped me to understand more about the character of Skye.

Skye's parents, Eirene and Henry, sailed westwards whereas Great Aunt Ellen has returned from the East. In the winter of 2006-2007 I watched Nick Broomfield's brilliant and disturbing film *Ghosts*, based on investigative research by Chinese journalist Hsiang-Hung Pai. *Ghosts* dramatises the journey of one young mother from Fujian Province in China to England. She came seeking work to support her child and elderly parents but never saw any of them again as she was drowned collecting cockles in Morecambe Bay. Her family was left to pay her debt to the smugglers and money-lenders.

Shotley is not far from Ipswich. During the winter of 2006 the bodies of five women were discovered in some of the beautiful areas around the town. They had been murdered and although I have known Ipswich since I was a child, I was as shocked as Rev. Wendy to discover that the town had a red light district. I gave myself the shivers wondering where the next body would be found or whether the murderer might be hiding in one of the many deserted, winter-covered boats.

Grim things happen in books and life but as far as I'm concerned they are always outweighed by the goodness, kindness and generosity of other people. Where to start when saying thank-you? I could start at the beginning by thanking my father and mother for buying *Peter Duck* so long ago and giving my two brothers and myself such a wonderful introduction to sailing. I could thank the Palmer family – (Edith) Ann, Greg and Ned – for being adventurous owners of *Peter Duck* from 1987-1999 and for letting me use their names in my stories. Ann's sister Eirene lent me her name too – it means 'peace'.

I must certainly thank my beloved partner, Francis, for changing my life by buying *Peter Duck* back into our family and then I thank my brother Ned, my niece Ruthie and my youngest children Bertie and Archie for making summer sailing such fun and for checking out so many of the *Strong Winds* trilogy's locations. (I freely admit to being very much less poised than Great Aunt Ellen when we were bumping up and down outside Lowestoft harbour entrance with all sails flapping and milk spilling in the cockpit.) I had better add that Erewhon Parva vicarage, Gallister High, the Floating Lotus and the Oriental Xpress are entirely fictional. As are all my characters – though not necessarily all of the boats.

Thanks to the people who have been generous with their special knowledge. Alec Reeve was the true inventor of OBOE. He was a brilliant and unusual personality whom I read about first in Andrew Wheen's book *From Dot-Dash to Dot-Com*. My friend Heidi shared experiences that she'd rather not have endured (as did many of the families I met when I worked for the Workers' Educational Association). Bertie Wheen did the binary conversion. Karen Lee named the Cantonese sea-cook. Peter Clay sent photographs of his yawl, *Nirvana*. Peter Dowden saved the book from two almighty howlers. Peter Willis and Andrew Craig-Bennett have been knowledgeable friends to me, my boat and my books throughout. I am particularly grateful to Christina Hardyment and the Executors of the Arthur Ransome Literary Estate for giving me permission to use the quotation from *Winter Holiday* in chapter ten. (And to AR for writing such an excellent book. If you like codes and communication systems, *Winter Holiday* is full of them.)

Working with Claudia Myatt has been a delight – especially when we were able to sit in the cockpit and discuss cover design while her son, James Crickmere, took *Peter Duck* storming out to sea. I continue to miss designer Roger Davies, who died shortly before the publication of *The Salt-Stained Book*, but working with Megan Trudell has been a new pleasure. Thanks to David Smith for his perceptive, professional editorial input and Francis Wheen, Frank Thorogood, Peter and Eleanor Dowden, Claudia Myatt, Megan Trudell and Ruth Elias Jones for dollops of the kitchen-table variety. Thanks also to Associated British Ports, Mattie Gardiner, Nicci Gerrard, Diana Heffer, Janine Johnston, Jan Needle, John Ravenscroft, Griff Rhys Jones, John Skermer, Gabrielle Wallington, Waveney District Council and all of the team at Signature Books for advice, help and kindness beyond the call of duty.

I am grateful, above all, to the readers who have ventured this far. I hope we'll meet again in *Ghosting Home*.

Julia Jones, Essex, 2011

Ghosting Home

When Donny saw which boat it was, slipping stealthily up-river in this dead hour between night and day, he crouched lower and motioned the others to do the same. No precaution could be too extreme. The *Hispaniola* had left her mooring.

Available Summer 2012